Also by Carolyn Brown

Dear Readers,

Welcome back to the Paradise, the old brothel in Spanish Fort, Texas, that became the setting for *Trouble in Paradise* more than two decades ago. *Sisters in Paradise* is the second book in the new trilogy about the seven sisters who grew up in the Paradise. *Paradise for Christmas* came out last fall, and *Coming Home to Paradise* is scheduled to be released next fall. I hope all y'all enjoy revisiting the old Paradise once again—this time in early summer when the flowers are in bloom and the gentle breezes ruffle the leaves on the ancient pecan trees. Ophelia and Tertia are waiting to get to know you better, and I can't wait for you to read their stories!

In reality, Spanish Fort is a little ghost town right on the Red River in north central Texas. In my mind, the Paradise is very real. Who knows what could happen to that little town if businesses keep moving into the area? Before long, it might even be taken off the list of Texas ghost towns.

I hope you all enjoy going back to Spanish Fort, Texas, and to the Paradise as much as I did, and that after you finish the last words in this book, you are already wanting to read another one.

Until next time,

Carolyn Brown

Sisters in Paradise

CAROLYN BROWN

Published by Sourcebooks Casablanca, an imprint of Sourcebooks
P.O. Box 4410, Naperville, Illinois 60567-4410
(630) 961-3900
sourcebooks.com

Cataloging-in-Publication Data is on file with the Library of Congress.

Printed and bound in the United States of America.
KP 10 9 8 7 6 5 4 3 2 1

*This one is for my daughter's group of friends,
who are prime examples of women empowering
other women: Amy Lee, CJ, Dana, Jayci, Jennifer,
Kristy, Sherri, and my daughter, Amy.*

Chapter 1

BOSSY. NOSY. SASSY.

Look up any one of those words in a dictionary or on the internet, and Ophelia Simmons was sure that her great-aunt Mary Bernadette's picture would be right there beside the word.

Aunt Bernie, as everyone called her, was pint-sized, but was living proof that dynamite came in small packages, and it didn't take old age settling in for her to speak whatever was on her mind. She had owned a bar in Oklahoma for more than sixty years, and everyone who came into Bernie's Place had to follow the rules posted on the wall right above the bar or else she would toss them out on their ear—or a lower part of their anatomy if need be. Rumor had it that she had taken her sawed-off shotgun from under the bar and fired it on more than one occasion to settle rule number one—no fighting in Bernie's Place—and that the holes in the ceiling testified that she was serious.

"I told you so." Bernie smiled as she slid into the passenger seat of Ophelia's pickup truck and fastened the seat belt that Thursday morning.

Ophelia grabbed a pair of sunglasses from the console and put them on. "You told me so about what?"

"Remember back at Christmas when I said that Ursula and Luna would be married before summer was over? Well, my prophecy is coming true," Bernie answered. "I've worked my magic on those two, and now it's time for me to go to use my powers on you and your sister. Tertia should be home tomorrow, and my new prediction is that I'll have both of you in serious relationships in no time."

"Hey, now!" Ophelia started the engine and drove down the lane to the highway. "Luna was already secretly dating Shane when you moved here, so you can't take credit for that."

Bernie crossed her arms over her chest. "You can think whatever you want. I know that it was my meddling that put Ursula and Luna right where they are today, and I do *not* intend to stop working my magic until I'm either dead or else have all you girls back here in Spanish Fort. Nope, that's not right. Not just here in town but settled down and either in a serious relationship or married. The Universe has told me that is why I'm here, and I don't argue with the Universe or doubt anything that it says."

"Why?" Ophelia was not worried about her aunt Bernie dying any time soon. Heaven was *not* ready for the likes of her, and the devil didn't want her for fear she would try to take over his domain and shove him out for good.

"Why am I not dead? Or why am I determined to get all seven of you sisters settled?" Bernie asked.

"The latter one," Ophelia answered.

"I owe your mama that much," Bernie said. "My sister

gave her my name, and then she gave you the same. Mary Bernadette." She poked a finger toward her heart. "Mary Jane," she said as she glanced in the side rearview mirror back at the Paradise, and then pointed across the console at Ophelia. "Mary Ophelia, so y'all are special to me. Plus, she has taken me in and lets me be a part of her family. I didn't know what I would do after I sold my bar, but your mama invited me to come on down to Spanish Fort and live with her. I thought about it a few days and decided I didn't want to be a burden." She stopped for a breath.

"You are not a burden," Ophelia argued.

"Thank you, darlin', but I was thinking about the day that all you girls came home and wanted your own rooms again, and besides I'm no spring chicken. Those stairs would have killed me when I got older. So, I bought my travel trailer and moved into the backyard."

Ophelia had heard the story before, just like so many more that Aunt Bernie told and retold. "I'm glad you're here, but now that Ursula is married, you *could* move into the house."

"Pepper likes his privacy, and so do I." Bernie dismissed the idea with a wave of her hand. "Mary Jane wants all you girls to settle down close enough to her that she can be a part of your lives. I know what it's like not to have family around me, and I like being here in among all y'all. Pepper and I plan to be here until we die."

"You've got..." Ophelia started.

Bernie waggled her finger at her niece and shot a dirty

look across the console. "I know I have other relatives. There's your grandmother, who is my sister, and my two other grandnieces, but Mary Jane has never been ashamed of me for running a bar, or for who I am. She loves me and all you girls unconditionally. That, darlin', is the difference between relatives and family."

"Why are you determined that Tertia and I are your next projects?" Ophelia asked.

"You will both be here. It's not so easy to work on Bo and Rae when one of them is in the Oklahoma Panhandle and the other one is in Nashville, but they'll both come home soon," Bernie answered. "First, I'll fix you and Tertia up, and then it will be Bo and Rae's turn. I have been communing with the Universe about them, and I know I'm getting through to it because Ursula is getting married this weekend in a little family ceremony, and Luna is having a big blowout the first Saturday in July. So, get ready for the ride, darlin', because you and Tertia are next."

Ophelia started to say something, then realized the turn to the winery was right in front of her. She braked hard enough to make Aunt Bernie use cuss words that could have cracked the front windshield. Gravel flew up around them, and the multitude of birds that had been sitting on the barbed-wire fence took to the sky in a blur. If Ophelia had been fluent in bird squawking, she was fairly sure that their swear words would have rivaled Aunt Bernie's.

"That sign should be bigger," she gasped.

Bernie laid a hand on her heart. "Girl, you about gave

me a heart attack. The deal I made with the Universe is that I would not die until I accomplish my mission for your mama. If you kill me before that time comes, then you're going to be in for a helluva lot of bad luck."

"Sorry about that." Ophelia said, "but you're going to be around forever if you think you're going to get all of us seven girls to come back to Spanish Fort."

"My petition is that you will all live in this county at the very least. I'm not asking for magic, just a little miracle or two," she said, "and I hope I do live for a few more years after this all comes to pass, so I can see Mary Jane's grandbabies at the Paradise. That way I can be in one of those generation pictures. When the baby is born, your grandma can come visit Spanish Fort. Her mother, my twin sister, the good one of the two of us, passed away before you were born, so I'll stand in for her."

Ophelia turned right at the sign pointing her back to the winery. "That's sweet, but I think I'll drag my feet in this relationship business just so you'll stay around for many more years. Maybe I'll even be the last one to get married and settle down."

"That's not playing fair," Bernie declared. "And besides you are thirty-one years old. Your biological clock has already started ticking." Bernie cocked her head to one side. "I do believe I can hear it clicking off the seconds."

"'All's fair in love and war,'" Ophelia reminded her as she parked in front of the winery.

Bernie shook her bony index finger across the console at

Ophelia for the second time that morning. "Yes, it is, and I don't lose in either one."

Ophelia motioned toward the building in front of them and changed the subject. "This is not what I expected."

"Seems like an omen to me," Bernie pointed at the sign in the window that says BRENNAN WINERY in a flourishing script with shamrocks and bunches of grapes circling around the lettering. "That looks downright romantic, doesn't it?"

"A sign doesn't mean anything," Ophelia argued.

"It does today," Bernie argued as she unfastened her seat belt, opened the door, and got out of the truck.

Another word that could be added to Bernie's long list was *spry*. The septuagenarian was halfway across the parking lot when Ophelia caught up with her. "We don't have to jog, Aunt Bernie," she said.

"I'm in a hurry to take a look inside, so either keep up or go wait in the truck…" She stopped and nodded toward a sign tacked up beside the door that said HELP WANTED in big bold letters, and under that in smaller type was: *Must apply in person. No online applications. Full-time work with benefits.*

Ophelia hustled to catch up to her aunt, but then Bernie stopped dead in her tracks and pointed to the sign.

"There's your answer to what you are going to do now that school is out," she said. "I just found you a job. You've been moanin' around about not wanting to go back to substitute teaching. Well, now you don't have to do that anymore. You can make wine. That sounds like a better deal to me, anyway."

"I don't know one thing about making wine," Ophelia declared.

Granted, she was so tired of running all over Montague County to work as a substitute teacher that she had actually considered reenlisting in the air force. Her captain had told her when she left last December that there would always be a place for her if she wanted to come back and fly drones or even teach a few classes in that area.

Bernie opened the door and marched inside. "You ain't dumb. You can learn."

Various kinds of wine filled small cubicles that covered one entire wall. A lovely brass tray with small bottles of wine sat on a round table in the middle of the room. Ophelia had visited more than a dozen wineries while stationed in California, and most of them were laid out just like this one. She wasn't a wine connoisseur by any means, but she did know the difference between a good red wine and a bad one. But if she was buying wine, she could pop into a convenience store and get a bottle of Boone's Farm Strawberry Hill for less than five bucks.

The bell above the door must have been hooked up to something in the back, because she and Bernie had only been inside a couple of minutes when a man entered the room from the back. His curly blond hair touched his shirt collar, and mossy-green eyes rimmed with thick lashes twinkled behind his round wire-rimmed glasses.

"Good mornin'." His deep Texas drawl was downright swoon-worthy. "I'm Jake Brennan, the owner of this little winery. What can I do for you lovely ladies?"

"I'm Bernie Marsh, and this is my niece, Ophelia Simmons. We're here to check on the reception hall for the Baxters on Saturday"—she paused and threw a glance over at Ophelia—"and to apply for the job you've got listed on the window."

"I'm proud to make your acquaintance, and I would love to talk to you about the job," Jake said.

"Do you let mean little Chihuahua dogs in your place of business?" Ophelia asked.

"I'm sorry, but no pets are allowed," Jake answered. "I've seen Remy's dogs and neither of them are Chihuahuas. Have they gotten another one and want to bring it to the reception? If that's the case, I can refund their deposit."

"I'm not talking about Remy and Ursula's dogs, but Aunt Bernie"—Ophelia glanced over at her aunt—"must be interested in the job you have posted on the window since she asked about it. However, she has a yappy little dog that barks at everything from the wind shaking leaves in a tree to crickets, and she would never leave Pepper alone all day."

Bernie narrowed her eyes and shot a dirty look toward Ophelia. "Pepper isn't mean or yappy. He's just little, and he has to take up for himself against those ornery cats at the Paradise. And besides, he wouldn't be coming to work with *you*."

"Well, I'm very sorry, Miz Bernie, but we have a strict rule about animals in a winery." Jake chuckled. "Do you have a pet that would keep you from applying for the job, Miz Ophelia?"

With his accent, Ophelia could have listened to Jake read *Moby Dick* without getting bored. She glanced across the counter and locked eyes with him. "I do not have an animal, but…" She hesitated. "I don't know anything about wine."

"Remy told me about Ursula's sisters. You are the one who spent a while in the air force and flew drones. Is that right?" Jake asked.

"It is," Bernie answered with a smug expression, "but since there's not much in this part of the world for her job skills, she's been substitute teaching all over the county since she came home last Christmas."

Jake tilted his head to one side and locked gazes with Ophelia. "Well, now, I expect if you can corral a bunch of kids, you wouldn't have any trouble at all waiting on customers. They'll probably flock in here just to see someone as beautiful as you are and, honey, if you can fly drones, you can learn the art of a cash register."

The heat of a scalding blush filled Ophelia's cheeks. This was the very last time she would go anywhere with her aunt, and she would warn Tertia of Bernie's plans as soon as they got back to the Paradise. "Thank you for the compliments," she muttered.

"She would be good at it," Bernie said, "and working here would be a perfect job for her."

Jake didn't take his eyes off Ophelia. "I can't believe that Remy hasn't introduced us. He mentioned that Ursula was one of seven sisters who grew up in the old brothel up the road from this place. Is that right?" Jake asked.

"Yes, it is," Ophelia answered.

"I've met Ursula," Jake said. "Do all the rest of the sisters have red hair?"

"Nope, just this one," Bernie answered.

"I'm standing right here." Ophelia's tone held an edge even in her own ears.

"Then open your mouth and talk to this handsome feller about the wonderful job he's offering you," Bernie scolded.

"Like I said, I don't know anything about making wine," Ophelia said.

"I've got three hired hands who help me with the wine making," Jake said. "What I need is someone to work up here in the front. Sell wine, host a few wine tastings a month, help with a small event when someone books the venue"—he nodded toward the room off to the left—"in that area where Remy and Ursula's reception will be held."

Bernie elbowed Ophelia.

"What are the hours?" Ophelia asked more to appease her aunt than to seriously think about the job.

"We are open Tuesday through Saturday from eleven to six. Closed on Sunday and Monday unless there is an event like a wedding. You will get an idea of what that entails tomorrow evening at your sister's party," he answered. "If you will consider the job, I'll remove the sign from the window. All you have to do is fill out some tax forms and show up Tuesday morning."

"Just like that"—Ophelia snapped her fingers—"you would hire me because I have red hair?"

"No, I would hire you because Remy has told me all about you and your sisters, and because anyone smart enough to fly drones would be an asset to my business," Jake answered. "And if you hadn't come around today to look at the reception room, I would have singled you out at the reception and talked to you about the job."

"Then why do you have a notice in the window?" Ophelia asked.

"I'll take applications, but..." he shrugged.

"But what?" Bernie pressured.

"The job is Ophelia's if she wants it," he answered.

Had the man fallen into one of his vats of wine? He knew nothing except what Remy had told him about her, and just because she could look at a computer screen and fly a drone did not mean she would be a good salesperson. Other than teaching a couple of basic drone-flying courses for the military, she had worked in a cubicle for years and only talked to one or two other people all night or all day, depending on her shift. She had no idea how she would even like working with people in a permanent job.

You grew up in a household with seven girls. You can be sociable, the niggling voice in her head scolded. *You need a job, or else you will be spending the whole summer listening to Luna fret about wedding plans or spending every waking hour with Bernie. Your choice, but don't whine if you make the wrong one.*

"I'll think about it," Ophelia finally said.

"Fair enough," Jake said as he headed over to open

double doors for them into a room that was already set up with tables. "This is the event room."

"How do you know Remy?" Bernie asked as she followed him.

"Met him when he came in last Christmas to buy some wine. He found out that I had some acreage next to his place." Jake stood to the side to let them enter first. "I just recently leased it to him so he can grow hay on it for his cattle. He invited me to attend the reception, but I will be working it since I don't have any help—yet," he said with a long sigh and a sly wink toward Ophelia. "I haven't had much of a social life since I opened the doors to the winery, so even though I'll be working, I'm looking forward to being there. Maybe you'll save the last dance for me?"

"If she don't, I will," Bernie said, "but I'm betting she'll say yes."

"Aunt Bernie!" Ophelia scolded.

Bernie poked her on the arm. "Then tell this sexy guy that you will dance with him."

"Okay, okay," Ophelia agreed. "I will save a dance for you."

Jake's smile lit up the room. "Thank you, ma'am. And just so you know, I'll take that help wanted sign down until next Tuesday."

"Why next Tuesday?" Bernie asked.

Jake followed behind her. "Ophelia needs time to mull my offer over. If she shows up Tuesday morning, or before, I'll show her the ropes. If she doesn't, I can put the sign back up. It's not a problem since we're closed on Sunday and Monday anyway."

"Thank you, sir," Bernie said.

"Not sir. Just plain old Jake," he said.

Ophelia's shoulder brushed against his as she passed by him. No way would she admit that she'd felt some vibes at his touch. If she did, Aunt Bernie would pile wedding books up outside Ophelia's bedroom door.

She touched her arm to see if it was as warm as it felt, but it was cool. "This is a lovely room."

"Thank you." Jake nodded. "The stage can be used for a live band or a DJ. Remy said that one of the sisters has a playlist ready for the evening and will be taking care of the music."

"Bo will be doing that," Bernie explained.

Jake stood just inside the door. "She's the one who's been in Nashville, right?"

"That's right." Ophelia's voice sounded slightly higher than normal, and goose bumps the size of the Wichita Mountains were still raised up on her arm. Remy must have been talking about the sisters a lot for Jake to know their names and what they did for a living.

"We have some generic centerpieces, if you want to use them," he went on. "Either yellow or red silk roses in bud vases."

"We'll be bringing our own, maybe this afternoon so that tomorrow won't be so rushed," Ophelia said, "but thanks for the offer."

"Well, I'm very pleased with this place," Bernie said, "and I'm glad Remy thought of it. The reception here will be great. I still think Mary Jane would have liked for her oldest daughter to have a big wedding, but Ursula did it the way *she* wanted and went to the courthouse a couple of weeks ago."

"Ursula would never steal Luna's thunder," Ophelia said.

"Ain't that the truth," Bernie agreed. "If she did, Luna would never forgive her, and heaven forbid that they would have a double wedding."

She shot a look over toward Ophelia and mouthed, "*Tick tock.*"

Ophelia ignored her. "Remy's mama, Vera, isn't comfortable in big crowds, so this is perfect."

"Y'all take your time. There's water bottles in the refrigerator through that door over there," Jake said as he started out of the room. "That bell is my cue to wait on a customer. Y'all look around all you want, and you are welcome to bring those centerpieces anytime today. The winery is open until five, but if you need to arrive later, I'll stick around after hours."

"Thank you," Ophelia called out as he hurried past her, and would be hanged if his arm didn't brush against hers again.

"You are very welcome." Jake threw over his shoulder.

"Well?" Bernie asked.

"What?" Ophelia answered.

"Are you at least going to think about the job?"

Ophelia wandered around the room, taking it all in. "I am, but not right now. This is Ursula and Remy's time to be in the spotlight, and I've got until Tuesday morning. I don't want to rush and make the wrong decision. This really is a lovely place for a reception, isn't it? The centerpieces we've made for the middle of the tables are going to look so pretty."

"And that stage is perfect for Ursula and Remy's first dance. I wonder what song they've chosen. What is going to be yours when you get married?" Bernie asked with a smug little smile on her wrinkled face.

"I'll play it for you on the way home," Ophelia answered.

"So, you have given it some thought?" Bernie asked.

"Maybe a smidgen. Are you ready to go?"

"Oh, yeah!" Bernie seemed to be so excited that she had a toe in the matrimony door that she almost skipped out of the room.

Jake waved at them from behind the counter as they slipped out into the bright sunlight. Aunt Bernie hummed all the way to the truck and did not say a word even after she had fastened her seat belt. Ophelia started the engine, backed the truck up, and headed down the dirt road.

"You are welcome, and now you can play your wedding song," Bernie finally said with a hint of a giggle.

"I'm welcome for what?" Ophelia asked.

"I overheard Remy telling Ursula about Jake needing help, so I asked Mary Jane to let us go look at the room today. I told you that I would help you find a man like Remy, and I just did, and honey, a stone-cold blind woman could see and feel the sparks that were hoppin' around between you two. They reminded me of Pepper when he wants a treat." Bernie giggled. "So, you are welcome that I helped you get a job, plus a new boyfriend. I'm getting good at this!"

"I only just met the man, and I damn sure don't believe in love at first sight. And like I said, you can't take credit for Ursula or for Luna," Ophelia argued.

"If I can't cuss, then you can't," Bernie snapped.

"I don't suppose you put a shot of Jameson in your morning coffee?" Ophelia fired right back.

"All right," Bernie crossed her arms over her chest and glared at Ophelia. "I won't tattle if you won't. Now play me the damn song. And for your information, Mary Ophelia, I gave Ursula a little push, and I shared my whiskey with Luna when she and Shane had their first big fight, so I do get to take credit for them." She stopped and sucked in a lungful of air. "So, put that in your pipe and smoke it. You ain't takin' my glory away from me."

"Push, nothing," Ophelia almost snorted, "you gave her a shove, but she and Remy just reignited a twenty-year-old crush, so it wasn't all your doing."

Bernie shook a finger across the console at Ophelia. "Don't argue with me. You'll see soon enough that I have relationship powers. Who do you think gave Remy and Ursula the matches to light that fire between them? And honey, I've got five more matches reserved for the rest of you girls, so stand back and watch me. I told you before, and I'll tell you again, and again, I know men. I ran the bar for decades, and I can spot a worthless SOB or a good man a mile away."

"Oh, really?" Ophelia raised an eyebrow. "So, Remy and Shane are good men."

"They're alive aren't they?" Bernie asked, "Any sumbitch—and cuss words said in this vehicle stays in this vehicle—who treats any of you sisters wrong will be dead men, because no one is ever going to hurt one of you again. That sorry sucker who caused Endora so much pain is lucky—for today anyway. I may still take care of him for what he did to her self-confidence. And since Martin is your biological father, I won't even say what I think of him, but he's lucky that he's not sitting on a barbed-wire fence in hell."

"Aunt Bernie!" Ophelia scolded.

"Don't you 'Aunt Bernie' me. I speak my mind whether folks like it or not," Bernie told her. "But for now, Martin and Kevin are safe because I have to take care of my precious little Pepper, but if he dies before I do, I don't mind spending the rest of my days in jail. You girls can all come to visit me there every Sunday and sneak bottles of whiskey in for me. That's saying that I get caught, which ain't damn likely. I know places up around Ratliff City where I can dump trash like Kevin and Krystal both for treating Endora the way they did." She leaned over the console and whispered, "*And* dead bodies, so that they won't ever be found, and it's really hard to prove murder without a body. Now play me that song."

Ophelia laid her phone to the side and pressed an icon to start her playlist. The guitar prelude started, and Bernie frowned. "You wouldn't dare play 'Smell Like Smoke'! That song talks about whiskey, and your mama would have a fit if..."

"If"—Ophelia butted in—"the words talk about getting drunk and sayin' that I'm not ashamed of where I come from—and that would be that I grew up in a former brothel. I may even come down the aisle to that song if you meddle in my romantic business."

She turned left into the pecan-tree-lined lane that led up to the Paradise.

"If you do, I will stand up on the front pew where I'll be sitting and dance to the song while you are strolling down the aisle," Bernie declared. "God knows it's more my song than yours anyway."

Ophelia was trying to think of a comeback for that when she parked her truck in front of the Paradise.

"You ain't got nothing else to say?" Bernie asked.

"Not about my wedding song, but..." Ophelia said, "if you want to exact a little vengeance upon Kevin for cheating with Krystal when he was engaged to Endora, I'll buy a drone and take care of him. We'll have an alibi that we were with family two hundred miles away from the scene. If you get caught, I'll break you out of jail and we'll hop a plane to some country that won't send us back."

"Well, crap!" Bernie said with a long sigh.

"What?" Ophelia asked.

"I can't let you do that since by then you'll be married and have a houseful of little kids that have pretty, mossy-green eyes. You'd have to leave them behind, and we could never come back. That would break Jake's heart as well as Mary Jane's heart," Bernie answered with a long sigh. "So, we'll just have to leave the vengeance to the Universe when it comes to Endora's old fiancé and her former best friend."

Chapter 2

OPHELIA TOOK A DEEP breath and enjoyed the fresh spring breeze filtering through the screened-in back porch. Texas still hung on to the last few pleasant days of spring before summer pushed it out and brought months of scalding heat. Her sister Luna had planned an outside wedding in July without remembering how blistering hot it always was during that time—even at sunset, which was when the marriage was to take place. Mary Jane had rented a huge air-conditioned tent for the reception so at least they wouldn't soak their pretty dresses with sweat before the evening was done.

Ophelia was thinking about how smart her older sister was to sneak off to the courthouse and just have a small reception at the winery, when she leaned her head back on the porch swing and dozed off. She dreamed that she was sitting on the sofa in her therapist's office. Folks often say that what happens in Las Vegas stays in Las Vegas. In the room where she managed drones, that would be an understatement. Telling anything that went on in that place could get a person thrown so far back into prison that sunshine would take days and days to even reach them. *Classified* meant that she didn't talk to anyone—except the military therapist—and that was mandatory. Her appointment was set for the first Monday of every month at eight o'clock in the morning.

"I can't do this anymore," she told the therapist. "I hate substitute teaching, and I've been offered a job in a winery."

The woman just smiled and nodded. "How does that make you feel?"

"Wake up." Tertia's voice penetrated the dream.

What was her sister doing in the therapist's office, and how much had she heard?

"Earth to Ophelia," Tertia singsonged. "If you don't wake up, I'm going to pour water on your head."

Ophelia opened her eyes slowly and then rubbed them with her knuckles. She hadn't been to a therapist since she came home, but she wondered if her dream wasn't telling her to find one close to Spanish Fort and make an appointment. "Where did you come from? You aren't supposed to be here until later."

Tertia sat down beside her on the porch swing. "You were mumbling in your sleep just like you used to do when we were kids."

"Welcome home." Ophelia straightened up and rolled her neck to get the kinks out, then gave her sister a sideways hug.

"I only just got here ten minutes ago," Tertia said. "I was so excited about coming home for good that I couldn't sleep, so I left Vega before daylight."

"Mama and Daddy are off buying groceries," Ophelia

said. "Luna and Endora are finishing up the last day of school. They'll be disappointed that they weren't here to give you the big huggy-huggy welcome home."

Tertia set the swing in motion with her foot, pulled her legs up, and wrapped her arms around her knees. "Aunt Bernie gave me the first hug, and Pepper barked at me, so I'm good. She said she will join us in the next few minutes. She had to take Pepper out to the trailer. You've been here since Christmas. Are you settled in yet?"

"Not really, but I'm workin' on it," Ophelia admitted. "Every now and then something will trigger a nightmare, but that doesn't happen very often anymore."

Tertia took a deep breath and let it out slowly. "I love the smell of home."

"Smells good now but wait until we spend a summer here. Remember how hot it gets, and how we say that we can actually smell the heat rising off the ground?"

Tertia tucked a strand of curly light-brown hair up into the messy bun on top of her head. "It won't be worse than the Texas Panhandle. And I don't have to think about going back to teaching in the fall. You can't imagine how free I feel."

"Oh, yes I can," Ophelia argued.

Bernie brought out three glasses of iced tea on a tray and set it on a table beside a nearby rocking chair. Once she had given one glass to each girl, she eased down into the white rocker, picked up Pepper, and set him in her lap. "Pepper whined when I started around the house, so I just brought him with me. I think he wanted to hear my news."

"And what's that, Aunt Bernie?" Tertia took a long drink of her tea.

"Ophelia has a job and a possible boyfriend, but don't worry, Tertia. Soon as I get her settled into a relationship, I'll go to work for you. We'll find a good man for her, won't we, Pepper?"

Tertia spewed tea out across the porch, sending it flying only a few feet from Aunt Bernie and Pepper. "What did you just say?" she sputtered.

"I do *not* have a job or a boyfriend!" Ophelia protested.

"And I do not *want* a boyfriend right now," Tertia declared. "I need to figure out what I'm going to do with my life before I even think about relationships. But it does sound like my sister is protesting too much, so tell me more, Aunt Bernie. Who is this man and what kind of job?"

Bernie glanced over at Ophelia. "His name is Jake Brennan, and he owns and operates the Brennan Winery, and he has a really sexy Texas brogue that goes with the way he fills out a pair of tight-fittin' jeans."

"He offered me a job that I do not know if I even want, and he is *not* a potential boyfriend, and you are right, I am protesting," Ophelia declared. "Next thing you know Miz Meddling Britches here will be picking out my wedding dress and ordering a wedding cake."

"What would Ophelia do in a winery?" Tertia took another long drink of her tea. "Does he use drones to fly over his grape arbors and scare off birds and grasshoppers?"

"No, but he needs someone to run the front office,"

Bernie answered. "She would sell wine and take appointments for events, and maybe even help with receptions or tastings if they're on a Saturday like the reception we're having tomorrow for Ursula and Remy."

"Sounds like a good job," Tertia rubbed her aqua-colored eyes and yawned. "If you don't take it, I might apply. I'm sick of teaching, and I really need this next year off to figure out what I really want to do. Just being a clerk might be the very thing to give me time to think about the future."

Ophelia narrowed her eyes at her sister. "If you want the job, then go for it."

Tertia shook her head. "On second thought, I promised myself a couple of months of doing nothing but helping with Luna's wedding plans. I need some time to sleep late and be lazy."

"And you are conspiring with Aunt Bernie to get me married off, aren't you?" Ophelia accused.

"Hey," Bernie protested. "I told you before, I'm on a mission, and I don't need any help. But since y'all mentioned the future, let me ask a question. What would either of you really like to do if you could do anything?" she asked. "What's on the top of your bucket list when it comes to jobs? Mine was always to own my very own bar, and I did that, so I scratched that off and celebrated with a bottle of Jameson the first day that Bernie's Place belonged to me. The top item on the list now is to get all seven of you girls settled so that Mary Jane and Joe Clay can enjoy their grandkids. I've got two down and y'all are the next ones that I'm going to help."

Ophelia shrugged. "Put me at the bottom of the list for that settling-down business. To answer your question, I know I don't want to do anything that's so classified and secretive that I have mandatory therapy sessions to be sure my job isn't depressing me. That said, I don't know what I want to do for the rest of my life."

"I love to cook, and I should have been a home economics teacher instead of a coach, but I got that softball scholarship, so..." Tertia shrugged and yawned again.

"But hindsight is the only perfect vision in the world," Bernie said.

"I know beyond any doubt that I do not want to teach," Ophelia said. "Subbing this past semester taught me that the classroom is not where I belong."

"Then why don't you try your hand at the wine place?" Tertia asked. "If you don't like it, you can always give two weeks' notice and find something else."

Ophelia glanced over at Aunt Bernie. Pepper was snuggled down in her tie-dyed skirt of pinks, blues, and purples with a splash of yellow scattered around. Several strands of Mardi Gras beads hung around her scrawny, wrinkled neck. Rings with different-colored stones decorated her fingers as well as her toes and her flip-flops were covered with fake diamonds.

"Are you admiring my jewelry?" Bernie asked. "I'll be glad to share any of it with you girls if you need it for a date."

"Thanks, but I was just thinking about how pretty you look today," Ophelia answered.

"Did you dress up because I was coming home?" Tertia asked.

"Yes, I did," Bernie answered. "I wore this every year in the bar when we celebrated Redneck Mardi Gras. I dragged it out special today to bring good luck to Tertia on her first day back home where she belongs, and to bring me good luck in my mission with you and Jake."

Tertia finished off her tea and stood up. "What is Redneck Mardi Gras?"

"Me and my regular customers couldn't go to New Orleans for Mardi Gras, but that didn't mean we couldn't celebrate. We played jazz music that night, and we drank hurricanes, and I even had some beignets in the bar to serve to all the folks who arrived to join in the fun for our Redneck Mardi Gras evening," Bernie answered.

Tertia took a step toward the door. "Thank you, Aunt Bernie, for dressing up for me today, but if you've got any good luck to spread my way, use it for a job, not a boyfriend."

Bernie twirled a set of purple beads and woke Pepper up. "I wore extra beads today so that I could do both." The dog growled, hopped down off her lap, and went to the back door.

"Don't you talk to me in that tone of voice, or you won't get your afternoon treats," Bernie scolded him.

"I'm going to unload my vehicle, get unpacked, and then take a twenty-minute power nap. But one more question, Aunt Bernie. What makes you think this Jake feller is the man for my sister?" Tertia asked.

"I'm an expert on men, and the way he looked at her said that it was more than her pretty red hair that had him interested," Bernie declared. "But hey, I don't mind introducing you to him if Ophelia isn't going to sit up and take notice of this opportunity. I'm thinkin' about going into the matchmaking business. I did pretty damn good with Ursula and Luna, and running a bar for all those years makes me an expert on which men would be good with what women."

Ophelia threw up her palms. "All right! All right! I'll talk to Jake some more about the job, but I'm not making any promises. You're right, Tertia. If I don't like working there, I can always quit and find another job or—heaven forbid—go back to doing sub work when school starts again."

"Yes!" Aunt Bernie did a fist pump. "Tertia, you can teach me that Zoom business so I can interview my clients. Maybe I'll even start up a wedding-planning business too. All y'all girls can help me get things started."

"We'll talk later about all that, Aunt Bernie. Thanks again for the good luck charms and for the tea," Tertia said.

"I'll come help you," Ophelia offered.

"I never turn down help," Tertia said.

"You're just running away from me because you know I'm right. I bet I'd make a dang good wedding planner and matchmaker," Bernie declared as she got up and headed for the back door to let Pepper outside. "I love walking in the fresh green grass in my bare feet. Reminds me of when me and my twin sister were kids. She has always been the good girl, and I have been the ornery one."

"I'm not running from you," Ophelia declared with a long sigh. "But I would like to know why you are so excited about me working in a winery, and why didn't you get all dolled up when I left the air force at Christmas?"

"You and Tertia have both sown your wild oats, and now it's time for y'all to settle down and…"

Tertia whipped around to face Bernie. "There are no *ands*, and I haven't sown wild oats anywhere. Plus, I need to find myself before…"

"Yeah, yeah, yeah," Bernie butted in. "I've heard all that before. Y'all both need to wake up and listen to your biological clocks. Look at what happened to me when I didn't pay attention," she scolded. "All of Luna's brides' magazines are stacked up on the coffee table in the living room. At least go flip through them and see if you can't get bit by the wedding bug."

"Never!" Tertia declared. "You can burn those magazines as soon as Luna and Shane's wedding is over. That is"—she winked at Ophelia—"unless *you want* to look at them. I'm doing fine without them."

"If you want help unpacking, you might consider choosing your words carefully the rest of this morning," Ophelia said in an icy tone.

Tertia turned to face her and just smiled in that annoying way she had always done when they were all just kids—that all-knowing, aggravating expression that reminded all of her sisters that she was the smartest one of the seven—which was just a figment of her own imagination. Everyone knew that Ophelia was the most intelligent daughter in the family.

"Oh, hush." Ophelia had meant what she had said. She might work for Jake Brennan, but there was no way she was letting Aunt Bernie run her life, or even take credit for anything romantic that might come along—or encourage her in this new notion about matchmaking and wedding planning either. When Ophelia found someone to fall into a committed relationship with, it would be of her own choosing, and she did not intend to tell any of the family about it until she was sure. Endora's experience had taught her to tread lightly in that area.

"It's just a job," Tertia said as she led the way through the house and out the front door.

"I know, and it seems like a good deal, but..." Ophelia answered.

"But you don't want Aunt Bernie to be right any more than I do," Tertia whispered.

"Probably," Ophelia admitted. "I'll talk to him a little more this morning. Mama wants me to take the centerpieces over there to put on the tables for the reception tomorrow. But first, let's get you unloaded and your things put away. What did you do with all your stuff from the apartment?"

"Boxed it up and sent it this way by a mover. It'll be here the first of the week. Daddy said there was room in the storage barn for my things, but to mark them because your stuff is out there too." Tertia opened both back doors and the hatch of her red SUV. "What time is the reception for Ursula and Remy?"

"One o'clock," Ophelia answered. "Can you believe that

they eloped? I figured Mama would be furious, but she just took it in stride."

Tertia picked up two suitcases and rolled them over the gravel parking lot toward the porch. "Ursula would have been a bridezilla, so I'm glad that she and Remy didn't try to have a huge wedding so soon after Luna's."

"You got that right," Ophelia agreed.

"Hey, Aunt Bernie means well, but don't let her goad you into doing anything that don't feel right," Tertia said when the two sisters were inside and started upstairs. "I sure don't intend to let her run my life. What we do with our relationships is our business, but my advice—which you can take or throw in the trash—is that you should at least consider the winery job. You don't like teaching, and there's not a lot going on in this little town."

"Thanks, Sister," Ophelia answered.

Ophelia rolled the truck windows down and sucked in a lungful of fresh spring air that blew through the cab. Tomorrow was the reception, and then Mother's Day—this year on May twelfth—and then if things were normal, it would start to get hotter and hotter.

Back when she had worked night shifts, which was more than half the time, she had slept during the day, and worked at night. She was at work before sunset, and at home asleep before sunrise most of the time. Until she came back to Spanish Fort, she had not even realized how much she had missed the simple things like watching all the colors of a Texas sunset or taking a walk in the brisk morning air.

She started her playlist and kept time with her thumbs on the steering wheel as Blake Shelton sang "Goodbye Time." That had been playing when she left California in her rearview mirror and began the long drive home to Texas. Even though it was a song about a woman leaving a man who loved her, and not a job that still gave her the occasional nightmare, the lyrics seemed appropriate for Ophelia's situation—especially the title.

She had turned onto the dirt road leading back to the winery when Kane Brown's song "What Ifs" began to play. The words talked about what if he was made for her, but like she had done with Shelton's song, she thought about the job she had been offered. What if she did not take it, and the love of her life walked into the shop to buy wine? Or what if she was helping clean up after a wedding reception and *the one* was sitting at a table all alone? Or what if Aunt Bernie was right, and those vibes she felt when Jake was nearby turned into something permanent?

"The chemistry I felt wasn't anything but the moment. Jake could very well be married or engaged," she muttered, pulled off to the side of the road, and turned off the engine. When she had been trying to decide whether to reenlist or not, Gina, her therapist, had told her to close her eyes and imagine how she would feel if she stayed in the service another eight years. After examining her feelings for a few minutes, she was supposed to remember what she had thought about, open her eyes, and then close them again and think about how she would feel if she went back to Texas to live.

Texas won that day.

She tried to use the same method to decide whether she wanted to take the job or to put in applications in Nocona or Saint Jo for summer work. She tried to think about how it would feel to work with someone like Jake, who made her more than a little breathless just thinking about his eyes and those muscles that strained the sleeves of his knit shirt emblazed with the Brennan Winery logo right above his heart.

His heart!

Was he a player? What did his past relationships look like? Joe Clay said that he was a good man, but maybe Jake had only shown his good side to the people around Spanish Fort.

Everyone has a good side and a bad one, according to Gina. No one is totally good or all evil. Ophelia tried to believe her when she pressed the button to send a drone payload on a target, but it seldom worked.

"Do I need a therapist again?" she whispered.

She had asked her mother that question when she had had the first nightmare after coming home, and Mary Jane had told her that she just needed time.

Her eyes opened wide, and everything was a blur until they adjusted to the bright sunlight. "It's just a job. He only asked for a dance to entice me to work for him. He's charming, but he was not necessarily flirting," she whispered as she started the engine. She drove the rest of the way to the winery and parked in the same place she had the day before. Before she could get her seat belt unfastened, her truck door swung open. Jake stood there with one of his signature brilliant smiles and motioned for her to get out.

"This is great timing. I was just coming out for a breath of fresh air," he said. "I'll help you get all these boxes into the reception room."

Her heart skipped a beat and then plowed ahead with full steam. Could she really work for a boss that affected her like that?

"Thanks," she muttered and slid out of the seat. "I never turn down help."

"Smart lady." He stacked a box on top of another and headed out across the yard.

Ophelia thought about trying to take two at once but nixed that idea when a visual popped into her head of stumbling on the porch steps and breaking what was inside. Mary Jane would never let her live it down if she broke all those wineglasses.

"What's in the boxes?" Jake asked.

"Stemmed wineglasses," she answered.

"You didn't need to bring your own," Jake said. "The catering service Mary Jane is using provides all that kind of thing."

"These are for the centerpieces." She carried the single box in her hands into the reception room. She set it down on the first table she came to and removed the lid. Mary Jane had shown her exactly how to place everything in the middle of each of the ten tables, so she got busy—three wineglasses with different stem heights turned upside down on the round mirror. A daisy under each glass, and a flameless candle set on the flat part of the wineglass.

"This looks so much like Ursula," she muttered.

"What was that?" Jake asked as he brought in the last box. "That looks really elegant. I'd like to take pictures to go in the book that I show folks, if you don't mind."

"I don't mind at all," she answered, "and I was just saying that this looks so much like Ursula."

"I don't know her so well, but I was thinking about a Saint Patrick's Day wedding that's on the books for next year. We could use the same idea, only put shamrocks under glasses and use green candles. Would you like for me to flip the switches on the candles about half an hour before the reception starts?"

Ophelia moved over to the second table. "That would be great."

He opened a box and followed her example of how to arrange the centerpiece on another table. "Do you need a long table set up for the bride and groom and their parents?"

"No, they just want to mix and mingle among the family and friends," Ophelia answered.

"What about the table for the cake?" Jake asked.

"A round one will do fine. We'll have cake and punch on it. Mini peach cobblers have been ordered instead of a groom's cake." She talked as she worked. "A simple luncheon of chicken Parmesan, breadsticks, and salads will be served. Then we'll have wedding cake, cobbler, and an assortment of bite-sized cheesecakes for dessert."

"That doesn't sound so simple to me," Jake said.

"What would you consider to be simple?" Ophelia asked.

"Finger sandwiches and chips and dips. A keg of beer and cookies," Jake replied.

"So, when you get married, will you have that?" Ophelia asked.

"Depends on what the bride wants. The wedding is her bailiwick. Keeping her happy and feeling cherished the rest of her life is my job," Jake said.

"That sounds pretty romantic for a guy," Ophelia said.

"Just speakin' the truth, ma'am," Jake told her.

Ophelia finished the centerpiece she was working on and moved to the next table. "You must have had some good parents to teach you that."

"I *have got* good parents. They've been together for up close to fifty years now and are still ranching," Jake answered. "I have two older sisters who live close to them, and I get plenty of sass from them not living within ten miles of where I was raised like they are."

"How *did* you wind up here?" she asked.

"Cheap land that would raise good grapes," he answered. "What brought you back to this area?"

"Family and good memories." She smiled at how easily that answer slipped off her tongue. "Before I forget"—she pulled a note from her hip pocket—"Mama said to remind you that the cake lady will be here at noon tomorrow and to ask if we need to be here."

"I will be glad to take care of that for you," he replied as he finished the last centerpiece. "You've been home since Christmas, right? I can't believe I haven't met you before now."

"Yes, and you've been here how long?" She pulled out a chair and sat down. Her sisters and Aunt Bernie wouldn't know how long the decorating job would take, and she was in no hurry to get home and answer all their questions.

He took a seat at the next table over from her. "Four years, but I'm just now to the point where I can sit down and relax for five minutes without feeling guilty. The first year, I was so busy with planting and building this place that I lay awake at night worrying about what all needed to be done. Then we got the grape arbors up, and there was some praying for a good crop. I made wine from strawberries, blackberries, and even watermelon during that time, but my main purpose was to develop a good red wine. This is the first year I've managed to produce one, and it's a small batch. I saved the first bottle for a special occasion on down the road."

"Such as?" Ophelia asked.

"Maybe for my wedding night, or when my first child is born," he answered. "What would you consider something extra special?"

"Probably the same thing," she told him. "So, you're not married or have children?"

"Not yet," he answered. "I was in love once, but I dragged my feet too long. Sally Jo and Tommy and I all grew up together down there close to the Louisiana border, on the same street. I loved Sally Jo from the time I was in the fifth grade, but I was afraid to speak my mind. Then she and Tommy fell in love when we were in high school. I was the best man at their wedding ten years ago. They have three little blond-haired daughters now, and I've learned to speak up rather than being shy."

"Regrets?" Ophelia asked.

"I got over it." He chuckled. "Fifth-grade relationships don't always last anyway. And my friends are happy, so I can't begrudge them that."

"I think I'll take that job you offered me," she blurted out.

"What made you decide right now?"

"It feels like the right thing to do," she replied.

He stood up, took a couple of steps, and held out a hand. "Shall we shake on it?"

He held her hand just a second longer before letting go. "Thank you, Ophelia. I'll tear up that help wanted sign."

"Thank you for giving me time to think about it," she said. "I should be getting back to the Paradise." Her voice sounded a bit breathless in her own ears.

The bell rang, letting them know that someone had arrived. "Want to stay long enough to wait on one customer and learn the ropes a little bit?" Jake asked.

"I'll be glad to," she answered.

He led the way back into the shop. "Hello, Miz Dolly. What can I get you today?"

"I need a nice bottle of wine to put in a basket," she answered and then smiled at Ophelia. "Oh, hello. I'm glad to run into you here today. Can you tell me what kind of wine Ursula and Remy like? I'm making them a basket of wine and cheeses to give them for a wedding gift."

"I'm sure they'll like anything you pick out," Ophelia answered. "Would you like to taste what Jake has out on the table today?"

"Oh no, honey." Dolly shook her head. "I'm a Jack Daniel's girl when I drink, but I give bottles from our local winery as gifts all the time."

"You and Aunt Bernie would get along very well," Ophelia said.

"Yes, we do," Dolly said. "I go to her trailer on Monday nights for a game of poker and a little nip of Jack or Jameson. There's four of us golden girls—that's what we call ourselves because we are all over seventy, and we love that old show. We have such a good time. If we weren't so old, we'd turn the old store building into a bar. That would sure enough bring folks back to Spanish Fort."

"It just might," Ophelia said. "I wish someone would do something with that old building."

"Call me if you need me, and holler before you leave," Jake said and left her alone with Dolly.

"So, you're working here?" Dolly asked.

"I guess I am," Ophelia answered, and it felt right.

Chapter 3

OPHELIA LAUGHED AT A bunch of kittens tumbling around in the yard. The grass was that lovely shade of green that only comes with spring in Texas, and all the kittens were variations of black and white even though their mother was a big gray tabby. She glanced over at Jake and was surprised to see crow's-feet wrinkles around his eyes and gray sprinkled through his blond hair.

"Wake up, wake up. You are giggling in your sleep. Are you dreaming?" Tertia's voice interrupted her sweet dream. "Seems like I had to wake you up when I first got home the other day. This is getting to be a habit."

"I don't want to wake up," Ophelia muttered and refused to open her eyes.

Tertia threw the covers off her sister. "It don't matter what you are dreaming about this morning. You've got to get up and help us with the final reception plans."

Ophelia opened her eyes and in a flash realized that she had been fantasizing about a man she hardly knew. But sitting beside him on the porch and seeing the two of them years into the future had made her feel all warm and cozy. She wondered what her military therapist would say about that. She would probably ask her how the dream made her feel.

She rubbed sleep from her eyes and silently answered the question. The dream made her giggle, not wake up in tears and drenched with cold sweat, like it did when she was ordered to push a button that would obliterate a building that had human beings in it. Whether those people had horns like the devil or halos like angels, they were someone's sons and daughters.

"Today is all about Ursula," Tertia was saying. "Mama made cinnamon rolls for breakfast, and everyone is just grabbing and going. Ursula is so nervous that she's queasy."

"The rock that we once knew as Ursula Simmons, and now as Ursula Baxter, is jittery?" Ophelia covered a yawn with her hand. "That's hard to believe."

"I know!" Tertia replied. "Who would have ever thought that *she* would let a simple reception get to her like this? Luna, who worried herself sick about upsetting Endora with her relationship with Shane, is plowing through like a trouper, making all kinds of decisions about flowers and cakes and all that for her wedding. Ursula, who never lets anything shake her, not even quitting her job and moving home, is nervous about going to a reception that won't be all that different than our Paradise Christmas party is every year. Doesn't make a bit of sense." Tertia stopped talking long enough to take a breath and then clapped her hands loudly. "Stop woolgathering and get out of bed!"

Ophelia was on her feet so fast that it made her dizzy.

"Good Lord! Why did you do that? I'm barely awake, and besides I'm still adjusting to not working at night."

"You've had six months to get used to that," Tertia said, "and you've had several minutes to wake up from whatever dream you were having. The way you were smiling tells me that there was a guy involved."

"Bite your tongue," Ophelia growled and headed out of her bedroom. There was no way she would ever admit that Jake Brennan was in her dream, or that she had felt so happy while she was wrapped up in a make-believe world.

"Stand still," Tertia scolded Ursula. "I can't get the curls in your hair if you're wiggling around like Endora's cats when they are playing hide-and-seek."

"What are you worried about anyway?" Ophelia asked. "It's just a reception, and then y'all can come home. Tomorrow we'll have Mother's Day dinner after church like we always do, and life can go on."

"I'm not worried," Ursula declared to all of her sisters who were crowded in her old bedroom. "I love Remy. I always have—from the first time I saw him when we were just kids. I'm just hoping this isn't too much for his mother. Vera doesn't do well in big crowds, and I don't want her to be overwhelmed."

Ophelia fastened all the buttons up her own sundress printed with daisies on a green background. "Vera will be just fine. Maybe a glass of wine would settle your nerves?"

Ursula shook her head. "No, thank you. My stomach wouldn't handle that so well, but I might have a glass of sweet tea."

"I'll go downstairs and get one for you," Tertia said. "Either of y'all want something while I'm making the trip?"

"Nope," Endora and Ophelia chimed in from across the room.

"Nope, what?" Aunt Bernie asked as she entered the room. "Remy is downstairs looking like sex on a stick in his boots and creased jeans. Girl, you better be glad I'm not thirty years younger or I'd take that man away from you." She stopped and stared at Ursula. "You look beautiful, darlin', and Tertia did a lovely job on your makeup. But she needs to touch it up, because you look green around the mouth."

"She's worried about Vera," Ophelia said.

Bernie drew her eyes down and tilted her chin up. "Vera is fine. She's not nervous at all and is looking forward to seeing some of the folks she worked with all those years. She looks lovely in her yellow dress, which is almost the same color as mine." She turned around slowly to show off her attire. "Mama always said that this was my best color, but I've got to admit, I like red or hot pink better. I'm still mad at you for not letting us at the very least go to the courthouse with you and Remy, but what's done is done. We get to have a party today, so that makes up for it a little bit. I forgot to tell the Universe that I wanted to attend your wedding. I made sure to take care of that with Luna's event."

Ursula stared at her reflection in the mirror. "Thank you,

but I have had second thoughts about even having a reception. Mother's Day with both our families could have been the reception."

"The bride should have what she wants for a wedding. The groom's job is to love and cherish her." Ophelia repeated Jake's words. "But the party is in full swing now, so you've got to go, and Vera will be fine with Remy there."

"Remy makes everyone feel at ease," Bernie said. "I did good when I picked him out for you."

"I believe I did the picking," Ursula said, "but thank you all the same. And thank all of you for all the support today." Ursula smoothed the front of her white eyelet lace dress, designed with a portrait collar and short sleeves. It fit her tall, slim body like a glove and stopped at the tops of white lace-up cowboy boots.

Vera poked her head into the room, and then came on inside. "You are so beautiful," she said as she crossed the room and gave Ursula a hug. "I've always wanted a daughter, and I'm so lucky to finally have one."

"You should have come over and let me know that years ago," Mary Jane said as she entered the room. "I have seven and would have been glad to throw a couple over the fence to you."

"I would have taken all seven, but in those days, I was too withdrawn to even make friends with you," Vera told her. "But I'm better now that Alan is in my life."

There was no doubt that Vera was Remy's mother. They shared the same color eyes, dark hair, and slim faces. She was tall and slender and had a brilliant smile that lit up the room just like Remy's did.

Tertia came in with a glass of tea in her hands and handed it to Ursula. "Sorry it took so long. Remy says it's about time for us all to head toward the winery."

"He will be totally speechless when he sees Ursula," Vera said, "but I guess we do need to get on out to the vehicles. We don't want to keep the guests waiting too long."

Mary Jane looped her arm into Vera's. "We are so lucky to have Remy in our family, but not only him—you and Alan as well."

"Same here," Vera smiled. "I'm not bringing as much family to the mix as you are, but I'm grateful for all of you. Now, we have a lovely day for the reception, and it wouldn't matter if it snowed or rained or if we had to deal with a tornado, I'm grateful to be able to have Mother's Day tomorrow with the family. I couldn't ask for any more than that for this wonderful weekend."

Ophelia wondered if Ursula was sad that their own biological father had opted out of even coming to the reception. He and his wife were in Aruba at her summer house until after July fourth. Ophelia hoped that when and if she decided to get married, he would be off on a trip, because Joe Clay would be the father who walked her down the aisle or up the steps to the courthouse. She hung back while everyone filed out of the bedroom and wrapped her arms around Ursula. "I love you, Sister."

"Love you, too," Ursula said.

Bernie put her hand on Ophelia's back and gave her a gentle push. "You've got to get out of here, or you'll make your sister cry. You don't want to have Tertia mad at you for messing up her makeup job even if it does make you look a little sallow. We need to follow everyone else out to the cars."

When Ophelia saw the way Remy looked at Ursula as she came down the stairs, her mind went back to the dream that Tertia had so rudely awakened her from that morning. If—and that was a gigantic if—she and Jake were to ever get together, who would be his best man? And which sister would she choose to be her maid of honor or matron of honor? Luna hadn't been able to decide on a maid of honor, so all six of her sisters would be bridesmaids. When Aunt Bernie pouted, Luna gave her the important job of sitting at the reception table to welcome the guests.

Remy took Ursula's hand in his when she reached the foyer. "Everyone, please gather around. We've got an announcement to make before we leave for the reception. We want to…" He looked over at Ursula. "You want to tell them or should I?"

"Go ahead," she whispered.

Tell them what, Ophelia wondered and then she remembered how her sister had claimed nerves caused her nausea. Ophelia's breath hung in her chest so long that it began to ache, and when she drew in more air, it sounded like a gasp.

"Thank you all for being here, but before we start getting hugs and go to the reception, we want you all to know that we have a special bottle of nonalcoholic red wine that Jake has prepared for Ursula and me. Ursula won't be using anything with alcohol for a while," Remy said.

"Why?" Endora asked.

"Because I'm pregnant," Ursula answered. "Our baby will be a Christmas present."

"Oh! My!" Mary Jane gasped and hurried over to wrap both Remy and her daughter in a three-way hug. "This is wonderful news."

Tears ran down Vera's face. "A daughter and a new baby! Alan, we *will* have to come back to see the new grandbaby next Christmas."

"Yes, we will, darlin'," Alan said with a wide grin. "We might even buy that little house down by Shane and Luna's place. That way we could spend part of the year here in Texas and the rest in Wyoming."

"And Vera can help me with my new matchmaking and wedding planning business," Bernie said.

"What?" Vera asked.

Bernie patted her on the shoulder. "That's a later conversation. Today is all about Ursula, Remy, and the new baby."

"I'm jealous," Ophelia whispered when she finally broke through the family enough to get in her hugs. "But it seems only right for you to have the first grandbaby since you are the oldest."

"You could have the second one if you would get on the ball." Ursula beamed.

"Luna will beat me to that, and she'll probably have

twins and make hers the second and third both," Ophelia said with a sigh.

"Or maybe we'll have twins and she'll have to just settle for third," Remy teased.

"That's something to unload on us right before we have to leave. We'd like to all stay right here and talk about a new baby coming into our family all afternoon," Joe Clay said, "but I can't complain. I've waited a long time to be a grandpa, and we can talk more about it when we get home from the party."

"Yes, we can, but we should be going. The early-bird guests are probably already at the reception," Remy said as he ushered Ursula out to his truck.

"Shotgun!" Tertia called out as she made a beeline for Ophelia's truck.

"You always do that," Endora grumbled.

"I'm just faster than you are," Tertia joked as she got inside and fastened the seat belt. "You've got to learn to think ahead."

Ophelia had already put the truck in reverse and had started to back up when Bernie came out on the porch, waving and yelling. Ophelia braked and rolled the window down. "Is something wrong?"

Bernie hurried down the porch steps and ran out across the yard. "I had to put Pepper out in the trailer, and everyone else has left. I don't want to drive myself, so…"

Tertia undid her seat belt and held the door open for Bernie, then got into the back seat beside Endora. Ophelia looked up in the rearview in time to see Endora do a little head wiggle and point at Tertia, who promptly stuck her out tongue at her younger sister.

Bernie settled into the seat and then nodded at Ophelia. "Let's get this wagon train headed south."

"Yes, ma'am," Ophelia said. "Can y'all believe that we're all going to be aunts when Ursula and Remy's baby gets here? A Christmas baby is so exciting."

"I'm going to be a great-great-aunt," Bernie bragged. "This is the best day ever. It's even better than the day that Bubba Thomas proposed to me, and I turned him down."

"Aunt Bernie!" Endora gasped. "Why did you do that?"

"Because he was a two-timin' sumbitch, just like your Kevin. Sorry sucker slept with my cousin. She got drunk and told me that he wasn't all that good in bed anyway," Bernie answered. "Was your Kevin at least good in bed?"

"Aunt Bernie!" Endora's tone went all high and screechy like Poppy did the time that Aunt Bernie accidentally rocked on her tail.

"You don't have to answer that or ever get married, darlin'. Sleep with 'em and tell them to leave before breakfast…" She giggled and then paused. "Unless they're the ones cookin' for *you*. Then keep them around until you finish eating."

Ophelia wondered if Jake knew how to make something other than canned soup or bologna sandwiches.

"I'd like to formally announce the newlyweds as Mr. and Mrs. Remington Baxter of Spanish Fort, Texas. Let's give

them a big round of applause," Jake announced when the
wedding couple entered the reception hall.

Ophelia clapped with everyone else, but she couldn't
keep her eyes off Jake. His dark-red shirt with the Brennan
Winery logo fit him snugly. His jeans hugged his body, and
his cowboy boots were polished and shiny. Everything about
him was so very different from her last boyfriend, who was
a banker and wore suits and loafers—and who never offered
to cook breakfast for her, not even once. That man looked
more like someone who made wine, and Jake looked like he
ought to be rounding up cattle or hauling hay.

Bernie nudged her on the shoulder. "He is definitely one
good-lookin' guy, and it's not hard to imagine him all tangled up in sheets. If Bubba Thomas had looked that good, I
might have forgiven him and married him just to get at his
body every night."

"Who are you talkin' about?" Ophelia asked.

"You know who," Bernie said. "Do you think you're the
only single woman eyeballing him? I'd be willing to bet that
he will have at least a dozen phone numbers tucked into the
pocket of them tight-fittin' jeans before everyone clears out
of here. If only"—she sighed loudly—"I was young enough,
I wouldn't put my number in his pocket. I would take them
jeans off real slow-like and…"

"Aunt Bernie!" Ophelia blushed.

Bernie shook her finger at Ophelia. "Don't you go fussin'
at me like Endora's been doing all day. Ain't a one of us women
in the family still a virgin. Sex is natural and it's a helluva lot

of fun, and you can't tell me you ain't been thinkin' the same thing about Jake. That scarlet color fillin' your cheeks is a dead giveaway. I was right about there being a new baby in the family by Christmas, and I'm predicting—again—that we'll have at least one more serious relationship by that time. I'm actually shootin' for two, but I'll be satisfied with one at a time, and"—she shook her finger at Ophelia again—"you can run from it, but your heart knows better. You know, I might start up one of them advice columns too."

Ophelia grabbed her aunt's finger. "Duroc pigs and Angus bulls will sprout wings and fly before I get married in only six months or even have a serious relationship. You better meddle in Tertia's love life if you want Santa Claus to bring another wedding to the Paradise, or get busy on that matchmaking business you've been talking about. I'm not going to be the cause of Mama having a heart attack from overworking. She needs a couple of years to get over this and Luna's event."

Bernie pulled her finger free, laughed out loud, and slapped her leg. "Your mama is strong and would dance a jig in a pig trough to have you girls all settled down. But what you said about pigs and cows is funny. Looks like Tertia ain't the only one in the family with a sense of humor. I can picture pigs and cows flying around in the sky above the Paradise. I'll have to get my shotgun out for sure and do some target practice if they light on the roof."

"Daddy would probably barbecue them if that happened," Ophelia said.

"He makes a mean barbecue sauce, so I wouldn't mind chowing down on some spareribs or brisket. Maybe we'll do that for your and Jake's wedding. Think maybe you could lasso him, just so I can see farm animals take to the sky?" Bernie teased and then pointed across the room. "They're fixin' to cut the cake and do the toast, and then the preacher will grace the food and we can all eat. I'm starving. How about you?"

"Yes," Ophelia nodded, but her mind was not on food. She stole another sideways glance across the room in time to see Jake pour wine from a bottle with a lovely label that had *Remy & Ursula* written in scroll on it.

The reception was lovely. The turnout was awesome. The news about the new baby was priceless.

Chapter 4

"You girls need to remember that not having a honey-moon is the price you'll have to pay for not having a proper wedding. I've always wanted to be a maid of honor for one of you girls. I could throw a really good bachelorette party, and yes, I'm hinting. Since Luna didn't want to hurt anyone's feelings and there's no official maid of honor, I will take the responsibility of planning a bachelorette party." Bernie said in between blowing bubbles on the bride and groom as they drove away in Remy's pickup truck.

Ophelia shivered at the thought of a party Bernie would throw and decided that when and if she got married, she and her fellow would go to Las Vegas and have an Elvis imper-sonator do the honors in a drive-thru chapel. "Tomorrow is Mother's Day, and they want to be there for Vera and Mama," she said, trying to steer the conversation in another direction.

It did not work.

"Someday when they are as old as I am, they'll wish they'd gone to an island with lots of pretty water and a sandy beach to make some wonderful memories," Bernie said with a long sigh. "Maybe go skinny-dippin' in the water with the fishes and make wild passionate love in the sand under a full moon."

"That's a pretty picture," Tertia said. "But Ursula wanted to be married and start a family more than she wanted a big wedding and a honeymoon."

"All right, all right!" Bernie said with a second sigh. "I suppose a baby coming along in a few months will make up for it."

"Yes, it will," Mary Jane said and turned to face Ophelia. "Would you stay behind and box up all the centerpieces?"

"Sure," Ophelia agreed. "Should I unload them in the barn with all the Christmas stuff?"

"That would be great," Mary Jane said. "One down, one to go."

Bernie raised an eyebrow and finally smiled. "Maybe three to go."

"Bring 'em on," Mary Jane said with a nod. "I just need a day or two to rest in between the ceremonies. Who's next after that, Aunt Bernie?"

Ophelia threw up both palms. "Not me."

"Or me," Bo said as she passed by on her way to her vehicle. "I'm close to being ready to throw in the country-music towel and come home, but I'll need time to adjust before I even think about settling down."

Tertia joined them and swatted a few bubbles that still floated in the air. "Or me! When, and if, I find someone, I'll tell y'all that I'm married the day after I drag my fiancée to the courthouse, and I don't even want a reception. All of this"—she waved her hand around to take in everything—"is not for me."

"Never say never." Bernie chuckled.

Tertia shook her head. "I might not say never, but I will say that I've got too much to do to even think about a boyfriend for a long time. I won't even realize that I've quit teaching until it's time to go back to classes in the fall. That's when I might get serious about looking for a job."

Ophelia nodded in agreement. "And we've got to concentrate on Luna's wedding, not on all the rest of us."

Joe Clay slipped his arm around Mary Jane's shoulders and pulled her close to his side. "Are you ready to go home, darlin'? I was thinking that we *could* go out for Mother's Day dinner tomorrow. This has been a big day for all of us."

"No, sir!" Tertia argued.

"We always make dinner for Mama on Mother's Day," Ophelia protested. "Back when we first moved to the Paradise, we made grilled cheese sandwiches and served them with potato chips."

"And ice cream and cookies for dessert," Tertia added.

Mary Jane looped her arm into Joe Clay's. "I've always loved seeing what you girls come up with for my special day. Speaking of food, please bring home all the leftovers from this party, and we'll have them for supper tonight."

"Will do." Ophelia sat down on the top step of the porch. Her truck was left sitting all alone when the dust from the gravel parking lot had settled. A sensation that she couldn't put into words told her that Jake had come out of the building long before he sat down beside her. "We were so busy at the reception that we never got our dance, but I believe you owe me one."

"Bo has left so we don't have any music," Ophelia reminded him.

He pulled his phone from his hip pocket, laid it on the porch, and stood up with an outstretched hand toward her. "I've always got music."

She put her hand in his and let him help her up. "I hope it's a slow one, because I'm too tired for anything fast, and I'm barefoot."

"Oh, darlin' lady," Jake whispered. "A dance with a lady as beautiful as you should always be slow. And I promise I'll keep you on the little stretch of soft grass I've babied to keep growing here around the porch."

His warm breath against her neck and his Texas brogue mixed together sent all kinds of heat waves through her body. He slipped his arms around her waist and pulled her closer to his body, and she caught a whiff of his cologne— something woodsy with a hint of vanilla.

The moment the guitar music started, Ophelia recognized the song "When I See You," by Aaron Watson. She had listened to it over and over again when it first hit all the country music charts. Someday, some guy would tell her that when he first looked at her, he could see everything he ever wanted, just like the lyrics said.

"Why did you choose this song?" she asked.

"I didn't really choose it for this dance," he answered.

"It's the first one on my playlist because I like it so much. The words remind me that there's a lady out there waiting for me, and when she finds me, everything will be all right. That, by the way, is the second song on my playlist."

She leaned back and looked up at him. "What is?"

"'Everything's Gonna Be Alright,' by Kenny Chesney," he answered.

"Oh," she said with a grin and then laid her cheek back against his cheek. "Do you believe that?"

"I do," Jake answered, "with all my heart and soul. How about you?"

"I believe that everything happens for a reason," Ophelia agreed as the next song started, and Jake kept dancing with her.

After the third song, he took a step back and turned off the music. He brought her hand to his lips and brushed a soft kiss across the knuckles. "Thank you for the dances. May they be the first of many that we share."

"I bet you say that to all the women," she teased.

He dropped her hand and shook his head. "Only the beautiful ones with red hair who have agreed to work for me."

"And how many is that?" Ophelia asked.

"Including you, that would be one," Jake said. "I've managed both the front and back of the winery since I opened the doors. You will be the first lady I've worked with."

"Do you think throwing another person in an all-male mix will work?" Ophelia asked.

"I hope so," Jake answered. "Could we just visit for a little while before we go back inside and gather up all the stuff? Weekends are pretty lonely, and it's such a lovely day to be outside."

Ophelia backed up a step and sat back down on the porch. "What are you doing tomorrow?"

"When I first get up, I'll call my mother and tell her happy Mother's Day since I can't be there for her holiday this year," he answered. "Then I'll probably watch whatever ball game is on television."

"You could go to church with us and then have Mother's Day dinner at the Paradise," Ophelia offered, even though she knew that Aunt Bernie would make more of the invitation than just friendship.

"I would love that," Jake agreed with a nod. "Will your whole family be there? Would they mind if I took a few pictures to send to my mama? She and Dad keep planning to make a visit up here, but something seems to always come up, and she would love to see that I've made some friends."

"We always take pictures for Mama's albums, so feel free to take however many you want," Ophelia answered. "You can even tell her that you had dinner in a brothel."

"I've already told her about the Paradise, and she would love to see pictures," Jake said. "Shall I meet you at the church? Is it the one in Spanish Fort, or do y'all go to another one?"

"Why don't you just pick me up at the house about ten thirty, and we'll go from there?" Ophelia asked. "And yes, it is the one here in town."

"Why, Ophelia Simmons, are you asking me for a date?" Jake flirted.

"Nope," she answered, but sucking on a lemon couldn't have wiped the smile off her face, "but I'm askin' you to go to church with the family and then come to Sunday dinner as my new boss and hopefully my friend."

He kissed her on the forehead. "That will do for a start."

Ophelia had never believed in love at first sight—maybe lust at first sight a few times. What if what she felt was nothing more than a flash in the pan of hot lust? If that was the case, then she'd have to get over it. No way would she have a booty-type relationship with her boss. If that happened, she couldn't even imagine the awkwardness between them when it ended.

Chapter 5

UNTIL OPHELIA'S THERAPIST TOLD her that being a middle child was a tough row to hoe, she'd never thought of holding that position in the family. She was the second born of seven, and the last four could actually be considered two since they were twins. When she questioned the silly idea, her therapist told her that she was the middle of the firstborn three, and as such, she was organized and able to entertain herself like most middle children. As a middle child though, she was prone toward being the one in the family who tried to fix everything, and that put her at risk for stress.

She had gone back to her on-base housing that night when she got off work and researched the personality traits of not only her but also her sisters. The two sets of twins were definitely the youngest in the family. Ursula, the oldest, was the bossiest, and her therapist was right—the middle child wanted to take care of everyone else. Tertia, the third child, was said to be the calmest of the siblings, always had a smile, and was often the jokester of the family.

"Spot on all through our lives," she muttered as she parked her vehicle in the Paradise driveway.

Tertia was sitting on the porch in a rocking chair with

Sassy curled up in her lap. She threw up her hand and waved. Ophelia returned the wave and then opened the back doors of her truck.

"How were things in Dallas, or did you go all the way to Houston?" Tertia asked.

Ophelia slid out of the seat. "What are you talking about?"

"It doesn't take two hours to pack up a few centerpieces, so I figured you made a wrong turn and went to Dallas," Tertia teased as she carefully shifted Sassy over to another chair.

"Only got to Denton before I figured I was going the wrong way," Ophelia threw back at her sister.

"Why? Were you analyzing that dream I disturbed this morning?" Tertia crossed the yard and picked up one of two boxes of leftover food in the back seat. "Where's all the centerpieces?"

"I already unloaded them," Ophelia said. "And I wasn't analyzing that dream. Jake and I danced after everyone was gone. He can two-step better than any cowboy I've ever been with," she answered and hauled the second box out of the back seat.

"Think Aunt Bernie has put a spell on him?" Tertia asked. "She's definitely trying to put one on you and me both."

"Who knows about that woman?" Ophelia whispered as they entered the house. "She seems to have one of those red phone lines straight to the boss of the universe. Think she's serious about this matchmaking, wedding planning, and advice for the lovelorn?"

"If there's a charge for her using that special phone, I bet her bill is sky-high. She might not be able to put Jameson in her coffee after she pays it, and you never know about her adventures. Right now, she's busy with you and Jake, so she might have to put the new businesses on hold," Tertia said and then raised her voice. "Supper is here, everyone! As long as it took Ophelia to bring it home, we'll have to scrape the mold off of it."

"Yeah, right," Ophelia grumbled.

"We'll talk more later," Tertia whispered.

"After that smart-ass remark, I may not speak to you for days," Ophelia shot back.

Tertia set the disposable containers of food on the counter. "You know you are dying to talk to someone about how dancing with Jake made you feel. I'll leave the light on for you. Don't knock or else we'll have everyone in the room with us."

"What are you two conspiring about, or should I say against whom?" Mary Jane asked as she turned on the oven.

"Ophelia danced with Jake, but don't tell Aunt Bernie," Tertia said out the corner of her mouth.

"Tattletale," Ophelia hissed.

"My lips are sealed," Mary Jane promised. "Y'all get on up to your rooms and change out of those pretty dresses. You don't want to have to send them to the cleaners after just wearing them one time. I'll put the food in the oven. This is a pretty special weekend. We had dinner served to us at the reception, and now supper, and I don't cook tomorrow."

Tertia wrapped her arms around her mother. "Mama, you know I love to cook, so I could take over the kitchen duties on a full-time basis. At least until I find a job."

"Done, without a single argument, and appreciated more than words can say!" Mary Jane agreed. "That will give me more time to write the book I'm working on."

"Think you will ever retire?" Ophelia asked.

"Nope," Mary Jane answered without hesitation. "Someday when it's time for me to step off this world and into eternity, I hope I have just typed 'The End' to the novel in my last contract. Then Joe Clay and I will lace our fingers together and sprout our wings at the same time."

"Don't talk like that," Ophelia said around the lump in her throat. "I can't bear to think of life without you and Daddy."

Tertia wiped tears from her eyes with a dish towel and then wrapped her mother up in her arms and gave her a second hug.

"Face the facts, girls," Mary Jane said. "We will most likely pass on before y'all do, which is the natural way of things. We grieve for our parents when they are gone, but if we lose a child, it's unnatural, and the grief is even deeper. So, I hope that Joe Clay and I go before any of you kids. But for now, get on upstairs and change into your jeans and T-shirts. Shoo…go on."

Ophelia made the hug a three-way, and then stepped back. "Yes, ma'am."

"Mama, will you leave me the right to be the boss in your will?" Tertia's grin didn't quite reach her eyes.

"You can all fight for the right," Mary Jane said and pointed toward the door. "If I have to tell y'all again to get out of the kitchen in your good clothes, I may ground both of you for the whole summer and write my will to say that Bernie is boss."

"Sweet Lord!" Ophelia gasped as she turned around and ran from the room with Tertia right behind her.

"Okay," Tertia said when she and Ophelia were at the top of the stairs. "Talk to me. Are you attracted to Jake?"

"Are you?" Ophelia crossed the hallway and opened her bedroom door.

Tertia followed her sister into the room and sat down on Ophelia's desk chair. "Why would you ask such a thing? But to answer, no, ma'am, I am not. I don't like blond-haired men."

Ophelia raised an eyebrow. "Why?"

"Probably because Noah Wilson had blond hair," Tertia answered with half a shrug.

Ophelia removed her dress and hung it up in her closet. "Who is Noah Wilson?"

"That smart-ass kid who was hateful about me living in an old brothel when we first came to Spanish Fort. I blacked his eye and had to stay in during recess for a week because of it. Never have liked blonds since then," Tertia answered. "Jake is sexy for sure, and his eyes are pretty, but he doesn't do diddly-squat for my hormones. How about yours?"

Ophelia fanned her face with the back of her hand. "Oh, honey!"

"Lust or love?" Tertia asked.

"I don't know which one it is yet." Ophelia pulled on a pair of jeans and a T-shirt with the United States Air Force logo on the back. "What if it's just attraction and things go south? Or if it works out to be real, and Aunt Bernie never lets me live it down?"

"Small price to pay to have that kind of love, don't you think?" Tertia asked. "I'll see you downstairs and we'll talk more later."

Ophelia stretched out on the bed and stared at the ceiling. "This is insane. I've only known Jake a few days," she whispered.

"I heard you say something about Jake. Who are you talking to?" Luna asked as she came into the room and lay down on the other side of the king-sized bed.

"I was talking to myself," Ophelia answered.

"Did you tell him that you would take that job he offered you?"

"I did," Ophelia admitted.

Luna patted her on the shoulder. "That's good. Y'all seemed to work well together at the reception. I hope that…" She paused.

"That what?" Ophelia pressured. "You look worried. Is something going on between you and Shane?"

"No, not between us, but with me," Luna said. "I'm afraid that after we are married, Shane and I will get tired of each other."

"That's normal bride jitters," Tertia said.

Luna raised an eyebrow. "How would you know?"

"I read about it in one of those bride magazines that Aunt Bernie has lying around everywhere. But go on," Tertia said. "What put that negative thought in your head?"

"Up until last week I was teaching all day, and he was overseeing the work on the new store and doing some fishing guide tours," Luna explained. "We only saw each other in the evenings and on weekends, and even then I was busy with grading papers and lesson plans. Now that I've left teaching, we'll be together quite a bit of the time, and I'm worried about us getting bored with each other."

Ophelia propped up on an elbow. "If that's all that bothers you, then, girl, you are home free. You and Shane have one of those relationships like Mama and Daddy have."

"Are you sure?" Luna asked.

Tertia nodded. "Yep, we are both positive, so worry about rain on your wedding day, not whether you and Shane will grow bored with each other."

"Thank you," Luna said with a smile. "I just needed some reassurance."

Ophelia gave her sister a quick hug. "You are stepping off into a lot of unknowns. It's natural that you would have some doubts."

"What?" Luna frowned.

"You have quit teaching, which was a job you were used to. You are getting married. You've lived with Shane for six months, but marriage is serious business. You are going to manage a store—again something new to you. And you are possibly going to start a family pretty soon. Any one of those would cause stress, but add them all together, and it's only natural you would worry," Ophelia answered.

"Do you ever regret leaving your job?" Luna asked.

"Sometimes," Ophelia answered honestly. "I knew that job, and I was good at it, but it was depressing enough that I was seeing a therapist."

Luna sat up in the middle of the bed and crisscrossed her legs. "Really? I knew what you did was classified, but…"

"It was that plus the working nights," Ophelia told her. "Coming home has been the best thing for me."

Luna threw her legs over the side of the bed and took a couple of steps toward the open door. "Me, too, and that goes for Endora as well. She's coming out of that horrible funk she sank down into after Kevin cheated on her. Her cats and working on her children's books have really helped her."

"Maybe Aunt Bernie is right," Ophelia said, "about all of us needing to come home and put down roots."

"I'm sure she is," Luna agreed and disappeared out into the hallway.

Ophelia needed to consider everything before things went any further with Jake. Maybe he was just out for a good time with no strings. She stood up and looked at herself in the mirror above her dresser as she ran a brush through her light-brown hair. "Do I want to waste my time on a chance that it could just be a two-consenting-adults arrangement?"

She stared at her reflection for several minutes and decided that she did not—not even for someone who could dance as well as Jake did.

Chapter 6

"You did good today, Ophelia," Bernie said as she helped set the table for dinner on Mother's Day. "Church is a better place to take a feller on a first date than a bar. I talked to Dolly and Gladys and Frannie, my poker-playin' buddies, and they all agreed that we'd be good at matchmaking. We all need something to keep us from getting stale and molding to the point that we have to go to one of those nursing home places. And Endora is helping me set up a Facebook page to get things started."

"It wasn't a date," Ophelia protested.

"You sat with him," Ursula said. "I could almost feel the vibes that were dancing around the pew where we were all lined up."

"What you felt was pregnant brain," Ophelia told her.

"Pregnant brain forgets things and gets all emotional, and honey, I could almost reach out and grab those sparks that lit up the sanctuary this morning," Tertia argued. "And y'all shared a hymnbook. You know what that means in a small town."

Luna pulled the roaster with the pot roast out of the oven. "Small town, nothing! This is nearly a ghost town, so it means even more. I bet all the little old ladies in the church will be looking at the calendar to see what month they need to pencil in a day to give y'all a wedding shower."

"Small towns," Ophelia groaned.

"Gotta love 'em," Bo said with a giggle. "I've lived in Nashville all these years, and I only know a handful of people. I love coming home to Spanish Fort. This place is like a reality soap opera. No wonder Mama and Ursula can write such great romance stories. All they have to do is look around them for ideas."

Ursula took glasses down from the cabinet and filled them with ice. "Thank you for that, Bo, and you are right. I've got the first book in my new historical trilogy done, and all the edits are finished. Now it's on to the second one."

"Second what?" Joe Clay led the parade of the rest of the family, plus Vera and Alan, into the kitchen.

"My second book, but y'all all take a seat," Ursula answered. "Happy Mother's Day again, Mama. You and Vera are the queens today. We should have gotten y'all some crowns to wear."

Joe Clay pulled out a chair for Mary Jane. "She's the queen every day in my book."

"But today she and Vera are both mamas," Ophelia said. "So, we all want to honor them."

"Next month we'll make Father's Day as special as this one is," Ursula reminded him as she carried a basket of hot rolls to the table.

"Will you make blackberry cobbler for me?" he asked.

"Yes, we will," Bo answered. "And we will make corn bread and red beans with ham."

"And fried potatoes?" Joe Clay asked.

"For sure," Bo promised.

Jake crossed the room and picked up a tray loaded with all the glasses of ice. "I'll take this, and"—he lowered his voice so that only Ophelia could hear—"thank you so much for inviting me. This is great."

Ophelia followed behind him with a bowl filled with ears of corn on the cob. "What?" she asked.

"All of this family stuff." Jake set the tray on the table and then placed a glass at each place setting. "Do y'all ever argue or disagree on anything? This seems like one of those perfect old television shows from way back when."

"Oh, honey!" She giggled, "Stick around long enough and you'll see some first-class arguments."

"I just might do that," Jake said.

"Do what?" Aunt Bernie asked.

"I was wondering if the sisters ever have disagreements," Jake answered.

"I could tell you some stories that would knock your socks off!" Bernie replied. "They're on their best behavior today since it's Mother's Day."

"And Sunday," Joe Clay added. "Mary Jane always said that Sunday was the day they had to be good girls."

Endora sat down in her usual place. "If you fight on Sunday, it makes Jesus cry."

"That's right," Mary Jane said with a smile and a nod.

"I heard that so much that it's branded on my brain," Tertia said.

When everyone began to take their places around the table, Jake nudged Ophelia on the shoulder. "Where am I supposed to sit?"

Bernie pointed to a chair. "Right here between me and Ophelia."

After Joe Clay said a quick grace, Bernie picked up the tea pitcher on her end of the table, filled her glass, handed it to Jake, and asked, "What part of Texas did you grow up in?"

"Down around Jasper," Jake answered. "My dad has a ranch, but my grandpa on my mother's side had a winery." Jake filled his glass and passed the pitcher on to Ophelia. "Things weren't so different in that area than they are up here. Sunday dinner is at my folks now since my grandparents are both gone. It's not as big as this except on holidays. My mama is one of eight children, so there's lots of cousins. Conor, the one who's about my age, will be joining me in the wine business here in Spanish Fort at the end of summer."

Ophelia didn't even need to see Bernie's face to know her brain cells were running around like Endora's half-grown cats chasing each other up and down the stairs. She leaned back far enough to see Bernie smiling and staring across the table at Bo, Rae, and Endora, kind of like a kid in a candy store. A new man was coming to town. Aunt Bernie was already deciding which sister was going to wind up with him. If Jake's cousin was as sexy as he was and made one of her three sisters get little shots of steamy desire every time they were near him, then Aunt Bernie might not have to work too hard on her next project.

Ophelia's hand was still tingling from Jake's touch when he passed the tea to her and took the basket of hot rolls that Bernie sent to him.

"Got to keep these going or else we'll get yelled at," she whispered.

"Sorry," Jake said in a low voice, "I was just enjoying the moment."

Another brush of the fingertips when Jake passed the bread to Ophelia, plus the comment he had just made, put a slight blush on her face. She placed a roll on her plate and sent the basket on around the table, and then took a long drink of her tea. The icy-cold liquid did very little to cool her down.

"Does Conor have blond hair and pretty green eyes?" Bernie asked.

"Nope, Conor has black hair and brown eyes," Jake answered. "He's shorter than I am, and on the shy side. I'm looking forward to having him live with me in the trailer. I'm finding that living alone is a bit lonely.

"You look like you are deep in thought. I've got a penny for them, or even a bottle of your favorite wine, if you are willing to share," Jake whispered to Ophelia.

"Sorry, they're not for sale today." No way would she tell him that he was and had been in her thoughts too often to count. "But if you'd like to sell yours to me for a penny, I'll dig one out of my purse after dinner."

"I'll take that penny, but I don't want to yell my thoughts

out over all the top of this noise. Don't get me wrong, I'm enjoying every moment of it, but how about we go for a drive?" Jake suggested. "We can talk when it's a little quieter than it is here."

Ophelia shook her head. "Not today. It's Mother's Day and we play games after we eat. Besides this is a special one. We're celebrating Vera and Mama both being mothers, and Ursula who will be a mother by the time the next Mother's Day rolls around."

"Tomorrow, then?" Jake asked. "I need to go to Wichita Falls and pick up supplies. We could leave midmorning, have lunch, and then pick up my order at the warehouse."

"I'd love to," she said.

"Pick you up at ten?" he asked.

"I'll be ready," she told him. "And you *are* invited to stay for games after we eat."

"Love to, but I've got to warn you, if it's poker, I'm really good," he said.

Shane raised an eyebrow from across the table. "Oh, really? So, you enjoy a game of poker?"

"Did I hear *poker?*" Remy asked. "I've been thinking about getting up a weekly game."

"Dang it, Vera," Alan said with a long sigh. "If these boys are going to get up a weekly poker game, we really should get serious about buying that house next door to Shane and Luna's place. I would love to get in on games with them."

"I can sure agree with that," Bernie said. "Vera can help me with my new business venture."

"What's that?" Mary Jane asked.

"Aunt Bernie is starting up a matchmaking thing on the internet," Endora said.

"I thought you were teasing," Ophelia gasped.

Bernie winked at her. "No, ma'am, I am not, but right now I want to hear more about this poker-night thing."

"I'm offering the Paradise for a weekly game," Joe Clay said.

"Why don't we have it at my place?" Remy suggested. "That way the ladies could have a girls' night and work on wedding stuff for Luna and Shane. How about Sunday nights, starting tonight?"

"Works for me," Shane said. "We don't plan to open the new store on Sunday, so I'll be free."

"Sounds great to me," Mary Jane said. "I can finish up my special day with all my girls and Aunt Bernie."

"And after the wedding, it will be a girls' night for us," Ophelia said.

"I don't suppose you're going to let women play?" Aunt Bernie said with a long sigh.

"They'd lose all their money if you were allowed in the game," Mary Jane answered with a giggle. "And besides we need you here to help us with wedding plans. If your hotline to the Universe or Fate or whatever power you have is right…"

"Of course, it's right!" Bernie butted in, "Living proof is right here at this table."

Ursula raised her hand. "Here I am, and thank you, Aunt Bernie."

"You are very welcome," Bernie replied with a nod.

"It's settled then," Remy said, and then leaned over and kissed Ursula on the cheek. "Is that all right with you, darlin'?"

"Of course, it's all right. I'd love an evening every week with all my sisters. Rae, you and Bo could join us with Zoom when you are back in Nashville and Oklahoma, and you aren't on police duty or playing a gig," Ursula said.

"Tonight, Alan can get to sit in on the game before we have to fly home in the morning, and I get to spend more time with all these girls," Vera said. "So, you're thinking of starting a matchmaking business, Bernie? I'm not sure I could be of any help, but I would like to hear more about it."

Ophelia stole a sideways glance over at Jake and was glad she had decided to work for him. That way she would get to know all his ways—good, bad, or somewhere in between—on a daily basis.

———

"Okay, spill the beans," Tertia said as soon as all the guys left that evening to go play poker.

"Who? Me?" Ophelia asked. "I thought we were going to work on wedding plans."

"We'll do that later," Tertia said. "Bo and Rae are leaving in the morning, and we all want to know what all those sly little looks were between you and Jake."

Ophelia put on her best innocent expression. "Y'all are imagining things. You've all got wedding fever and you want to transfer it all over to me rather than accept the fact that you want to be in Ursula or Luna's shoes right now."

"I agree with Ophelia," Bernie said, "but that doesn't mean I don't want her to tell us how she feels about Jake."

Ophelia held up her palms. "Jake is going to be my boss starting Tuesday morning. At best, right now, we could be friends. I'm going with him tomorrow to Wichita Falls to pick up supplies for the winery. End of story. Let's move on to something else. Like whether we're going to have nosegay bouquets for us girls, or if we'll each carry a single rose."

"All right," Bernie said with a sigh and a shrug. "If you won't talk about Jake, then it just means that you are attracted to him, and you are covering it up, because you don't want to admit that my juju is right."

"Aunt Bernie," Mary Jane said in a scolding tone, "a woman would have to be stone-cold blind not to be attracted to Jake. That doesn't mean there's a budding romance."

"Not me," Tertia said. "I don't like blond men."

"Or me," Bo added. "I dated a man who wore glasses a few years back. Three dates in, I figured he was a controlling jerk. I've never been attracted to men with glasses or even contacts since then."

Ophelia poked Bo on the arm with her forefinger. "That's kind of mean to judge all men by one fool who had trouble seeing."

"Don't judge *me*," Bo snapped. "Tertia doesn't like blonds, so what's the difference?"

Mary Jane slapped a hand over her mouth to cover up

a giggle. "Mother's Day is officially over when my girls start to get snippy, but I sure appreciate y'all being nice most of today."

Tertia rolled her eyes and wiped imaginary sweat from her forehead. "It was tough, Mama, and I bit my tongue so many times that I've had to grow a new one."

"And to think I couldn't wait for you to come home," Ophelia groaned.

"I'm having second thoughts about coming back with all this going on," Bo said. "Reckon the police department up in the Oklahoma Panhandle needs a singin' cop, Rae?"

Bernie reached over and patted Bo's arm. "Don't you worry, darlin'. I'm taking care of Ophelia and Tertia. By the time you get here, it'll just be you and Endora in the house."

Vera nudged Mary Jane with an elbow. "This is the best Mother's Day ever. Alan, let's drive past that house for sale and get the Realtor's phone number off the sign. We can live here in the winter, maybe from Christmas until after Mother's Day, and then live up north through the hot Texas summer and into fall."

"Shane already got it for me, and we can look at it this afternoon at three," Alan said. "And I like the idea of spending half our time here in Spanish Fort."

Ophelia glanced over at her mother. "We argue. We agree. But we keep it in the family."

"Yes, we do." Mary Jane agreed.

Chapter 7

OPHELIA AWOKE TO THE aroma of cinnamon wafting up the stairs and into her bedroom on Monday morning. She rubbed the sleep from her eyes and sat up on the side of her bed. Even after six months, she still had trouble sleeping at night and usually had to figure out where she was—her apartment or in a tent somewhere when she was deployed to teach a class, or in a tiny office surrounded by technical equipment. The latter was where she stared at a screen for hours and took care of the things that gave her nightmares. After a quick trip to the bathroom, where she splashed cold water on her face and whipped her red hair up into a messy bun, she padded downstairs in her bare feet.

Bernie raised a coffee cup and greeted her from the end of the table. "Good mornin', sleepyhead."

"Mornin'," Ophelia said on the way to the coffeepot. "Where is everyone? I thought that Tertia was in charge of the kitchen."

"Rae and Bo left an hour ago. Rae's dropping Bo off at the airport, and then driving on up north by herself," Bernie answered. "I'll be glad when those two realize that they belong here. Tertia said last night that today was a DIY breakfast—*do it yourself*—because she was worn out from the reception on Saturday and then Mother's Day. Mary Jane and Joe Clay had oatmeal, and then he went out to the barn to work on the gazebo he's building for Luna's wedding, and she went to her office."

"Endora?" Ophelia asked as she made herself two pieces of toast.

"She took Ursula's advice about writing a children's book and is up in her room working on it," Bernie answered. "Your mother said if anyone disturbed her or Endora today that it better involve blood or broken bones. I wanted her to show me more about how to navigate Facebook, but I wouldn't go against Mary Jane for anything."

"Wise woman," Ophelia said.

"You are leaving with Jake at ten thirty, so eat fast," Bernie said. "You don't want to be late on your first date, or on your first day at work tomorrow."

"Yes, ma'am." Ophelia gave her aunt a snappy salute. "But like I've said a dozen times already, it's not a date."

"Don't you get sassy with me," Bernie shot back at her. "I heard that story before from Ursula. Sit down right here beside me and I'll give you some pointers on…"

"Good Lord!" Ophelia said with a long sigh. "I think I can figure out how to talk to Jake all by myself while we drive to Wichita Falls and back. Why don't you work on Tertia's romance instead of mine?"

"Don't worry, darlin'," Bernie said with a smile. "Soon as I hear you and Jake are dating, I'll start working my magic on her. I want to be able to say that I'm a successful match-maker when I interview my clients."

"Magic don't work on me," Ophelia declared. "I'm immune to it, so bypass me and Tertia and go right to Endora."

Bernie finished off her coffee, stood up, and refilled the cup. "I'm saving her for last so that she can have more time to heal. Bless her baby heart, she's making progress in getting closure and moving on, but she's not to that final stage of acceptance."

Ophelia wondered if *she* would ever get past the night-mares and into the final stage of accepting that what she had done was really for the greater good.

———

Bernie had a captive audience in the kitchen and was telling Tertia a story about something that had happened in her bar when Ophelia tiptoed out onto the front porch. She sat down on the porch swing, but she didn't put it in motion. If Bernie heard even the slightest squeak, she would be outside in a flash with lots of advice for the first date.

"It's not a date," Ophelia said under her breath. "I don't care if Ursula did say that same thing and then ended up married to Remy. We have different stories."

She stopped arguing with herself when she heard a truck driving up the lane. She shaded her eyes with the back of her hand, and as soon as she was sure it was Jake, she stood up and headed out into the yard. Jake parked and was out of the vehicle with the passenger door open for her before she even made it to the bottom porch step.

"Good morning," he said cheerfully.

"Mornin' to you," she said.

Heavy dew still lay on the grass, but she was too busy looking at the way Jake's faded jeans fit to notice anything else. She put one foot on the running board and started to hoist herself up, but the wet sole of her boot slipped. She tried to grasp something—anything—to keep from falling, but there was nothing to wrap her hands around. Then suddenly, Jake scooped her up into his arms like a new bride and lifted her into the passenger seat.

"Can't have you hurting yourself on our first date," he said, chuckling.

"My middle name is not Grace," she muttered as she fastened her seat belt and glanced back toward the porch to be sure that nosy Bernie hadn't come outside the minute she realized that her niece had left the kitchen. So far, so good.

He closed the door and jogged around the front of the truck, slid in behind the wheel, and started the engine. "So, what is your middle name?"

"Ophelia," she answered breathlessly. "First name is Mary, and before you ask about our unusual names, Mama named us after whatever heroine she was writing about at the time of our birth."

"I wasn't going to ask," Jake said, "but I'm glad you offered up the information."

"Everyone asks," she protested.

"On my birth certificate I am Patrick Jacob. That's not so unusual, right?" he asked, but didn't wait for her answer. "My sisters pester me all the time about having a common name. My older sister is Murphey and the one who's just a year younger is Haisley. Mama just knew they were boys, so that's the only names she and Dad had picked out. Since they couldn't agree on anything for a girl, they just used what they had. I'm used to girls having unusual names."

"How much older than you are they?" Ophelia asked.

"Murphey was fourteen when I was born, and Haisley was thirteen. I was one of those *oops* babies, but I'm the third so I'm the charm, and besides they finally got a son," he answered. "My first memory is when Murphey got married and Haisley started college the next week or so."

"How did that make you feel?"

"I figured out that crying and hiding in my bedroom wouldn't fix things," he answered. "What's *your* very first memory?"

"That would have been when Daddy took Mama to the hospital late one night. Grandma Marsh came to stay with us girls, and Mama said she would bring home a surprise for us. We all thought it would be kittens, but the next day, they came back with twin girls—Bo and Rae. I would have been between three and four, and I already had two sisters. I would have much rather had a kitten," Ophelia answered with half a chuckle.

"Mary Jane had five girls in about four years?" Jake's deep voice raised an octave or two.

"Mama had seven girls in just under six years because Luna and Endora were born a year later, almost to the day. My father wanted a son, so when Ursula was born, they decided to try again, and got me two years later. No luck, so they decided that—like you said—the third would be the charm, and they got Tertia almost two years after that. They gave up on ever having one after that," Ophelia explained.

"But?" Jake asked as he made a right-hand turn in Nocona and headed west.

She smiled across the console at him. "Birth control failed, and they got twins—Bo and Rae. My father had a vasectomy as soon as they were born, but he didn't go back to get things checked. One year later they got the second set of twins in the summer before Ursula started first grade. My parents divorced a couple of years after that, and Mama managed to raise us as a single mom, and still put out three to four books a year."

"Do you see your father often?" Jake asked.

"Maybe once a year if he and his wife can fit us into their plans," she answered. "But like another old saying goes, 'What the eyes don't see, the heart don't grieve.' Daddies don't just see their kids when it's convenient. They are there for them no matter what—when they fall off their bike and scrape their knee, when they cry over their first boyfriend breaking up with them, when they go to father-daughter dances with them, and they even buy an old van to take the whole family to sporting events and all over the county to see the Christmas lights."

"My dad is like that," Jake said. "I guess I should appreciate him more for the memories that I have."

"That's what Joe Clay did for us girls, and that's why we call him Daddy," Ophelia said. "Look!" She pointed at a sign. "Did you see that billboard for another winery?"

"There's more than a dozen within a couple of hours driving distance of mine," Jake answered. "I visited all of them before I finally decided to buy land in Spanish Fort."

"I had no idea there were so many," Ophelia said. "I went to several when I was stationed in California, but never realized there were any close to Spanish Fort. You said we were going to Wichita Falls for supplies. What do you get over there?"

"Sugar mainly," Jake answered, "but today I also need to buy wine yeast. I've got a deal with a farmer just over the Red River in Terral, Oklahoma, to buy watermelons when they're in season, and with some more local farmers to buy elderberries and strawberries as it all gets ripe."

"How many people work for you?" she asked.

"Four when you start tomorrow. Three guys help me in the back where we make the wine," he answered. "But I'd rather talk about you today than the winery," Jake said. "You mentioned being disappointed because you got two more sisters instead of kittens. I saw a dog and a couple of cats over at your house when I was there. Are any of those yours?"

"Nope..." she answered. "Yes..." She paused again. "Maybe."

Jake chuckled again. "Which one is it?"

"Pepper, the Chihuahua belongs to Aunt Bernie. Endora was allergic to dogs when she was a little girl, but Aunt Bernie says that there's something about a dog of that breed that folks aren't allergic to. Personally, I think Endora grew out of her allergy, if it ever even existed, but if she wants to believe that she can be around Pepper, then who am I to argue? The two yellow half-grown cats belong to Endora. Sassy is the house cat, and we all claim her, so no, the dog isn't mine. Yes, on Sassy," Ophelia explained. "It's complicated. How about you? Do you have pets?"

"A mutt that adopted me when I moved here," Jake answered. "He's ugly as warmed-over sin, but he's good at chasing possums, raccoons, and every other grape-eating animal out of the arbors."

"Luna and Shane have two dogs and one is named Mutt. He's not a pretty feller either, but he's a good watchdog."

Could this really be a date? Getting to know each other sure made it feel like one. However, she didn't have the angst in her gut like she'd always experienced on first dates before. Talking to Jake about her family and learning about him seemed natural and comfortable.

Chapter 8

AN ADRENALINE RUSH CAME with Tertia's last days of school: telling her students goodbye, the long drive home from Vega to Spanish Fort, and getting there just in time for a wedding and then hearing about the new baby. On Monday morning she woke up totally drained and having second thoughts about her decision to give up her job and move. She dragged herself downstairs, poured a cup of coffee, and sat down at the table with Aunt Bernie.

"Where is Ophelia?"

"She's already gone with Jake," Bernie said. "I thought you were going to make breakfast every morning."

"I told you last night that today was DIY breakfast. That stands for—"

"I know what it stands for. I keep up with all that kind of stuff. If I didn't, I would never be able to read a text message," Bernie snapped. "Dam…dang it! I meant to tell her not to do anything I wouldn't do when she left."

"That leaves a green light on about anything," Tertia said.

"One down—that would be Ursula—and one to go—that would be Luna. Now that my work is done there—"

"Thank God, but not until July. Luna could still call the wedding off right up to the last minute." Tertia interrupted her aunt as she poured herself a bowl of cereal and sat down at the table to eat.

"She will not!" Bernie declared in a defiant tone. "I need a perfect record to launch my new career on, and there's you and Ophelia. I figure four will be a good start."

Not rolling her eyes took every bit of Tertia's willpower. She just couldn't see a woman pushing eighty being a matchmaker or a wedding planner. "I've only been home a few days, Aunt Bernie. I'm barely over all the worry and excitement of quitting my job, and the weddings and everything else that's happening."

"How long has it been since you dated anyone? And I don't mean a one-night stand," Bernie asked.

"I don't do one-night stands, and let's just say it's been a while." Tertia wondered if she and Ophelia should just say they were dating. The idea was good but then she remembered that Aunt Bernie had owned and operated a bar. The woman could probably spot a fake boyfriend from a mile away.

"Do you hear that?" Bernie cocked her head to the side.

"What?" Tertia asked.

"It's a ticking sound," Bernie's expression was dead serious, but her eyes twinkled.

"I don't hear anything," Tertia replied and strained her ears even more.

"It's your biological clock, and since you can't hear it,

it's my job to listen for you," Bernie told her. "I hear the minister at our church is retiring real soon, and talk has it that the hiring committee has their eye on a young man in hopes that he will build up the church. Maybe you'd make a good preacher's wife."

"Good God, Aunt Bernie!" Tertia said with a giggle. "Not a one of us sisters would make a good preacher's wife. We're all too independent for that, and besides, what man of God would want to marry a woman who lives in an old brothel?"

Bernie cut her eyes around at Tertia. "What if he's really, really good in bed?"

"Sweet Jesus!" Tertia gasped. "As soon as I finish my cereal, I'm going for a long walk to shake this conversation from my head."

"Don't bother inviting me to go with you," Bernie declared. "I did enough walking behind a bar to do me for years. From my trailer to here and back again is enough for me. Besides Pepper's little legs would be worn out on a walk that long, and he would pout if I left him at home. He's taking his morning nap out on the trailer porch right now. He loves to soak up the sun."

"Good mornin' to y'all," Endora said cheerfully as she entered the kitchen and headed straight for the refrigerator. "I'm ready for a glass of iced tea. It's already getting warm out there."

"Where have you been?" Bernie asked.

"I walked to the old store building and then came back. I love my morning walks, but pretty soon I'll have to go out a little earlier to beat the heat," Endora answered. "Either of y'all want a glass of tea?"

"Love one," Bernie said.

"No, thank you," Tertia said.

Endora poured two glasses and set one before Bernie before she took a seat. "My morning walks are my alone time to think about my children's books. Pepper, Sassy, Poppy, and Misty are the main characters in it. I've outlined half a dozen stories and almost have the first one done about when Pepper and Sassy adopted Poppy and Misty because they needed a good home. Pepper and Sassy hate each other, but they agree to be civil when the babies are around."

"Pepper is getting a new collar with fake diamonds on it when the book comes out. He will walk on the red carpet with me when the children's movie hits the big screen," Bernie declared. "Let's take our tea out on the screened porch, and you can tell me more about your new ideas while your sister goes on her alone-time walk."

"I don't mean to be selfish with my time when it comes to my walks," Endora said. "Remy has been Ursula's writing muse. My walks are mine, and I want to have at least three books done by the time school starts back. No offense, Sister."

"None taken," Tertia said. "I understand."

Endora and Bernie disappeared out to the screened-in back porch, and Tertia went the opposite way—out the front door and down the lane. When she reached the end, she had a decision to make. Go right and maybe drop in on Ursula?

No, that wouldn't work. She and Remy had taken Vera and Alan to the airport that morning. Left it was, then. Maybe to the old store like Endora had done, or perhaps she'd just walk all the way to Luna's place and check on how the new store building was coming along. That would be a good bit of exercise. Now that she'd left her job as a coach where she was used to running with the girls every day, she would have to do something to keep toned up.

She hadn't gone twenty yards when a truck pulled up beside her. Luna rolled down the passenger-side window. "Where are you off to this morning?"

"Escaping Aunt Bernie. Supposedly, she can hear my biological clock ticking," Tertia answered. "Are you aware that she's talking about putting in a matchmaking business? Maybe we should tell her the competition is pretty stiff. There are already dozens of sites out there, from getting farmers to senior citizens together."

"I'm well aware, and Endora thinks it's a great idea. Bernie will have something to keep her busy and out of our lives," Luna answered.

"Oh, honey," Tertia said with a sigh, "she'll always have time for that."

"You want to go to Nocona with us?" Luna offered. "We've got to get dog food and another gallon of paint for the construction crew, and I hear the snow-cone stand opened this week."

"Sounds good, but I'll take a rain check," Tertia said with a wave. "Y'all have fun."

She hadn't gone but a few more steps when a car passed her, honked, and then backed up. Bernie's poker friend Dolly yelled, "You need a ride, darlin'?"

"No, thanks," Tertia said. "I'm just out for a walk this fine morning."

"Treat them young legs good," Dolly said. "Time will come when they'll refuse to take long walks, and that stuff called cellulite will make them look like cottage cheese. Don't get over there in that tall grass. Chiggers are everywhere this year."

"Yes, ma'am," Tertia nodded.

How did Endora manage to think about her books at all? Tertia wondered as she kept going until she reached the old store building. She started to sit down on the steps but remembered what Dolly had said about chiggers. The grass and weeds were at least knee high around the porch, but the weathered park bench pushed back against the wall looked like it might not break down if she sat on it. She studied the faded bricks that covered the old building, and the cracked porch. It would be really nice if someone would come along with some money and use the space for a museum—maybe for old oil-rig equipment or photos of the cattle drives that came through that area after the Civil War. Surprisingly enough, the windows were still intact, and no one had kicked in the door. If the foundation was still good, the building might be good for any number of things.

She left that idea behind and let her mind wander to her sisters. The ones that had moved back to Spanish Fort seemed happy. Luna was all involved with the new store she and Shane were building, and of course her upcoming wedding. Ursula had a new husband, a baby on the way, and deadlines to keep her busy. Ophelia was going to work for Jake the next morning. Endora had finally found writing and illustrating children's books to take her mind off the horrible breakup she had gone through. Bo would be coming home soon, and Tertia wouldn't be surprised if Rae didn't follow right after her.

"I need to think about me, not my sisters," she muttered.

A hummingbird flew past her to the wild rosebush at the end of the porch. With its little wings fluttering, it started to suck the nectar out of the yellow roses. Tertia sat so still, hardly breathing, so the little thing wouldn't fly away. Sunrays made the green on its back look like emeralds. Then a truck pulled over right in front of the store and scared the bird. Tertia did not need a ride, and she didn't want to talk about chiggers or dog food. She was instantly aggravated at whoever had scared away her hummingbird.

"Good Lord!" she whispered under her breath when she recognized the tall man walking toward her as Noah Wilson.

"Hello, the store," he called out and then shaded his eyes with the back of his hand. "Tertia Simmons, is that you?"

"Hello, Noah," she said but there was no warmth in her voice.

"I heard you were back in Spanish Fort," he said as he crossed the lawn. "I stopped by the Paradise, and one of your sisters told me that you were out for a walk."

Tertia was glad that he said one of her sisters and not her aunt, or else Bernie would be ready to make up a wedding registry.

A tight-fitting T-shirt hugged his muscular body, and his coaches' shorts had the Saint Jo mascot on the leg. His blond hair was feathered back in a perfect cut. Ten years had been good to Noah, but there was still a bitter taste in her mouth when she thought of the way he had teased her. She hoped that the chiggers made a fine meal on his bare legs.

He sat down uninvited on the porch step. "I can't believe I found you just sitting here at the old store building."

"Were you looking for me?" she asked.

"Yes, I was," he answered. "We need a head softball coach and an assistant girls' basketball coach over in Saint Jo. Would you be interested?"

No foreplay about *How have you been? What have you been doing since we graduated more than ten years ago? Are you still peeved at me for being a jerk when we were in school?* Just right to the point.

"I'm surprised that you'd even ask me," Tertia said. "I moved back to the Paradise, which you will remember is an old brothel. Wouldn't that be a terrible thing for your students?"

"Good grief!" Noah frowned. "You're still pouting over that schoolyard argument we had. You blacked my eye. Wasn't that enough?"

"I don't pout," Tertia protested. "What do you do at Saint Jo?"

"I'm the high school principal," he answered. "The superintendent and school board would have to approve…"

She held up a hand. "Stop right there. No need for you to waste your breath on any more explanations. I'm taking a year off from teaching. I don't know what I want to do, but I know I'm burned out with coaching and teaching."

"Have you got any plans?" Noah asked.

"I'm going to find myself. Find something I love to do," she answered.

"That's what I plan to do too. I have to work a few more weeks to fulfill my contract, but then I'm done," he said, "and I hope I made the right decision."

"If you aren't going to work at the school, then why are you offering me the possibility of a job?" she asked.

"Before I leave in July, I promised I'd help find a new girls' coach," he said with a shrug. "You sure you won't at least think about it?"

"Absolutely positive," she answered. "What dream are you chasing?"

"My grandpa passed away last year and left me a lot of property here in Spanish Fort, plus a pretty good stock portfolio," Noah replied. "You'll think I'm crazy, but with a new little convenience store going in right close and a vineyard down out west of town…" He paused.

Tertia's curiosity was piqued. "I won't judge you, so spit it out unless you're thinking about putting in a brothel, and then all bets are off."

"I like the idea of building Spanish Fort up again, so...I am thinking...about..." Noah stammered.

How could this man be a principal and deal out discipline when he stuttered about something as simple as his dream? Tertia must have had an exasperated expression on her face because he finally took a deep breath and let it out slowly.

"Okay," he said, "I want to put a café in Spanish Fort. I like to cook. Please don't laugh at me."

Tertia did not laugh or even smile, but it was hard to wrap her mind around the star of the football team wearing an apron and flipping burgers or stirring a pot of beans. "That's a wonderful idea. Where are you building it?"

"I wanted to convert this old building, but it wasn't feasible, so..." he paused. "You don't think I'm crazy to build a café this far out?"

"'If you build it, they will come,'" she quoted.

"Good point, and I hope you are right," Noah said. "And for the record, Tertia, I apologize for all the hateful things I said when we were kids."

"Apology accepted, but I'm not ready to say sorry for blacking your eye," she told him. "You didn't tell me where you are building it."

"Fair enough, but maybe you will be sorry someday," Noah said with a smile. "I'm building it right across the street from where we are sitting. My folks moved to Wichita Falls to one of those senior citizens' gated communities when Dad retired last year. They gave me their house and the two acres that it sits on. It's..."

Tertia butted in. "I know where you lived as a child—right across the road from the Paradise."

"You sure don't forget easily, do you?"

"No, I do not," she admitted. "Spanish Fort just might grow enough not to be approaching ghost-town status, but I have to admit, I'm a little jealous."

Noah's eyebrows shot up. "Of me doing something kind of foolhardy?"

"No, of you following your dream and hoping for the best," Tertia admitted.

"What's your secret dream?" Noah asked. "Evidently, you weren't happy with teaching, or you would have stayed until you were old enough to retire."

"I don't have one," Tertia admitted. "But I'm happiest when I'm in the kitchen."

She could practically see the gears turning in Noah's head. "You are teasing me to get back at me for my smart-ass remarks when we were kids, aren't you?"

"No, and what does liking to cook have to do with something that happened all those years ago?" Tertia frowned and stood up.

"If I can't hire you as a coach, how about as a cook for my new café?"

"I thought you were going to be the cook," Tertia said.

"I am, but I can't be on duty from six in the morning until eight at night," Noah answered. "And I need help designing the café and figuring out all kinds of things. Since we both like to cook, maybe we could share thoughts about how to set up the kitchen, whether to use booths or tables, what to put on the menu—that kind of thing. I'd gladly put you on payroll starting anytime you want."

Tertia studied Noah's face. Either he was a really good poker player or else he was serious. "Why don't you ask your wife to help you? How is Wanette going to feel about you working so closely with a woman?"

Noah gazed out across the road at the empty lot. "I'm not married anymore. Haven't been for two years."

"I'm sorry," Tertia said.

Noah shrugged. "That's water under the bridge, and I've moved on. So has Wanette. She's remarried and living in California."

The football star and the head cheerleader were supposed to be a match made in heaven. Evidently, it wasn't, but unless Wanette had drastically changed since high school, Tertia couldn't imagine her being happy with a cook in a tiny town café—not even if he owned the business.

Noah stood up. "I should be going. If I give you my phone number, will you call me?"

"Why would I do that?" Tertia asked.

"Just to talk about café stuff," Noah replied. "Everyone else that I've talked to thinks I'm crazy—even my folks. They tell me that I'm putting my money into something that will stand as empty as this old store within six months. It's nice to have someone to visit with that has a positive outlook."

Tertia pulled her phone out of her shirt pocket and

handed it to him. "Put your number in there and grab mine. You can call me when you want to talk."

He handed it back in a few seconds. "Thank you."

"Sure thing," she said.

"Can I give you a ride back to the Paradise?" Noah asked.

"No, thanks, I need the exercise." She smiled up at him.

Noah returned the smile. "Okay, then. See you around."

He got into his truck, waved out the window, and made a U-turn to get back on the road headed south.

"Wipe that grin off your face, Aunt Bernie. Not even your precious Universe has enough power to fix me up with Noah Wilson," Tertia whispered.

Chapter 9

"DID YOU HAVE A good walk? Did Noah Wilson find you?" Bernie asked from the porch.

Tertia knew better than to beg any higher power—God, the Universe, or Fate—for a whole day without her aunt's meddling, but a couple of hours would be nice. She stopped at the end of the porch steps, and Sassy came out to meet her with both of Endora's half-grown kittens, Poppy and Misty, trailing along behind her. Ever since Endora claimed the poor little orphaned yellow babies as her own, Sassy had taken them under her wing. The trouble was, so did Pepper. When the kitties were around, Sassy and Pepper were peaceful. But if they weren't, then they still growled and hissed at each other.

She stooped down to pet each of the cats. "They're spoiled almost as rotten as Pepper."

"No animal is as spoiled as my Pepper," Bernie declared.

Tertia thought she was home free from having to discuss Noah Wilson, but then Endora came out onto the porch and sat down in a rocking chair beside Bernie. Before Tertia could argue with Bernie about which animal was most spoiled, Endora asked the same two questions that Bernie had.

"She'll try to change the subject and talk about Pepper and the cats," Bernie said.

"I had a wonderful walk, and you are right about needing to go earlier in the day. Noah Wilson wanted to offer me a coaching job at Saint Jo. I turned him down," Tertia answered.

The rest of what she and Noah discussed was classified, as Ophelia would say, or maybe it was need-to-know, and no one, especially Aunt Bernie, was on the need-to-know list right now.

"I can't believe he would even..." Bernie huffed. "He's not the man for you, Tertia darlin'. I did *not* tell the Universe to put him in your pathway."

"Why?" Tertia sat down on the top step and all three cats crawled up in her lap. "What's the matter with Noah?"

"Once a bully, always a bully," Bernie declared. "I won't have one of my girls in a relationship with a man who said such ugly things about the Paradise and your mama."

"Aunt Bernie, Noah was just a little boy at the time. He and Tertia were still in grade school. And besides she gave him a shiner, so they're pretty well even. You need to be focusing on finding someone else so you can go into your new business with four perfect couples. There's no way that Noah and Tertia would ever be good together," Endora said and then turned to Tertia. "Since you turned down a position so close to home, I guess you really must be tired of teaching. I wish I had the courage to quit like you and Luna."

"Then just do it, Endora. Stay home for a year and work on your children's books. They seem to bring you a lot of pleasure," Bernie said, and then whipped around to face Tertia. "I've been around enough men to know that that bullying nature will rise, so Noah Wilson is off-limits for you, Tertia. I'll get out my potion book and brew up something to put in his coffee if you bring him around here. I'll ask the Universe to find a decent boyfriend for you, but"—she shook her bony forefinger at her niece—"I won't have Noah Wilson set foot on this porch."

Tertia figured that the Universe that Bernie was always talking about had been good to her that day. Her aunt wouldn't be trying to fix her up with Noah, so she was home free. "That's settled," she said, "so let's move on. I've got five minutes before I need to go fix lunch. Endora, it doesn't take courage to quit teaching for a year. You just have to write a resignation letter and clean out your room."

Endora pulled a ponytail holder from the pocket of her jeans and flipped her blond hair up off her neck. "And how would it affect me? If my books don't sell, would I feel like a failure like I did when my fiancé and best friend betrayed me? I don't need any more stress, or ever want to go through that kind of pain or anger again."

"At first you would have a feeling of euphoria," Tertia answered.

"Kind of like getting lucky?" Bernie covered Pepper's ears. "Ever since I took him to the vet and had his little jewels removed, he gets depressed when he thinks about all the sexy little Chihuahuas out there that are missing his pickup growls."

"Aunt Bernie!" Endora scolded.

Bernie removed her hands from the dog's ears. "Well, he does and, honey, these days getting lucky means I make it to the bathroom on time. But, I still have my memories of those wonderful nights when it meant so much more."

Tertia giggled and then laughed out loud. "Darlin' sister, it's better than"—she lowered her voice and glanced over at Pepper—"than getting lucky. I was absolutely overjoyed about the idea of not having to go back to school in the fall. Then this morning, I started sweating bullets worrying about whether it was a mistake to come back here. But that long walk convinced me that there are a lot of options out there. Look at all of us who were teachers and then realized we didn't want that job anymore—Ursula, Luna, and now me. If we can do it, you can too."

"But you won't have the problem of moving," Bernie said. "You're already living here. Are you tired of what you are doing?"

"Not really tired of it, but maybe bored. I'm just not as excited about teaching as I was in the beginning," Endora admitted.

"What excites you?" Tertia asked.

Endora bit her lower lip, like she had always done when she was nervous. "My children's books, but what if…"

Bernie set Pepper down on the porch. "Follow your heart. It won't ever throw a *what–if* into your mind. That's the enemy of your happiness. Shake them cats off your lap, Tertia, and let's go inside and make some dinner. Joe Clay's still out in the shop working on that wedding project. Remy came over to help him while Ursula works on her writing, and Joe Clay is bringing Remy with him for lunch. Mary Jane always comes out of her office for an hour-long break at noon."

Tertia carefully set Misty and Poppy off her lap, and they immediately ran over to bump noses with Pepper. Sassy growled down deep in her throat, and then holding her head and tail both high, she marched across the room with both kittens right behind her.

Endora got up from the rocking chair and opened the door. "Yes, Your Majesty. You and the babies can come inside with us, but you and Pepper need to learn to get along even when the babies aren't around."

"Ain't goin' to happen," Bernie said as she followed the cats into the house. "Pepper is afraid if he lets Sassy into his life that I might like her better than I do him."

Tertia brought up the rear of the parade. She had been listening to Endora worry over what she should do about teaching and listening to her aunt forbidding her to be interested in Noah. But all she could think about was getting to be a part of building a restaurant right there in Spanish Fort.

———

Ophelia got back to the Paradise in the middle of the afternoon, and since no one was waiting on the porch—as in Aunt Bernie—to question her, she figured she was home free. She held her breath as she eased the door open in hopes that it didn't squeak. She heard her mother pacing the floor and the sound of a few Sunday school swear words—*dang, fizzling lousy thing,* and a few others that Ophelia had heard many times. That meant the characters in her mother's newest work in progress weren't behaving, or else her muse was sleeping on the job.

Ophelia tiptoed up the stairs and even remembered to avoid that one step near the middle that always creaked and had almost made it to her bedroom when Tertia's door opened. Her sister put a finger over her lips and then motioned for her to come into her room.

"What's going on?" Ophelia asked.

A soft southerly breeze billowed out the curtains covering the open balcony doors. Tertia fought them back and closed the doors, then sat down on the edge of the bed and nodded toward the rocking chair.

"You are beginning to scare me," Ophelia said. "What has happened since I left a few hours ago?"

"I went for a walk right after you left," Tertia answered. "Dolly Devlin is having iced tea on the screened porch with Aunt Bernie. If I leave the doors open, they can hear every word we say. I know because I've been eavesdropping on their conversation about starting off their business with Melody Gold. They were going to pair her up with Noah Wilson, but then they figured out that the two of them were distant cousins. As you know, other than us sisters, everyone seems to be connected someway to each other here in Spanish Fort, so now they are thinking about Quinton Denton."

"Good Lord!" Ophelia gasped.

"At least if they're working on Melody, then they might leave me alone," Tertia said and then went on to tell Ophelia every detail of what had happened, including Aunt Bernie's reaction to Noah Wilson. "And"—she paused for a breath— "Noah Wilson is Dolly's husband's cousin's son. Dolly says that he was a spoiled brat as a child, but when Wanette left him, he had a tough time moving on, and that he's really grown up the past couple of years. Her words, not mine."

"Well, Sister, it's not like he dropped down on one knee and proposed," Ophelia said. "He just offered you a job, not a diamond ring. From what you said, he needs a friend and a colleague to help him plan and get his café going. It would give you something to do this summer, and remember what you told me about quitting if I don't like the job?"

"Yep, and I guess if his bullying side comes out like Aunt Bernie thinks it will, or if I flat out don't like working with him, I can always walk away," Tertia said with a long sigh. "But how am I going to even do that much without Aunt Bernie pitching a fit?"

"Secretly, until you figure out if you really want to work with Noah," Ophelia answered. "Don't I remember you saying something about loving to cook? Sounds like Aunt Bernie's Universe might be smiling down on you."

"One more thing." Tertia sighed again. "I promised Mama I'd take over the cooking this summer."

"You said that Endora was sympathetic, right?" Ophelia asked.

"Yes."

"Then how about we bring her in on the secret?" Ophelia suggested. "She could help with meals when you need to be away, and you can always say that you are helping me out at the winery that day. Us sisters have always stuck together, but remember, you'll have to come clean about the whole thing if and when you decide to really go to work with Noah full time."

Tertia popped up on her feet, crossed the room, and hugged Ophelia. "Let's go talk to Endora right now."

Ophelia was glad for the distraction, but most of all because Tertia was so involved with her own problem that she didn't even ask about the trip with Jake. Like two kids sneaking around behind their parents' backs, the sisters peeked out of Tertia's bedroom door and then tiptoed across the hall.

"Dammit!" Tertia swore under her breath as she whipped around so fast that she almost knocked Ophelia down.

"What the…?" Ophelia groaned.

"Old habits and all that crap," Tertia whispered. "Endora took over Ursula's old bedroom for her office last week. That's where she will be."

Ophelia reached the door across the hallway first and didn't even knock before entering. Endora stopped humming and looked up from her sketch pad. "Y'all look like a couple of canaries that got out of the cage. Oh, wait a minute!" she exclaimed and wrote a few lines in a nearby notebook. "There's another idea for a book. The canary gets out of the cage, and Misty and Poppy almost eat him when Pepper steps in and tells them that wouldn't be nice."

"Great idea," Ophelia closed the door behind her. "But we need your help."

"You can say no, but please keep my secret if you do," Tertia said.

Endora laid her pencil to the side. "I can keep a secret. Sit down and tell me what's going on."

"It all started with the walk this morning," Tertia said, and then gave her sister a short version of what had happened. "I don't plan on falling in love with Noah, or even dating him. He's not my type, but..." She paused and shrugged.

"You don't want to suffer the flak that Aunt Bernie will dish out, right?" Endora asked. "I can help steer her away since she and her cronies are all interested in finding Melody a husband right now. Poor girl has wedding-dress fever. I recognize the symptoms because I was afflicted with the same when I was first dating Kevin."

Endora motioned toward the rocker beside the closed balcony doors. Ophelia sat down in it, and Tertia perched on the edge of the bed.

"Aunt Bernie is the tip of the iceberg. Ursula and Luna will tease me unmercifully after I made that comment about not ever dating another blond-haired man," Tertia said just above a whisper. "Like I said, we won't be dating, and I'd like to test the waters before I tell the rest of the family."

Endora nodded and said, "I understand, and of course I'll help. It's kind of like frenemies, right?"

"That's right," Tertia agreed.

"Tell you what," Endora said. "I'll make this easy by suggesting that I take over supper duties each night until summer starts. That leaves you with the afternoons free. This makes me feel like old times when we conspired together against that sorry preacher man who had his eye on our mama."

"Kind of does, doesn't it?" Ophelia said with a smile and then nudged Tertia. "When are you going to call Noah and tell him that you'll talk to him?"

"Maybe tomorrow," Tertia answered. "I need to sleep on it first, but"—she paused—"thank you both."

Endora's eyes twinkled. "Now it's your turn, Ophelia. Tell us about your trip with Jake today. Were you nervous?"

"Not one bit," Ophelia said. "I wasn't antsy like I usually am on a first date, and he was easy to talk to, but even with Aunt Bernie telling me over and over again that this was a date"—she raised one shoulder in a half shrug—"it didn't feel so much like a date, other than…"

"Other than what?" Tertia asked.

"There was a little moment when I slipped on the truck's running board and almost fell. He caught me, and maybe there were some little sparks, but then it could have just been that I was saved from the embarrassment of falling at his feet," she answered. "Besides we all know that it's not smart to start up a relationship with your boss. That can create all kinds of problems."

"It could get awkward," Tertia agreed, but she was thinking of her own situation more than Ophelia's.

Endora stood up and rolled her neck a couple of times. "There, that got the kinks out. Sometimes I get so involved with my books and illustrations that I sit too long. I'm glad y'all are being smart about Jake and Noah."

"It's kind of the chance of a lifetime," Tertia said as she rolled up on her feet. "To get to be in on the building of a café from start to finish and then cook for a living. That would be my dream come true."

"Then go for it," Endora said.

A noise at the door made all of them jump. Ophelia visualized Aunt Bernie with her ear plastered to the door and listening in on their conversation. Then she pictured Pepper scratching on the wood, and Bernie giving him a look that would melt Lucifer's horns. She held her breath when Endora eased it open and let it out in a whoosh when Sassy and the kittens hurried inside, jumped up on her bed, and curled up in Ophelia's lap.

"They're spoiled rotten and fickle," Tertia said. "They were in my lap before dinner and purring like *I* was their favorite human."

Endora picked up Poppy by the scruff of the neck and sat back down in her office chair. "They bring me lots of happiness. I may just grow up to be the crazy old cat lady who lives in an old brothel and writes children's books that won't sell."

"Oh, honey," Tertia said. "Your books are not going only sell; they're going to be bestsellers."

Endora rolled her eyes toward the ceiling. "From your

mouth to a publisher's checkbook. Mama asked her agent, and Norma said to send in the first one completed, and she would see what she could do."

Tertia headed for the door. "That's a start."

"Kind of like what y'all are doing with your new jobs?" Endora said.

Ophelia gently laid Sassy and Misty off to the side. "How's that?"

"Five of the seven of us sisters have gotten a new start this past six months. Let's make the most of it," Endora said. "I think that's why Aunt Bernie has a bee in her bloomers about this new business. She's worked all her life, and she's finding retirement isn't so much fun."

"Amen," Ophelia and Tertia said at the same time.

Chapter 10

SINCE OPHELIA WASN'T SURE what she should wear on her first day of work at the winery, she dressed in a pair of jeans and a knit shirt. She checked her reflection in the mirror on the back of the door and decided her jeans and shirt were far too casual. She would be working in a winery, not a fast-food joint. She went back to the closet and tried on a pair of navy-blue dress slacks and a hot pink silk blouse. When she turned around and looked in the mirror, she shook her head—way too stuffy.

Of all the sisters, Ophelia had never been the indecisive one. Metaphorically speaking, she didn't sit on the fence and worry for hours about which side to take on any issue that came up. She made a decision—like she did in her sophomore year of high school to go into the air force—and didn't look back. So, why was getting dressed for work such an ordeal that morning?

Another trip to the closet netted a yellow gingham-checked sundress. She remembered it being cold in the winery, so she topped it off with a lightweight denim jacket. She twisted her curly red hair up in a messy bun and held it there with a big white clamp. With her plain white sneakers in her hands, she made her way down the stairs.

When she reached the bottom step, Luna was coming in the front door with Aunt Bernie right behind her. They both stopped and stared at her. Bernie frowned when she saw the shoes. Luna shook her head at the jacket.

"What?" Ophelia asked.

"You should wear jeans, and I bet Jake has shirts with the winery logo on them for you to wear," Luna answered.

"Those shoes do *not go* with that dress," Bernie said. "You need to wear high heels."

Ophelia sat down on one of the two ladder-back chairs beside the hall tree and put her shoes on. "I'm going to be on my feet all day, so I'm wearing something comfortable. If Jake wants me to wear jeans and a logo shirt, he can give me one and I will wear it tomorrow. But today this is what I'm wearing."

"You never was one to take advice," Bernie said with a long sigh and turned to face Luna. "Talk some sense into her. She's so bullheaded that she won't listen to me, not even about something as serious as her biological clock." She raised one bony shoulder in a shrug and headed toward the kitchen with Pepper prancing along behind her like he was leading the Thanksgiving Day Parade in Saint Jo.

"What have my dress and shoes got to do with relationships and babies?" Ophelia asked.

"Actually, I think you look cute," Luna whispered, "kind of like a Sunday school teacher."

"Good Lord!" Ophelia growled. "But you aren't going to talk me into changing into jeans with reverse psychology."

She tied her shoes and stood up. "What are you doing here so early?"

"Endora called, and I came to tell Tertia that I'm in on her secret about Noah." Luna answered in a low voice. "And so is Ursula. You know very well that Endora and I share everything, and it didn't seem right to leave Ursula out. Since we all know Tertia can say that she's coming to my place or Ursula's as well as to the winery. That way..."

"What are y'all whispering about?" Tertia asked as she made her way down the stairs.

Ophelia slung her purse over her shoulder. "I've got to get to work. I don't want to be late for my first day on the new job. Luna can tell you what's going on."

"Tell me what?" Tertia asked.

Ophelia waved and hurried out the door. Not even Aunt Bernie could win a battle with five of the sisters banding together. Bless the old gal's heart. She would have to commune with the Universe awhile longer. Ophelia giggled when a visual popped into her head of her aunt dancing around a black cauldron and chanting something about a clock not working properly. She shook the image from her head. Thinking like that meant that Bernie was rubbing off on her.

The commute would have taken only five minutes from the Paradise to the winery if she hadn't slowed down when she turned off the two-lane highway onto the gravel road, so it took a little longer. She didn't notice the CLOSED sign in the window until she walked up on the porch. Rather than going back to her vehicle, she sat down on the top step and started thinking about her outfit. Did she really look like a Sunday school teacher? And if she did, would that throw bad vibes toward anyone coming into the winery that day? Would they take one look at her and feel guilty about buying alcohol?

All those thoughts flew out of her head without answers when she heard the unmistakable whirring sound of a drone. When she first came home last Christmas, she had mistaken the sounds of the washing machine and Joe Clay's table saw for drones coming to exact punishment on her for what she had done. Yes, it was sanctioned by the United States government, and she had been deemed psychologically fit for the job, but that didn't wipe out the adrenaline rush when she heard a noise that sounded like a swarm of bees.

She looked up in the sky, expecting to see only big white fluffy clouds, but sure enough, there was the little demon, hovering right over her head. Immediately, her chest tightened, and her breath came out in short gasps. This was no dream. It was real. She couldn't look away from the thing, but she couldn't figure out whether she was looking at a camera or a small load of explosives on the underbelly. Somewhere some person was sitting in front of a camera, either looking at a picture of her or else had their finger on a button ready to turn Jake's winery into a pile of ash. She squinted against the bright sun and was so engrossed in figuring out what the silver thing was carrying that she didn't hear the front door open.

"Good mornin'," Jake said.

His deep voice startled her so badly that she bent forward and covered her head with her hands. The buzzing sound got fainter and fainter as it flew away.

"Are you all right? What scared you so bad?" he asked as he sat down beside her.

She raised up and managed a weak smile. "I'm fine. I heard a buzzing noise and thought a bee was attacking my red hair."

"What you heard was that drone up above us," he said. "It's been flying around these parts for a week. I suspect that it's from one of the wineries down around Saint Jo that is looking at what the rest of our vineyards look like. Did you fly that kind of thing when you were in the service? Is that what scared you? You are pale as a ghost. Let's go inside, and I'll get you a bottle of water or a glass of wine. Whichever one you need."

"I'm good. Pale is my norm, but I might like a bottle of water when we are inside." She managed a weak smile. "I'm the only sister with red hair and a buttermilk complexion. The hair comes from Aunt Bernie. They tell me that my great-grandmother was also a redhead and had pale skin like I have. And I talk too much when I'm nervous, so I'm shutting up now."

Jake stood up and extended a hand. "You look very pretty today, and I'm sure glad you wore comfortable shoes. And honey, your voice is so soothing that I could listen to you read one of those old-fashioned phone books to me."

Ophelia put her hand in his and allowed him to pull her up to a standing position. "Thank you."

"You are trembling," Jake said.

"There were no bees," Ophelia admitted. "I don't like to admit that I still have some scars left over from the job I did in the service. I can't give you details, but it involved doing things that go against my nature. That drone brought back some bad memories."

"Well, darlin'…" He gave her hand a gentle squeeze. "I hereby declare that working at Brennan Winery will erase all those memories."

The heat from his hand to hers and the smile on his face almost made her believe that he could be right. "Are you sure about that, or did you travel to Ireland and kiss the Blarney Stone?"

"I did kiss it a couple of times, but not in Ireland." He chuckled. "I drove my grandparents out to the Texas Panhandle to a little town called Shamrock. There's a real Blarney Stone out there that was sent over from Ireland."

"My sister Tertia just moved from that area, and she and I visited that small town," Ophelia said. "And before you ask, yes, I did kiss the stone."

Jake opened the door. "I'd say that since we both put our lips on the stone and since we are working together, this should be our lucky summer. The winery will make lots of money, and your ugly memories will fade and die. Today you look every bit the part of a lovely Irish lass. My grandfather would have told me that I got the gold at the end of the rainbow when I hired you."

"Because I have red hair?" she asked.

"For that and other reasons. My grandmother had red hair before it turned gray. I miss them both very much." He removed his glasses and cleaned them on the tail of his T-shirt.

Ophelia had always thought of Aunt Bernie being an extra grandmother, and even with her meddling, she would miss the old gal when she was gone. "Thank you for those compliments, and do you really think that kissing a big round rock can bring us good luck?"

"I think that having someone like you here in the winery is going to bring me even more luck than the gift of gab could ever do," he answered. "Right now, I want you to meet the guys who work with me."

He crossed the room, opened the door, and yelled, "Hey, everyone, can y'all come on up here and meet Ophelia?"

In just a few seconds, three men ranging from young to old paraded into room. "Guys, this is Ophelia. She's the lady I told you about who is going to run the front of the store. Ophelia, this is Rodney, Frankie, and Lester."

"Pleasure to meet you," Lester said.

Frankie and Rodney both nodded.

"I'm glad to meet all of y'all," Ophelia said with a smile.

Lester was a short man with a rim of gray hair around an otherwise bald head, and a thick gray mustache. Frankie was taller, maybe the same height as Ophelia, and had brown hair, brown eyes, and arms that looked like they could bench-press one of Remy's Angus bulls. Rodney's red hair was that burgundy color that was all the rage among women those days. If he walked into the shop and wanted to buy a bottle of wine, she would ID him for sure.

"Welcome to the winery," Frankie said. "We'd love to stay and visit, but we need Jake to test a batch of watermelon wine that we've got going."

"There'll be plenty of time later," Ophelia said.

"That's my cue to get to the back," Jake said. "If you need me, just hit the intercom button right there"—he pointed to a place beside the cash register—"and yell right loud. I'll come running. We've got a batch of strawberries going so I should get to the business in the back room. Oh, and there's a key on a Brennan Winery fob over by the cash register. It's for you to keep so you don't ever have to sit on the porch and wait for me to open up again."

Ophelia wondered what he'd meant by that statement about her bringing him good luck, but not for long, because for the next couple of hours she was steadily busy selling bottles of wine as fast as she could ring up the sales. At a few minutes past noon, Rodney came in the front door with two boxes of doughnuts in his hands and set one down on the counter.

"May I help you?" Ophelia asked.

"Hey, Miz Ophelia," Rodney said with a grin. "Jake sent me out to get doughnuts for our break time. He'll be up here in a minute. You might want to put on a pot of coffee if you have time."

"I can sure do that," she said. "And thanks for the dough-nuts, but where is the coffeepot?"

Ophelia wondered if having red hair of any shade was a

prerequisite for working for Jake, but then she remembered that Lester had gray hair and Frankie's was dark. She looked around the winery but didn't see a coffeepot anywhere.

Rodney pointed toward the door leading into the reception hall. "You'll find it in the kitchen behind the stage."

"Thank you," she said and started in that direction.

"No, ma'am," Rodney called out as he disappeared into the back. "Thank you! We haven't ever gotten doughnuts for break before now. See you around."

Before the coffee was done dripping, Jake brought in the box that had been set on the counter. He smiled and said, "Today we have doughnuts to welcome you to Brennan Winery, and to celebrate getting a really good batch of strawberry wine bottled up and set in the cellar to age."

"Well, thank you," Ophelia said. "It's already been a busy morning. Is that normal for a Tuesday?"

Jake got two mugs and two plates from the counter, then added a couple of forks. "Nope, it is not. I usually only see a couple of people on Tuesdays. The doughnuts are on a table in the reception room. We can take our coffee out there, and please feel free to make it whenever you want. We keep a pot brewing in the back room all day."

She filled two mugs and handed one to him. "Are the rest of the crew joining us?"

He headed out of the kitchen. "I asked them, but they like to take their breaks out in the yard when it's pretty weather. There's a picnic table back there, and Lester smokes."

He set his coffee on a nearby table beside the pink box

and pulled out a chair for her. Then he sat down beside her. "So how has the first hour gone? Did you get bored? I meant to tell you that…"

She held up a hand. "I didn't have a lot of time between customers, but when I did, I dusted the shelves and swept up the crumbs that folks let fall on the floor when they tasted the wine, cheese, and crackers."

"That's great," Jake said. "I hate to dust, and usually only clean on Saturday or Sunday afternoons when the shop is closed."

"Well, now you'll have those afternoons free." She took a sip of her coffee. "Do all three of the fellows I met this morning live around here?"

"Nope, they all live north of Nocona," he answered. "Lester worked with the construction crew that helped build the winery. Frankie is his son and Rodney is his nephew. Lester and his son had worked at a winery down around Galveston before they moved up in this area. Rodney is taking online college courses at night to be a teacher, so I won't get to keep him but another year or so."

He opened the box to reveal an assortment of doughnuts— sprinkles, green sugar on top of cake doughnuts, glazed, and maple iced—and motioned for her to choose first.

She picked up one with multicolored sprinkles. "Did Rodney drive all the way to Nocona for these?"

"Yep, he did," Jake replied. "Too bad we don't have a pastry shop in town. Maybe I should buy the old store and put one in. It's probably big enough for that."

"How would you ever manage to do both a winery and a pastry shop?" Ophelia asked.

"I hear you've got another sister or maybe two coming home this year," he said. "Think one of them would want to get up at three in the morning to make doughnuts? They could be off work by noon."

"I kind of doubt it," she said. "But that is a good idea. It would put another business in town, but come on, Jake. In practically a ghost town?"

"Hey, other people drive all the way to Nocona for doughnuts. If there was a shop in town, they wouldn't have to do that. And if we sold cakes and pies as well, it could be profitable," he argued.

Jake picked up a chocolate doughnut, dipped the edge into his coffee and then bit into it, chewed, swallowed, and took a sip. "My grandpa ate doughnuts that way. Granny fussed at him for it, but it didn't stop him."

"So does my dad, Joe Clay," Ophelia said, still amazed at how comfortable she was with Jake. "He says it's the only way to eat them. And he dips cookies and graham crackers in milk."

"That's a man who could be my friend," Jake said.

"He's been mine since I was a little girl." Ophelia finished off the last bite and picked up a maple iced one.

"Little girl?" Jake asked.

"He came into our lives when we moved to Spanish Fort. Ursula is the oldest sister and she was about twelve, or maybe nearly thirteen. Anyway, Mama wanted to raise us girls away from the big city life. She read an article about the old brothel and decided to drive up here and look at the house. The elderly lady who had lived in it for fifty years died, and her grandchildren that inherited it wanted a quick sale. Mama got it at a good price and moved us into the place just like it was."

"Was that a good thing?" Jake asked.

"Not in our minds. There was one electrical outlet in each of the seven upstairs bedrooms, one sink in the bathroom, and no closets. Mama reminded us that we had been whining for our own rooms, and now we had them. Then she told us to be patient. She hired Joe Clay to remodel the Paradise. He didn't want to do it at first, but she offered him room and board in addition to his wages. He didn't know that the deal came with seven girls," Ophelia answered with a giggle. "He had just retired from the military, and he didn't even like kids, but we changed his mind. He became a fantastic daddy and friend to all of us."

"Is your father dead?"

"No, he's alive and well, and he is a very wealthy doctor, but his wife has more money than Midas. She married him, not his family, so we don't have a lot of interaction with him."

"So, Joe Clay is the reason you joined the military?" Jake asked.

"Yep, he is, and Mama is the reason that Ursula and now Endora are novelists. Ursula writes romance and Endora is working on children's books," Ophelia answered. Talking about her sisters was a lot easier than revealing things about herself.

"And you are my good luck charm, so that makes you more important than all your sisters," Jake said.

"Good grief! Is that a pickup line?" she teased.

"No, it's the truth, but if it was, how would it be working?" His eyes twinkled and his smile lit up the room.

"Pretty good," she answered at the same time the bell above the door rang announcing another customer. "Break time is over. Thank you for the doughnuts and coffee."

"Anytime," Jake said. "I'll clean up here."

A man who was thoughtful, romantic, and wasn't afraid of dirty dishes. Aunt Bernie would hop up on her soapbox and sing his praises to the top of her lungs.

———

"I need something to do. I thought maybe I would take over supper duties if it's all right with Tertia," Endora suggested at the dinner table that Tuesday. "I don't want to get all up in Tertia's business, but sometimes I need an outlet after working on children's books all day."

Tertia could have hugged her youngest sister. Not even Aunt Bernie frowned at the idea. "I'm good with that."

"I don't care how you girls divide up the jobs." Mary Jane passed the bowl of potato chips around the table. "I'm just grateful y'all are taking on some of the chores so I can help more with the wedding plans and still not miss a deadline."

Bernie took out a fistful of chips and sent the bowl on to

Endora. "That's a wonderful idea. Tertia will have more time to date once I find a suitable feller for her. I need to get onto that project soon, or Noah Wilson might try to wiggle his way into her life. We can't have that—no, sir!"

Tertia swallowed a mouthful of tea quickly so that she didn't spew it across the table at her aunt. "I keep telling you that I'm"—she sputtered—"not ready to even start down that path. Maybe in a year, but not now."

"In a year you could be in a relationship and expecting the second grandbaby to arrive here at the Paradise," Bernie argued. "When I'm dead and layin' in my casket, you'll be sorry you didn't have children before I kicked the bucket, and that I didn't get to help train up your daughters to be sassy like me."

"What if I have all sons?" Tertia asked.

"Joe Clay can take care of teaching your sons to be responsible young men"—she shifted her gaze over to Tertia—"and to help them learn that being a bully has consequences. But remember this, I'm already old, and Joe Clay and Mary Jane ain't getting no younger. You want to raise your kids without grandparents or me, either one?"

"Aunt Bernie, don't talk like that," Endora scolded.

"I agree with Endora," Mary Jane said with a shiver. "I don't want to think about you not being here, so we'll hear no more about caskets or death."

"That's right," Joe Clay said. "But that said, Mary Jane and I are sure looking forward to being grandparents."

"Please don't die, Aunt Bernie," Remy said. "Ursula

would be so sad if you were to pass away. She was crying last night wishing all the family was here together."

"Yes, I was," Ursula said with a nod.

"Ursula just has a case of pregnant brain," Mary Jane chuckled. "Hormones are what cause the weeping."

"See!" Bernie snapped and shot Tertia another dose of stink eye. "Other people in the family listen to my advice." She turned to face Remy. "Most of my influence with the Universe has been in another direction, trying to take care of Ophelia and Tertia, but I can ask that Bo and Rae get so miserable that all they can think about is the Paradise."

"I don't want them to be unhappy," Joe Clay said.

Bernie tipped up her bony chin and smiled. "Sometimes just a little unhappiness makes a person appreciate the joy that they find at the end of a rainbow."

Tertia pushed back her chair and stood up. "Endora, will you help me bring out the dessert? I made a pan of brownies—just plain ones with no dusting of Aunt Bernie's magic powders—and thought we might top them off with some ice cream."

"Glad to," Endora answered and followed her sister into the kitchen.

"Do you think Aunt Bernie really has marijuana gummy bears in her trailer?" Tertia whispered as they put a plate of brownies and half a gallon of ice cream on a tray.

"I wouldn't put anything past her," Endora answered. "I'll be super careful not to let her near the food when I'm cooking."

"Me too," Tertia said, "and thank you for doing this. I owe you."

Endora picked up the tray and winked at her sister. "Don't worry about it. I *will* collect sometime in the future."

Tertia didn't have a single, solitary doubt that her sister was dead serious, despite that cute little wink that reminded her so much of how Endora used to be before she had gotten her heart broken.

Her phone pinged right after she sat back down at the table. She pulled it out of her pocket, but before she could even glance down at it, Bernie shook her long, bony forefinger at her.

"If that's Noah Wilson, you can text him back to drop dead."

"I expect if he wanted to talk to Tertia, he would call on the house phone," Endora said. "How would he get her cell phone number?"

Smart girl! She hadn't told a lie or even stretched the truth a little.

"Maybe he's got one of them phones that steals phone numbers from just being close to another one," Bernie argued. "Bullies grow up to be con men, and he did stop and talk to her today."

Tertia held the phone out for everyone to see. "It's Ophelia telling me that she wasn't coming home until the shop closes. Jake keeps sandwich makings at the winery, and they don't take a lunch break until about three."

Bernie smiled so big that her wrinkles deepened into

crevasses. "I've gotten three good men right—Remy, Shane, and now Jake—so listen to me when I tell you that Noah Wilson isn't the one for you."

"Thank you," Remy said. "I needed all the help I could get, and Ursula and I appreciate whatever you did for us."

Tertia shoved her phone back into her pocket. "What if Noah is just my boss in my dream job, and we never date or even become close friends?"

"Not even!" Aunt Bernie snapped.

Joe Clay passed the brownies over to Mary Jane. "Dream job? I believe I missed something."

Tertia raised her shoulder in half a shrug. "My favorite memories are when I helped Mama in the kitchen. I always thought I'd like to be a chef."

"I wanted to be an actress," Endora said.

"What did you want to be when you grew up, Aunt Bernie?" Remy asked.

"I wanted to own a bar," Bernie answered, "and now I want to run a successful business where I match up couples and make them live happily ever after."

Mary Jane took a brownie off the plate. "How did you buy your bar? I never heard that story."

Bernie smiled. "I won it in a poker game."

Tertia's phone pinged again, but she ignored it. No sense in tempting fate a second time.

"Who would put their bar up as stakes in a card game?" Joe Clay asked.

"A drunk fool who thought a straight flush would beat

a royal flush," she grinned. "His name was Buford Clifford, but everyone called him Slim."

"What did you bet?" Remy asked.

"A night in my bed with whoever won the game." She giggled. "I was down to my last dollar and didn't have anything else to wager."

"Aunt Bernie!" Endora gasped.

"Honey, with the hand I had, I knew I wasn't going to bed with any of those fools. I won the bar, a thousand dollars, and this ring in that game." She held up her hand to show off the ring they were all familiar with—a pretty emerald in a filagree setting. "It's brought me good luck ever since the night I won it, and I told the undertaker to bury me with it. I might need a little more luck to get past them pearly gates."

Thank you! Tertia rolled her eyes toward the ceiling. Steering Bernie away from the Noah Wilson topic had been pure genius, so Endora wasn't the only one she owed that day.

Chapter 11

TERTIA KNOCKED GENTLY ON her mother's office door and then peeked inside to see Mary Jane in her recliner with a notebook in her hands. "Mama, you got a minute?"

Mary Jane laid the notebook aside and motioned toward a second recliner. "Always."

Sunlight flowed through the open window, and a slight breeze fluttered the sheer curtains. A jar candle threw off the aroma of vanilla, her mother's favorite scent, and blended with fresh air and the smell of the rosebushes in the backyard. Since she had been a little girl, Tertia could always depend on her mother to give her good solid advice.

She eased down into the chair and popped the footrest up. "Noah called and wants me to meet him at his folks' house across the street to give him some ideas about the café he's going to build right here in Spanish Fort."

"Go," Mary Jane said.

"But…"

Mary Jane popped the footrest down and laid a hand on Tertia's knee. "I'll tell you exactly the same thing I've told all seven of you sisters for your entire lives. Follow your heart. Do you want to go talk with Noah about a café?"

Tertia nodded. "But I don't want to fight with Aunt Bernie. She has her heart *set* on me not having a thing to do with Noah. She's really adamant about the issue. What if I cause her to have a heart attack or a stroke?"

"You can't follow her heart," Mary Jane said. "You have to pay attention to yours. Meeting with him, even working with him eventually, does not mean you are going to fall in love with him and marry him next week, does it? And besides you were just kids when you had that fight at school. You've both grown up and are in a far different place in your lives than you were then."

"How does a woman get to be as wise as you are?" Tertia asked.

Mary Jane pointed at the messy bun on top of her head. "These gray hairs that sprout up daily are marks of wisdom."

Tertia rose up out of the chair, took a couple of steps, and bent to give her mother a hug. "Thanks, Mama."

"Anytime," Mary Jane said. "Is this why Endora is taking over supper duties?"

"Yes, ma'am, but I'll help her when I don't have to be away in the afternoons," Tertia answered.

"Do all of your sisters know about that?"

Tertia nodded. "All but Rae and Bo."

"I'm proud of you girls for sticking together," Mary Jane said. "Now go on and meet with Noah. Who knows? Your generation could knock our little community right off the almost-a-ghost-town register. And one more thing before you go, honey. Don't worry about Aunt Bernie's heart.

She's strong as an ox and will probably outlive every one of us." She lowered her voice to a whisper. "And if a miracle occurred and you and Noah did get into a relationship, she would declare that it was her reverse psychology that caused it and take full credit."

"I wouldn't be a bit surprised, but none of you have anything to worry about in that area," Tertia said as she left the room and closed the door behind her.

Sassy and Misty were sitting beside Mary Jane's office door, so Tertia had to slip out quickly to keep them from sneaking inside. She sat down on one of the ladder-back chairs to put her shoes on, and both cats rubbed around her legs, purring the whole time. Then Pepper came from the living room with Poppy right behind him. Evidently, the kittens were choosing sides that morning. One with Poppa Pepper, and one with Mama Sassy. But if Pepper was in the house, that meant Aunt Bernie was probably in the kitchen or on the screened porch.

Tertia wondered if this was a sign. She had never seen Poppy and Misty more than a couple of feet away from each other, but then Luna and Endora had always had that twin thing too. Did this mean that there were two sides to everything, like Tertia's mama had preached to the girls while they were growing up? She scolded herself for trying to find a sign in everything, one that would convince her that she was doing the right thing. Her mother had just told her to follow her heart. What half-grown cats and a Chihuahua did or didn't do had no bearing on what Tertia's heart was telling her to do.

Poppy went to the front door and meowed loudly. "You have to stay in the house or else you will try to follow me. Endora would never forgive me if you followed me and got hit on the road."

Tertia slipped outside and hurried down the lane until she came to the end. Turning left would take her to the old store and, if she went on around the corner, to Luna and Shane's house. Right would take her to the school and in the direction of Nocona. Walking across the road would take her down a short lane to the house where Noah grew up.

His father worked in Nocona, so he took him to school every morning, and his mother picked him up in the afternoon, so he never rode the bus with her and her sisters.

Memories surfaced of when she and her sisters caught the bus right where she stood.

"That was probably a good thing," she muttered as she crossed the road and walked up the short lane to a brick house. Noah's truck was sitting in the circular driveway, and the front door was open. A grown gray and white cat lounged on the porch steps, and a cage with a cockatiel inside hung from a chain between two white porch posts.

"Hey!" Noah opened the door and waved. "I've been keeping a watch out for you. Come on in. I've got things spread out on the dining room table. The contractor needs a general idea of how big I want to make this café before the end of the week, so he can work up an estimate, and something don't seem quite right. I'm so glad you came over. I need help."

The cat didn't even open an eye when Tertia walked up onto the porch, but the bird gave out a wolf whistle that caused the cat to sit up and growl. "Evidently, they aren't best friends."

"Nope." Noah chuckled. "The cat was my dad's pet, and the bird was Mama's. The place where they moved doesn't allow pets, so they are part of the inheritance deal on this place. The cat's name is Higgins because Dad loved the old *Magnum P.I.* series, and the bird is Rocky. Mama inherited him from my grandmother when she passed away, and Granny liked *The Rockford Files.* Higgins would eat Rocky if he got a chance. Rocky would gladly peck the cat's eyeballs out."

"Sounds like Pepper the Chihuahua and Sassy the cat over at the Paradise, except when Endora's kittens are around. They seem to get along in front of the children." She stopped in the living room and scanned the place. Lawn furniture was scattered in front of a small television sitting on a wooden apple crate. Through the archway she could see a long table with eight chairs around it and a crystal chandelier hanging above it.

"There's as much contrast in my house as there is between a cat and a bird." Noah chuckled. "Mama could take her living room furniture to the new place, but the dining room stuff wouldn't fit, so I inherited it with the house—like the smart-ass bird and the lazy cat. Got to admit they are growing on me, though, and they are company."

Tertia walked to the table and looked at the big sheet

of butcher paper. "Kind of like my Aunt Bernie. At first all of us sisters wondered what Mama was thinking, letting her move her travel trailer onto the Paradise property with Pepper. But now we don't know what we'd do without her most days."

Noah joined her at the table. "Most days?"

"Aunt Bernie thinks she has a hotline to the Universe and spends a lot of her time meddling in our lives, and now she is determined to extend her expertise out further by playing matchmaker like those places on the internet," Tertia admitted. "She's practicing on me these days."

"I believe that some folks really do have a hotline that lets them see into the future. I should have listened to my grandmother." Noah chuckled again. "She told me not to marry Wanette. According to her, I should have gotten one of them nose rings to make it easy for Wanette to lead me around. She came to the wedding, which surprised me, and even had her picture taken with us. As soon as the divorce papers were signed, she burned it."

Noah, bless his heart, didn't know he was digging his own grave. If Tertia listened to Aunt Bernie, she wouldn't even be looking at his rough drawings on white paper. "Aunt Bernie would have had a bonfire and danced around it, singing to the top of her lungs, if she'd been in your granny's shoes. Now, tell me more about this drawing. What am I looking at?"

"It's a very rough draft of the old store, but when I got to figuring out the size of tables for four and maybe booths along this wall"—he pointed—"it would only seat about thirty people tops. I think we should enlarge it to accommodate at least fifty."

"I agree, and maybe lengthen it out a little," Tertia suggested. "What do you think about putting a small store in this part where the guests pay out. Maybe sell some locally made jelly and relishes, and T-shirts with the café logo?"

Noah nodded more with every word. "That's a great idea. I was in a little place like that up in northern Oklahoma. I bought pickled okra and some plum jam. It would only take a few more feet and involve putting some shelving along the walls. We might even have some key chains with our logo on them, and maybe some mugs or glasses for sale. The promotion would be great."

"You *could* give away a key chain if the bill came to more than like fifty dollars," Tertia said. "That would encourage folks to bring their friends and family to the café."

"Wonderful idea. I like it a lot." He picked up a metal square and added a few feet to the length and to the width of what he had drawn, then erased two lines. "Now, should the kitchen be across the back or down the side?"

"Definitely across the back," Tertia answered without hesitation. "And remember to add in two restrooms somewhere."

"Ahh," his mouth twitched, "I thought we'd just throw up a couple of outhouses in the backyard."

"That will be fine if they will pass inspection," she shot back at him. "You should have the builders cut a quarter moon on the guys' door, and a star on the ladies'. But think about whether or not your customers want to go outside in the rain or snow to use the facilities."

"I can see that you are still just as funny as you were back when we were in school," Noah said. "But you might have an idea there. We could make the bathrooms rustic-looking with what looks like outhouse doors on the stalls and old galvanized basins for the sinks."

"So, it's going to be kind of rustic instead of crystal-chandelier fancy?" Tertia asked, amazed that he remembered her for anything other than a black eye.

"That was my idea," he answered and then added another few feet to what would be the front of the building. "I'm glad you remembered bathrooms, and it would be best if they weren't near the kitchen, so we'll put them up here near the checkout counter."

"Will the customers pay at the counter or at the table?" Tertia asked.

Noah combed his blond hair back with his fingertips. "Food at the table, and retail items at the counter."

"What's this?" Tertia picked up a square of red construction paper.

"Those are tables, and the yellow ones are chairs."

She laid twelve of the red ones out and then started putting the yellow ones around them. "That's forty-eight, and you've got plenty of room for someone to push back chairs from this table and this one without causing a problem. I like that arrangement."

"I wouldn't have thought of that either," Noah said. "Man, I'm glad you agreed to come help me out today."

"You are welcome," Tertia said. "What are you naming the place?"

"Either the Old Store Café or the Red River Café," he answered. "Which one do you like best?"

"That should be your decision," Tertia told him.

"What sounds catchier to you?" Noah pressured.

"Old Store Café," she answered without hesitation. "Shane and Luna are tossing around ideas for their new store, and one of them is the Red River Place. I told them to just call it the Beer, Bait, and Bologna Store, since it will have convenience store items, bait to fish with, and a place to buy beer and wine."

"Don't forget fishing licenses," Noah reminded her.

"*Bait* covers that," Tertia told him.

"Beer," Noah groaned. "I'm a terrible host. I was so excited that you came over that I didn't even offer you anything to drink. I've got beer, sweet tea, and several kinds of soda."

"I would love a beer," she answered without looking up from the drawing. She was missing something—she could feel it in her bones.

He left and returned in a minute with two longneck bottles of icy-cold beer, twisted the top off one, and handed it to her. "You are studying that awfully hard. What's the matter?"

She took a long drink of her beer and then set it down on

the table. "I feel like we are missing something important, so I'm going over the rough notes you have written on the side here."

Noah removed the cap from his beer and took a sip. "I see it now. We've got to have a food prep center. If we add four feet to this side, we could slip a prep counter into the kitchen."

"That's why the kitchen didn't look right," Tertia agreed. "What are you going to put on the outside? Siding? Rough cedar?"

"Distressed red brick so it will look like the old store," Noah answered and pointed to the front. "A couple of park benches on the porch, and a handicap ramp on one end. We'll start off with a gravel parking lot, and if things go well, we'll pave it in another year or two."

"Looks like my work here is done, then," Tertia said.

"Not until you finish your beer," Noah told her. "Come on into my fancy living room and sit a spell on one of my lawn chairs."

Tertia remembered Bernie pitching a hissy fit when she caught Endora about to pour out half a bottle of wine after the Paradise Christmas party. According to her, it was an unforgivable sin to pour out any kind of booze—be it beer, wine, liquor, or even moonshine—so, Bernie couldn't complain if Tertia visited with Noah long enough to finish her bottle of beer, now could she?

She followed him from the dining room table to the living room and sat down in one of the chairs. She had taken a small sip when Higgins—no, that wasn't right; the bird was Rocky—squawked out something that sounded like, "Put on your britches. We got company."

"Dad used to yell that to Mama when someone pulled up in the yard. That will be my contractor. You might remember Justin Davis, who went to school with us. Henry is his father, and he's the one who is going to build the café," Bernie said.

"What happened to Justin?" Tertia asked.

"He developed a software program, sold it, and retired to an island last year. I heard that he actually bought the whole island and is developing it into a fancy retreat," Noah answered as he headed for the door. "Just goes to show there's more money to be made in being a nerd than in teaching and/or coaching."

She held up her beer. "Amen to that."

"Come on in, Henry. I think we might be ready to show you our plans," Noah said and led the tall, lanky man back to the dining room table. "Tertia, will you join us?"

She set her bottle on a plastic end table and stood up.

"So, this is the *we* you were talking about," Henry said. "You are one of the Simmons girls, aren't you?"

"Yes, sir," Tertia answered. "I'm Tertia. I was in the class with your son, Justin."

"I remember you very well," Henry said. "Justin had a bit of a crush on you back then."

"Oh, really?"

"Yep, but he was too shy to say anything, and then he

went to that fancy science school for his junior and senior year and met Iris, the girl he eventually married. They're out on an island now."

"Tell him I said hello next time you talk to him," Tertia said.

"I sure will," Henry said with a nod. "Now show me what y'all have come up with."

Tertia stood back and let Noah explain what he wanted. Henry nodded with each idea and only made a couple of suggestions. One was that Noah add a few more feet all around to give the kitchen more room, and the other was that the porch should be the same size as the one on the old store building.

Noah made a few notes on the bottom of the butcher paper, rolled it up, put a rubber band around it, and handed it off to Henry. "I think we are ready to go to the next step."

"I'll take these to the guy who draws up the drafts for me and get back to you in a week. If you're in agreement, we can start construction right after that. Do you want a wooden porch like the old store had in the beginning, or a concrete one?" Henry asked.

"Wooden," Tertia said so quickly that she wondered if she'd even said the words out loud. "I'm sorry if I overstepped. I just see it with a wide wooden porch and the park benches out front for folks."

"You didn't overstep, and I agree," Noah said, "and I plan on putting a sign up above the porch like what's over at the old store now."

"Still thinkin' about covering the building with old-lookin' red brick on the outside?" Henry asked.

"Yes, sir," Noah answered. "Now that we got that settled, could I get you a beer or a glass of sweet tea?"

"No, I better be getting on back. I've got an appointment with some folks that I'll be contracting things out to, like plumbing and electrical, but thanks for the offer," Henry said. "Tertia, tell Bernie that my wife, Frannie, sure does enjoy getting together with her and Dolly and the other girls in their Sunday school class every week."

"I will," Tertia said with a smile, even though she wanted to groan. Any notion that she could keep her meeting with Noah a secret was nothing more than a whim. Bernie would have her soapbox out and polished up to crawl up on it and fuss at Tertia as soon as Henry got home that evening. He would tell his wife, and she would call Bernie and Dolly. Before nightfall, rumor would have it that Tertia and Noah were dating.

Tertia glanced over at Noah. He would make a fine cover model for one of her mother's romance books. Maybe one of those stories about enemies becoming friends and then lovers.

"What?" Noah asked. "Did you remember something else? I can always call Henry."

"No, I'm just surprised that you want to be a chef," she answered.

"Not a chef, a cook." He grinned. "Chefs make dishes I can't pronounce. I want to be a country cook. Which one do you want to be?"

"A cook if that's the definition." She smiled.

Enemies to friends—friends to lovers.

Maybe friends in time, but that third step wasn't going to happen.

Chapter 12

THE COOL EVENING BREEZE made it a perfect night for Tertia to sit out on the balcony and watch the sunset. The scent from the rosebushes mixed with the lingering aroma of the fresh bread that Endora had baked for supper wafted up to her as she thought about the last few days. She had met with Noah on Tuesday afternoon and had expected Bernie to fuss at her the next morning. Or Thursday, and now it was Friday evening—and not a word from her aunt about Noah Wilson.

Ophelia came out of her room a couple of doors down and sat down in the chair next to Tertia. "Hey, girl."

"Hey, right back at you," Tertia said. "I thought you had a date tonight."

"Nope, tomorrow night," Ophelia said. "Aunt Bernie has already been giving me all kinds of advice about it, and you are welcome."

"For what?" Tertia asked.

"She's been so busy gloating about fixing me up with Jake that she hasn't had time to think about you and Noah," Ophelia answered.

Endora stuck her head out of another door. "Are y'all spilling tea without me?"

"Not really," Tertia answered. "I wouldn't let Ophelia tell me about her week at work until you got here."

Endora dragged a chair over to where her sisters were, dropped it on the other side of Ophelia, and sat down. "Okay, I'm here. Did something juicy happen? But wait, before you tell us about Jake, how do you figure that Aunt Bernie hasn't been up on her soapbox about Noah yet?"

Tertia stretched up one arm and bowed her head. "Thank you, Jesus, for that miracle."

Endora hopped up and moved a few feet away.

"Where are you going?" Ophelia asked. "I thought you were interested in spilled tea."

"I am," Endora answered, "but I see a dark cloud over there in the southwest. Lightning could come out of it and zap Tertia for what she just said. I don't want to be so close to her if it does."

"And they say Tertia is the funny sister," Ophelia said. "Besides, the miracle will be over by morning."

Endora returned to sit in her chair. "What makes you say that?"

"Look at the vehicles parked in front of Aunt Bernie's little trailer. See that silver Caddy? That's Frannie's car. I bet she waited to tell her about Noah and Tertia until tonight at their senior women's Sunday school class meeting."

Tertia groaned and laid the back of her hand on her forehead in a dramatic gesture. "You are probably right. Frannie would want to see Aunt Bernie's expression when she got the news!"

"Yep," Ophelia said with a serious nod. "Those old gals meet on Fridays to do more than talk about the lesson for their Sunday morning class."

"They play poker, drink Jameson, and spill enough tea to flood that trailer," Endora added. "And tonight, they have some really juicy gossip about you helping Noah. Maybe you should go stay with Luna or Ursula for a few days until Bernie cools down."

"Maybe tonight they will really talk about their lesson for Sunday." Tertia groaned.

"If you believe that, then I've got some of that ocean-front property up in Wyoming to sell you," Ophelia said. "But that's tomorrow's battle. Tell us how many times Noah has called or texted since you saw him. And when are y'all getting together again?"

"To discuss the café of course, since this is just a business venture and has nothing to do with friendship," Endora added.

"I didn't count the times he called or texted, and this really is a business venture with a possibility of a job when the café is built," Tertia replied. "Right now, I'm just consulting on a new café. Ophelia is the one with the date tomorrow night. She should be telling us about her week. Did she and Jake sneak a few kisses beside the coffee machine?"

"We did not!" Ophelia protested.

"Okay, then, where are you going tomorrow night, and what are y'all going to do?" Tertia asked.

"Jake is cooking for us at his trailer and then we're

going to watch a movie. I'll be home by midnight," Ophelia answered. "Or maybe I'll spend the night, skip church, and sit on his porch all day Sunday, just so I don't have to be here when Aunt Bernie lights into Tertia. You don't have to worry about lightning from the sky, little sister. Aunt Bernie will bring something even worse when she finds out that Tertia has been seeing Noah."

"I'm not seeing Noah," Tertia protested. "I'm working with him, mostly by phone. I only saw him one time."

Endora wiggled her forefinger at her sister. "You had a drink with him, so that counts as a date. And now I'm going back to my room. I'm working on the last rough draft illustration for book number one."

"You should do one where Pepper and Sassy go to church and create havoc chasing each other." Tertia was glad to turn the conversation away from her and Noah.

Endora stood up. "I'll put that in my idea book for a later date."

"I'm going inside to watch some reruns of *Justified*. I can't decide if I like Raylan the hero or Boyd the villain the best. Want to join me?" Ophelia asked.

"Nope," Tertia answered. "I'm just going to sit out here and be ready to dash out to Aunt Bernie's trailer with a water hose when the gossip sets it on fire."

"Call me if you need any help," Ophelia said as she headed back to her room.

Tertia's phone vibrated, and she slipped it out of her hip pocket to find a picture of Noah's face. She hit the green icon and smiled back at him. Before the FaceTime started, she reminded herself that she was a grown woman and had been making her own decisions for more than a decade.

———

Tertia made a breakfast casserole and French toast for breakfast on Saturday morning, but it didn't do a thing to soften Bernie's expression when she came through the back door. Poor little Pepper had to trot to keep up with her, and he flopped down flat on his fat little belly in the middle of the floor.

"See what *you* have caused," Bernie growled. "Pepper might have a heart attack."

"Me?" Tertia asked.

Bernie shook her finger at Tertia. "Don't give me that innocent look. You know exactly what I'm talking about, but"—she sighed loudly—"you are a grown woman, and if you can't take my advice about men, then you'll have to sleep in the bed you make—and believe me, I will say, 'I told you so,' when you are whining about making a mistake."

"What's going on in here?" Mary Jane asked.

Joe Clay squatted down to pet the dog. "Looks like you just ran a marathon, old boy. Or were you just chasing a squirrel up a tree?"

"He was trying to keep up with me," Bernie declared. "I walk fast when I'm upset, and your third daughter has just plumb jacked my blood pressure up the stroke level."

"How did she do that?" Joe Clay asked.

Bernie didn't have a real soapbox, but a lot of stomping and creative cussing went on when she crawled up on her virtual one and answered the question.

"We raised all our girls to be independent and make their own decisions," Joe Clay said. "I trust that Tertia knows exactly what she is doing, so don't get your underbritches in a wad, Aunt Bernie."

"What will be, will be, and what…" Mary Jane started.

"And what won't be, might be anyway," Bernie finished the sentence. "Your grandmother started that saying. But I'm tellin' all y'all right now, Noah is not the man for Tertia, and I will ask my Universe to help her open her eyes and realize that."

"Thank you for praying for her," Mary Jane said with half a smile.

"I'm not praying," Bernie declared. "That's a God business. The Universe is something different. But since I can't change her mind, and she won't listen to me, then she will have to face the consequences."

Tertia took a couple of steps to the side and hugged her aunt. "I promise this is a business deal, not a love affair. Are you ready for breakfast? I made your favorite French toast."

Bernie stuck her nose in the air. "Yes, I am."

"What's going on in here?" Ophelia asked.

Endora dropped down on her knees and laid her hand on Pepper. "He's alive, thank goodness. He can't die before I finish my series of books about him and the cats."

Sassy came around the corner with Misty and Poppy

trailing along behind her. She stopped, fluffed up her tail, and glared at Pepper. The dog hopped up on his short little legs, bristled, and growled down deep in his throat.

Poppy ran over to him and bumped her nose against his. The two of them left the kitchen and headed toward the foyer, but they cut a wide swath around Sassy and Misty.

"Pepper isn't in a good mood, and neither am I," Bernie answered. "But you're going to tell me all about your date tonight, and that will make me feel better. At least you are smart enough to listen to me." She sent a dirty look toward Tertia.

"Who told her?" Mary Jane whispered as she poured two cups of coffee and handed one to Joe Clay.

"The Universe?" Joe Clay asked out of the corner of his mouth.

"Only if it's named Frannie," Tertia answered. "But I can breathe easier now that she knows. I won't have to feel like I'm sneaking around."

"Is that a good thing or a bad thing?" Joe Clay chuckled.

Mary Jane tiptoed and kissed him on the cheek. "Both, darlin'. There's a little bit of intrigue and excitement with the sneaky business, but it could take all the fun out of the relationship, and that would be bad."

"Why?" Joe Clay asked and then nodded. "You don't have to answer that. I understand. Bernie would gloat."

"Yep," Tertia agreed.

"What are y'all whispering about?" Bernie asked.

"They're discussing the possibility of my date tonight

being a mistake, since I work for Jake," Ophelia answered and slid a sly wink over toward her sister.

"No, it's not a mistake," Bernie declared. "It's going to turn out to be a happy-ever-after just like I fixed for Ursula and Luna, and I'm layin' the groundwork for Melody and Quinton. Both of them are Sunday school teachers so that should be a match literally made in heaven."

"Thank you," Tertia mouthed, and then removed the breakfast casserole from the oven and set it on the table beside the platter of French toast.

Joe Clay pulled out a chair for Mary Jane, and when she was seated, he sat down at the head of the table. "This looks amazing. I'm so glad your mama taught all you girls to cook. Now, Ophelia, tell me about the wine business. Has your first week been good or have you gotten bored?"

Tertia could have kissed her dad when he changed the subject away from Ursula's date and the café business that she and Noah were into.

"Good," Ophelia answered as she poured herself a glass of milk and sent the jug around the table. "I wasn't bored for even one minute. In between customers, I stock the shelves, be sure there's a couple of kinds of wine for tasting, and each morning I dust the shelves."

"Don't want there to be a little dust on the bottle," Mary Jane laughed.

"Hey, that song was on the jukebox in my bar," Bernie said. "One old truck driver used to play it over and over again. He said it reminded him of his younger days, when he would steal a bottle of wine from his uncle's cellar to impress his girlfriend."

"Whew!" Tertia fanned herself with the back of her hand. "That David Lee Murphy is one good-lookin' cowboy. I could dive right into his blue eyes and live there forever."

"When I get over my mad spell, I will ask the Universe to send you a happy-ever-after guy that has dark hair and clear blue eyes," Bernie said.

"Awww"—Tertia flashed her brightest smile at her aunt—"you still love me."

"If I didn't, I wouldn't be mad," Bernie snapped. "Did I tell y'all that I won a hundred dollars at the poker game last night? Of course, I've already put a ten in my purse to put in the missionary envelope on Sunday. I promised God if he'd let me win, I would do the right thing. Seems like ten percent is right."

Mary Jane nodded. "That's sweet of you, but why didn't you talk to the Universe?"

"Because there's no way to pay the Universe back when it does something good," Bernie answered.

Universe. Fate. God.

Tertia wondered which one was working on her behalf, or if maybe they had all joined forces and were going to make her eat her words about not ever dating a man with blond hair.

Time would tell, and no matter what happened, Aunt Bernie would either take the credit or say, "I told you so." Neither of which really mattered to Tertia that morning because that afternoon she was going over to Noah's house to talk about a rough draft of the menu for the café.

Chapter 13

THE LAST HOUR OF the workday always passed like a sleepy snail crawling through maple syrup. Whether it was a weekday or Saturday, it was still the same. Ophelia had sold several bottles of wine, but after the last customer left, she was alone. She dusted. She swept the floors. She cleaned the inside of the door window. At five thirty she put away the leftover wine and the cheese and crackers from the tasting table.

She was staring at the clock when Jake came in from the back and leaned on the counter. "I sent the guys in the back room home. Want to close up a little early?"

"You are the boss," she answered.

Before she could even nod, the door opened, and eight women pushed their way into the shop. They all appeared to be about Ophelia's age. Four were blonds with blue eyes. One was a brunette. One had blue hair, and the other two were sporting a pink streak in their platinum hair.

"Hello, we're here to taste a little wine, and maybe buy a lot for Darlene's bachelorette weekend," the brunette said, pointing toward one of the blonds.

"Y'all are welcome to look around while I set up a little

tasting." Ophelia hurried back to the kitchen area. She prepared the dome-covered crystal dish with cheese and crackers and carried it out to the shop, then went back and brought out the three half-empty bottles of wine and a sleeve of disposable tasting cups.

Most of the pack were choosing wine from the racks, but Miss Blue Hair had cornered Jake between the wall and the end of the checkout counter. Her right hand was splayed out on his chest, and she was looking up into his eyes. He took a step back, but she moved with him and leaned into him even closer. Poor man looked like he was the only bunny rabbit at a coyote convention.

"Darlin'," Ophelia called out as she set the wine on the table. "We have strawberry, watermelon, and blackberry. Maybe you could get some sample bottles of red and white from the back."

"Is this your man?" Miss Blue Hair slurred her words.

"That is my man," Ophelia answered as she set the bottles in the tub of ice still on the table.

"After what happened to me, we don't flirt with married men," Miss Brunette growled. "Come on over here and pick out your bottle. We're each buying at least one."

"*Thank you*," Jake mouthed toward Ophelia as he practically jogged to the back.

"Have y'all been out all morning?" Ophelia took her place behind the counter.

"Yep," one of the pink streaks answered. "We started at nine o'clock in Saint Jo, hit two wineries there, and then drove over here. We each bought a bottle at each place. This is our last stop."

Miss Brunette poured a small cup of blackberry wine. "We're going to Dallas tonight to celebrate Darlene's last weekend as a single woman." She swirled it around a couple of times and then smiled. "This is amazing. I'm buying two bottles. One for the party and one to take home."

The rest of the women gathered around the table. In just a few minutes, all the wine was gone, the cheese and crackers were gone, and more than a dozen bottles were on the counter ready for Ophelia to ring up.

"Hey, sorry I took so long, but I had to make up some samples," Jake said as he returned with a wooden bowl filled with tiny bottles of red and white wine.

"Those are so cute," one of the blonds said. "I'll buy them all and we can all take one home to remember tonight."

"If we don't crack them open and drink all of them on the way to Dallas," Blue Hair said with a giggle.

"Don't worry about them," Brunette whispered. "I'm pregnant so I'm not drinking. I volunteered to be the designated driver."

Jake set the bowl on the counter and stayed on Ophelia's left side while the women lined up to check out. "That's good, but don't speed. It's the driver who gets the ticket and who will be fined if there's an open bottle in the vehicle."

"Even if it's a little bitty thing?" Pink Streak asked.

"Yep," Ophelia replied as she checked them out one by one. "Are you speaking from experience?" Darlene asked.

"Possibly," Ophelia answered. "That will be forty-three dollars and nine cents for you."

Darlene whipped out a credit card. "Daddy says I have to give this back tomorrow before the wedding, so just charge it all to him."

"Hey, this is *our* party for you," Blondie Number Three protested.

"Y'all bought at the last places. This one is on me as a thank-you, and on my daddy for not letting me keep my cards after I'm married," Darlene said.

"Girl, you are marrying the richest oil man in Texas. You don't need your daddy's credit cards anymore," Brunette told her. "But that said, thank you, and now we can go on to the spa resort."

Ophelia rang up the total and handed Darlene the receipt to sign. The woman scribbled her name across the bottom and pushed it back across the counter. "I'm so ready for a mud bath and a massage," she said as she started toward the door.

Blue Hair looked over at Jake and sighed. "Maybe another time."

Ophelia followed them to the door and locked it behind them. "Well, that sure helped today's sales."

"Thank you," Jake said with a smile. "Not only for the sales, but for helping me out with that woman."

"You can't tell me that women don't flirt with you," Ophelia said.

Jake came out from behind the counter, removed his

glasses, and wiped them. "Not like she did. Did that really happen?"

"Yes, it did, and you are welcome." She glanced up at the clock shaped like a wine bottle. "It's five minutes after six. Are we ready to go now?"

"Definitely!" He crossed the floor and opened the door. "I'll pick you up at seven."

"I could just drive to your place," she suggested.

He shook his head and followed her out onto the porch. "This is a date. I will treat you with respect, knock on your door, and meet the parents even though I've met them before now. My mama would come all the way up here just to give me a tongue-lashing if I let you drive over here, or if I honked and expected you to come out to the truck."

"My dad will appreciate that. I'll see you soon. Are you sure you don't want me to bring dessert?" Ophelia took a step off the porch out into the bright sunlight.

"Positive," Jake waved and went back inside to lock up.

She waved back, hurried over to her truck, and grabbed her sunglasses from the passenger's seat. She glanced down at the dashboard. Day: May 19. Time: 6:13. Temperature: 89 degrees. The weatherman had said they could be in for a storm that night, but all the numbers she was looking at said he was wrong.

Ten days ago, she had met Jake for the first time, and even after such a short time, she felt like she had known him for years. From day one on the job, she had been comfortable, not only with what she was doing, but with Jake and the guys who worked for him making wine. When she went home at the end of the day, she didn't feel like pulling her hair out like she did when she had battled children or teenagers all day.

"Thank you for meddling, Aunt Bernie," she muttered as she drove away from the winery. She had just turned down the lane toward the Paradise when she saw Bernie and Pepper walking toward her. "Speak of the devil, and she shall appear," she whispered. Bernie usually took Pepper for his afternoon walks out to the back side of the property so he could chase squirrels. Could she be planning to cross the road and confront Noah?

Ophelia braked and rolled down the truck window. "Where are y'all going? Need a ride?"

"Nope," Bernie answered. "We're going up to the end of the lane, and…"

"And what?" Ophelia's thoughts went to all kinds of horrible things.

"I don't plan on burning down Noah's house," Bernie snapped. "I don't want to be in prison when you and Tertia are finally settled like Ursula and Luna."

"Sure you don't want a ride?" Ophelia asked. "Endora probably has supper on the table."

"Thank you, but Pepper and I will finish our walk," Bernie said. "Supper is on the bar, not the table, and I've already eaten."

"Okay, then, see you at home." Ophelia drove slowly to keep from throwing dust back on Bernie and Pepper. She kept an eye on the rearview mirror to be sure that her aunt didn't cross the road and have a showdown with Noah, and then parked in front of the Paradise. When she got out of her vehicle, she saw that Bernie had turned around and was coming back toward the house.

"Whew!" She removed her sunglasses, wiped a few beads of sweat from her forehead, and then tossed the glasses back into the car through the open window. She was on her way across the yard when she saw a movement in her peripheral vision.

"Hey," Tertia yelled as she came around the end of the house with all three cats trailing behind her. "Clam chowder is in the slow cooker on the bar."

Ophelia stopped at the bottom of the steps. "Thanks. Are you on your way over to Noah's?"

"Nope," she answered. "Why do you ask?"

"Aunt Bernie is headed this way," Ophelia answered.

"You don't think…" Tertia gasped.

"No," Ophelia answered, knowing exactly what was in her sister's mind because she had thought the same thing just minutes ago, "but she might stand on this side of the road and make demands that the Universe send him another woman to talk to about the café business."

"I'm glad that things are going well with you and Jake, but I wish she would put her powers, as she calls them, more to work on Melody and Quinton and leave me out." Tertia sighed and sat down on the top porch step. Sassy crawled up in her lap, and the orange kittens snuggled up together at her feet.

Ophelia reached down and petted Sassy, then eased down beside her sister. "When are you and Noah...?"

"Supper tonight. We're driving over to Nocona to a little café that is kind of like what he's building. We've been talking about menus and specials, so we want to check out how they do things," she answered. "You have a date with Jake, right?"

Ophelia nodded. "He's cooking over at his place, and we're watching a movie afterward. I'll be home by midnight."

"Ahh, a man that is sexy and cooks too. Do I hear your biological clock purring?" Tertia teased.

"Nope, that's three cats," Ophelia answered.

"I guess it is. Hopefully, Aunt Bernie will be asleep by then. I'll wait for you on the screened porch," Tertia whispered and then nodded toward the lane where Bernie and Pepper were coming toward the house.

"I'm going inside to get dressed," Ophelia said.

"Some sister you are, leaving me to deal with her alone," Tertia groaned.

Ophelia laid her hand on her sister's shoulder and gave it a gentle squeeze. "You've got Sassy and the kittens. Maybe all the purring they are doing will distract her, or maybe Pepper will be in a bad mood, and she'll have to chase him down when he goes after Sassy." She took her phone from her purse and held it like a microphone. "In this corner we have the Ball-Busting Bernie and her ferocious animal, Red-Hot Pepper. And in this one we have the Terrible Tertia with three tigers ready to go to battle with the dog. I'm putting my money on four against two. Don't let me down."

Ophelia's phone rang just as she was ironing the shirt she planned to wear that evening. The phone was in her purse across the room, so she rushed in that direction, stumped her toe on the rocking chair, and used enough of the colorful language she had learned in the service to almost melt the glass panels in the doors leading out to the balcony. She managed to grab the phone on the fifth ring, just before it went to voice mail. She figured it was Tertia and didn't even look at the picture that popped up on the screen.

"Give me a minute. I'm not through cussing a rocking chair," she gasped.

"O...kay..." Jake said. "What did the chair do to you?"

"It got in my way," Ophelia answered.

"From your tone, I will remember not to get in your way." Jake chuckled. "I'm calling to tell you that the electricity is out in my trailer. It happens pretty often when there's a storm or high wind like what is whistling through the trees right now. Our supper plans will have to change. I thought we would drive over to Muenster and eat at a little German restaurant that I like. I can still pick you up in a few minutes if that works for you."

"I love Rohmer's," Ophelia replied, "and I'll be ready."

"Great," Jake said. "See you then, and I hope your toe gets better and you forgive the rocking chair."

"Thanks, but I'm slow to forgive and even slower to forget."

"I'll remember that." Jake said and ended the call.

Ophelia laid the phone down and turned to find her mother headed for the ironing board. "I came up here to put away some towels and smelled something burning." She ran across the room and set the iron off of the shirt. "I hope you weren't planning on wearing this tonight or ever again. I guess we could cut the sleeves out…" she peeled it off the board and it ripped across the back, "Nope, that won't work either."

"Dammit!" Ophelia stomped the floor, and then plopped down on the edge of the bed and grabbed her aching foot. "I should just stay home tonight and not even come downstairs for supper. The stars are lined up against me. First, I came close to breaking my toe, and now I've burned up my favorite shirt. And this rotten high wind has knocked out the electricity in Jake's trailer so he can't cook. We are going to drive over to Muenster instead, and I'd looked forward to just having an evening with him."

Mary Jane unplugged the iron and then sat down in the rocking chair. "Darlin' daughter, all relationships require work. You can't expect things to be perfect. You have to overcome whatever obstacles get thrown your way to get to that pot of gold at the end of the rainbow. Quit your whining and choose another shirt. You will have the drive over there and back with just the two of you, and Rohmer's is a special place. The coconut pie will make you forget about all these hurdles you had to jump over to get there."

"But now I've got to choose a whole different outfit," Ophelia huffed.

Mary Jane stood up and patted her daughter on the shoulder. "Wear that cute little sundress with the shamrocks on it, and your green sweater." She headed out of the room and turned back. "And a pair of high heels."

"But my toe..." Ophelia groaned again.

"Is going to hurt no matter what shoes you wear," Mary Jane told her.

Chapter 14

THE DOORBELL RANG PROMPTLY at seven o'clock, and Ophelia's breath caught in her chest when she opened the door. His jeans were creased and stacked up perfectly on his boots. The green in his plaid shirt matched his eyes. The scent of his shaving lotion and a drop of water on his blond hair testified that he hadn't been out of the shower very long. She had a fleeting vision of both of them in the same shower, but she quickly blinked it away before she blushed.

"Wow! Just plain old wow!" Jake said. "You look amazing."

"Thank you," Ophelia said. "I was thinking the same thing about you. I would invite you in to meet my folks, but Mama is in her office and Daddy is still out in his shop working on things for Luna's wedding."

Jake opened the storm door. "Then we can go?"

"Yes, we can." She picked up her purse from one of the ladder-back chairs. She looped her arm into his, and together they headed toward his truck. He opened the passenger door for her and was about to close it when Pepper came around the end of the house in a flash, growling and snapping like he was as big as a grizzly bear. He latched on to Jake's pant leg and shook it as if he was trying to kill it graveyard dead.

"Pepper!" Bernie screamed right behind him. "You stop that right now!" She grabbed him, but he hung on to the pant leg until she popped him on the nose with her fingertip. "You've been a bad boy. There will be no extra treats for you tonight." She shifted her eyes over to Jake. "I'm so sorry. Did he tear your jeans?"

Jake glanced down at his pant leg. "Looks like they're okay to me. Just a little wet spot, and that will be dry before we get to the restaurant. I'm just glad he's not as big as a pit bull. He would really be dangerous then."

"You are a good man, Jake," Bernie said, but she was looking right at Ophelia the whole time. "You two get on about your date, and I will talk to Pepper about his attitude."

"Yes, ma'am." Jake nodded and closed the passenger door.

Bernie set Pepper on the porch and shook her finger at the dog. She was giving him a heated lecture when Jake settled in behind the steering wheel. Ophelia couldn't hear the words, and she couldn't read lips, but she kind of felt sorry for Pepper.

"I'm so sorry about that," Ophelia said. "Last time you were here, Pepper was nice. I never thought of him attacking you."

"Maybe he was mad at the cats. Seems like they have a love-hate relationship." Jake chuckled and nodded toward another truck pulling up beside his. "Looks like Noah is here. Are he and Tertia going out?"

"Not as in a date," Ophelia said. "They're going to check out a couple of diners this evening to get ideas for menus."

Bernie gave Noah's truck a look guaranteed to turn it into an iceberg. Noah got out and took a couple of steps toward the porch, and Pepper strutted down the steps and met him halfway. Noah was scratching him behind the ears when Tertia came out of the house. Bernie said something under her breath, and Tertia just smiled and gave her a hug.

Ophelia tried to bite back the laughter, but it escaped.

"What's so funny?" Jake asked.

"Aunt Bernie does not want Tertia to have anything to do with Noah, not even if it's just working for him in his new café when it's built, and Pepper is being nice to him. She loves *you* and the dog attacks you like you are the enemy," she explained.

"Well, then." Jake chuckled as he drove down the lane. "I guess I have to win Pepper over, and Noah has to do the same with Bernie. I believe that I have an easier job. Why does Bernie feel that way about Noah?"

"No doubt about you having an easier time," Ophelia agreed and went on to tell Jake about the fight between Noah and Tertia when they were in elementary school. "Aunt Bernie is of the opinion that 'once a bully, always a bully.'"

"What about the fact that Tertia blacked his eye?" Jake asked.

"That was self-defense, and she gets a standing ovation," Ophelia answered.

"Man, I'm glad I didn't live here back then." Jake chuckled.

Ophelia glanced across the console and tried to picture

him as a little boy, but it was impossible. When he turned to look at her, she pointed out the driver's side window. "Looks like the weatherman might be right."

"Yep," he nodded. "Maybe it will pass us on the south."

"We can hope," Ophelia agreed.

Dark clouds had gathered over the southwest, and a streak or two of lightning flashed through the evening sky as Jake drove a few miles west and then caught the road to the south headed toward Nocona. The ache in Ophelia's toe reminded her that she should have worn something other than high-heeled shoes. Then smoke wafted into the truck, and she remembered the burned shirt.

Jake pointed to a lonesome old scrub oak tree standing out in a pasture to their left that was ablaze but still standing. "Looks like lightning got that one. Good thing it's not beside a house."

"But..." Ophelia cocked her ear to one side. "I was about to say something about a grass fire being close by, but I guess it's the tree. I hear sirens."

A mile down the road, the Nocona Fire Department truck sped past them. "With this wind, a spark on dry grass could cause a wildfire," he said. "You ever been close to one of those?"

She nodded. "Twice. Daddy had to plow a fire break all the way around the Paradise. The blaze didn't quite make it up that far, but we could see it coming over the hill and eating everything in front of it. I remember Ursula saying that it looked like it was dancing toward us."

"As the crow flies, that burning tree is probably only a mile or two from my grape arbors." Jake's tone sounded worried.

"Do you want to go back and check on them?" Ophelia asked.

"Not since the fire trucks are here," he answered. "Everything should be fine."

He turned onto Highway 82 when they reached Nocona and headed west. The sign on the outskirts of town said that it was twenty-two miles to Muenster. The clouds had completely obliterated the sun, and streaks of lightning zigzagged through the sky more often than before. Ophelia wasn't afraid of storms—never had been—but common sense said that no one should be out in weather like this. She would have been a lot more comfortable eating bologna sandwiches and watching a movie at Jake's house.

"Did you see many tornadoes down in Jasper?" she asked.

"Oh, yeah!" he answered. "Seemed like I spent half of every spring in the storm cellar. Mama and Granny were terrified of storms, so they would shuffle us kids down into the shelter every time the weather got bad. We had two sets of bunk beds down there, so we would just go to sleep until it blew over. How about you?"

"They call our area Tornado Alley," she answered. "We didn't have a cellar the first year we were in the house, but by the next spring, Daddy had built a fancy one for us. We thought going to the cellar was a party. There is still a bookcase down there, and Mama always throws snacks in a tote bag to take with us. There's no electricity, but we could read by lamplight, and we thought that was so cool."

Jake slowed down when they went through Saint Jo, and then picked up speed on the far side of it. The sign there said that they were only nine miles from Muenster. Ophelia's stomach growled loudly at the thought of the coconut pie at Rohmer's.

"Hungry?" Jake asked.

"Starving, and be warned, I'm not a bit bashful when it comes to food," she told him.

"That's another reason I like you, Ophelia," Jake said. "I always feel like I've chosen the wrong place when I take a woman out to eat and she barely touches her food."

"Then you and I are going to get along just fine," she said.

Jake didn't have to slow down at either traffic light in Muenster. They pulled into the parking lot just in time to see a ball of fire rolling across the porch and then disappearing into the yard.

"What is that thing?" Jake asked. "It looked like a tumbleweed on fire."

"It was ball lightning," Ophelia answered. "It's really rare, and I've only ever seen it one other time. That was out near Vega where Tertia taught school. I don't understand how it happens, but it's got a lot of power. Knocked me square on my butt when I saw it on the balcony of her apartment."

"I'm going to take it as a good sign," Jake said.

Big drops of rain splatted against the windshield. Ophelia wished once again that they were back at Jake's trailer. Even without electricity, she would be a lot more comfortable there.

"Guess we'd better hurry up before the downpour." He was out of the truck in a flash and opened the door for her. He took her hand, slammed the door, and they ran onto the porch—only to find a handwritten note taped to the inside of the window that said the restaurant was closed due to no electricity.

Jake kept her hand in his, and they were both soaking wet by the time they got back to his truck. He reached over into the back seat and brought up an orange and black throw with the Texas Longhorns logo on it and handed it to her. "Wrap this around you."

"You are as wet as I am," she said. "We can share."

"I've got a denim jacket right here." He grabbed it from the back seat and put it on over his wet shirt. "I'll turn on the heat, and we'll warm up pretty soon. Maybe we'll even be dry by the time we get you back home."

Ophelia used one corner of the fluffy throw to dry her hair. It would soon be so frizzy and poufy that she would look like a mop that had been hung out upside down to dry. She knew she should have paid attention to the signs—her aching toe, the ruined shirt—and stayed home that evening.

"Where would you like to go for supper now?" he asked, and then took off his glasses and pulled out a napkin from the console to dry them.

She took her phone from her purse and did a little research, then called the number for Sonic. When they answered she asked if they had electricity and if they were open, and then she ended the call.

"Sonic," she said. "They're open, but only for drive-through orders. It's raining too hard for the car hops to take food to the cars."

"I love burgers, but this is not the way I'd planned our first date," Jake said.

"Sometimes plans get changed," Ophelia said. "It's only a few blocks from right here. Let's hurry before they lose electricity too, and Jake, it doesn't matter if we eat in your truck, or at a table with candles and cloth napkins. That you haven't told me that I look like a cross between a drowned rat and a poodle dog right now makes this a good date."

He flashed a brilliant smile at her. "Darlin', you are beautiful even with wet hair and muddy high-heeled shoes."

"You might need to wipe those glasses a little bit more, Mr. Brennan." She grinned back at him.

"We're close enough that I can see you fairly well without them." His smile widened even more, and his eyes twinkled. "To the Sonic, it is, then. I'll drive and you can navigate."

"I can do that." She pulled the blanket up around her shoulders and shivered.

"Want my jacket?" he asked.

"No, the heat is kicking on pretty good. I'll be fine in a few minutes," she answered.

"Think our second date will be better?" he asked as he drove away from the restaurant and followed her directions to the drive-in burger joint.

"You think there's going to be a second date?" she asked.

"I hope so, and maybe the next one won't be underwater. Look at that! Not a single vehicle at the Sonic."

"Most people have the good sense to stay in out of this kind of weather," she said.

"Only the brave and the beautiful venture out on a first date when the weatherman has issued a tornado warning," he joked as he drove up to the window. "Do you know what you want?"

"A double bacon cheeseburger, double fries, a chocolate shake, and an order of soft pretzel twists," she said without even a moment's hesitation.

He relayed the order to the teenager inside. "And please double that," he said as he passed a bill to her.

"Yes, sir. Drive around to the next window and we'll get that right out to you." The cashier took the money and started to make change.

"Keep it, and you have a good night," he said.

"You too," she said with a broad smile. "And a tornado warning isn't something to get all worked up about. When the weatherman says we're under a tornado watch, we begin to check the skies. If the sirens blow, then it's time to take shelter."

Jake drove up a few feet to the next window. Another teenager handed a sack and two drinks out to Jake, and he drove around to a stall and parked. The rain was coming down in sheets, and pounding so hard on top of the truck that it sounded like bad drumming. He opened the bag and handed half the food in it across the console to Ophelia, along with a paper napkin.

"I told my mother that I would rather have had the evening at your place than go out to a fancy restaurant," Ophelia admitted as she removed the wrapper from the burger.

"And what did she say?" Jake asked.

"That we would have the ride over here and back to talk," Ophelia answered and took a bite. "This is so good!"

He took a bite, chewed, and swallowed, and then said, "That's because you were starving and half-frozen from that cold, wet rain. And Miz Mary Jane is right, you know. I wanted to impress you with a nice dinner, but spending time with you is what I really wanted."

"Mama is always right, and I bet I don't ever forget this date," she told him.

"I won't forget any date I have with you," Jake said.

"Is that one of your best lines?" she teased.

"Just the truth, ma'am. Just the truth," he answered.

Chapter 15

THE DRIVE FROM SPANISH Fort to Nocona took less than half an hour, but Noah and Tertia talked about the café all the way, so it went fast. Noah made a left-hand turn off the highway and parked in one of the several empty spaces on the street where the small café was located. "Looks like the bad weather is keeping folks at home this evening."

"Maybe so," Tertia agreed. "Those clouds are dark, and we're supposed to have heavy rain tonight, and here it comes." A couple of drops hit the windshield with enough force that they sounded like hail instead of rain. "If we hurry, we might not get wet." She slung open the door and jogged across the sidewalk and to the wooden door opening into the café.

Noah grabbed the handle just as she did, and his big hand wrapped around hers. Hot little tingles traipsed up and down her arm. She jerked her hand free and told herself that she could not—would not—be attracted to him.

He slung the door open and stepped aside to let her enter first. "I'm sure glad there's an awning over the sidewalk."

She stopped inside the door and glanced around the dining area. "Me too, or we would both be soaked."

"Hopefully, the storm will pass over while we're eating, and the stars will be out before we have to go back outside." He seemed to take the whole place in with one sweep of the eyes, and then whispered, "It's not nearly as impressive as the one we are building."

"*You* are building. I'm just along for the journey." Tertia could still feel the warmth of his breath on her ear and neck even after he took a step back. Lord, have mercy! Why did she have to have this sudden attraction to Noah Wilson?

"Hey, this is a joint effort," Noah argued. "You've been like a partner, and I'm still hoping that you will stick around to cook for me once the place is built. Which brings me to the next question. Starting tomorrow afternoon, could you come over to my place right after lunch each day? I'd like for us to start testing and writing down our recipes—especially for the daily specials. I figure we can cook up one in an afternoon and then have it for supper."

"No problem," she said. "How many ideas do you have?"

"I've got a notebook full right now, but I'm open to ideas for more so we don't get in a rut. I figured we would need to have fourteen to twenty tested and ready. Some would be seasonal, like baked potato soup and chili," he answered. "We can switch them out depending on the weather and our moods."

"There you go with 'we' and 'our' again," she said. "I haven't decided whether or not I want to commit to a full-time job this fall. I gave myself a year to figure things out, not three months."

"Until you say absolutely no, then I'm going to hope that this is a 'we' and an 'our' thing," Noah said. "I've never known anyone as easy to talk to as you are, and you share my enthusiasm, so we'll make wonderful partners in this venture."

"Does any of that surprise you?"

"Yes, it does," Noah answered. "When we were kids, you were way too smart and pretty to talk to me. I should have pulled your braids instead of saying what I did about the Paradise. Looking back, I think I was just trying to get your attention."

"Your black eye testified that you got it."

"Yep, it did," he agreed. "And my mama grounded me for two weeks because I was rude to you. She said I could take one week off the punishment if I walked across the road, knocked on your door, and apologized. I was too proud to do that, so I had to be miserable for the entire time."

"I got a week for punching you in the face," Tertia said. "I wasn't given the choice of apologizing, and if I had, I wouldn't have done it. I thought you deserved the black eye."

A middle-aged woman finally appeared from a back corner and smiled. "Y'all sit anywhere, and I'll be right with you. Sorry you had to wait. I didn't hear you come inside. Nasty weather out there."

Noah motioned toward the nearly empty room. "Booth or table? And Tertia, I did deserve that punch in the face. My grandpa used to tell me the hardest lesson I would ever learn was when to keep my mouth shut. I remembered that every day for the next two weeks."

"Doesn't matter to me where we sit," she answered. "Are you thinking about whether we want someone to seat the guests or let them sit where they want?"

"Yes, ma'am." He led the way to a booth in the back corner. "If you will sit beside me, we can both see the whole place."

She took a small notebook from her purse and wrote *Hostess or not?* at the top of the first page.

"What do you think?" she asked.

Her shoulder was against the narrow wall on one side, and on the other, Noah's shoulder was pressed against hers. Lightning flashed in long streaks outside the window at the end of the booth, but it wasn't throwing off any more electricity than Tertia felt. The thunder that followed was nothing compared to the thumping in her heart.

She gripped the pen tightly because her hand was trembling and wrote *Pros and cons* on the second line.

"It would easier if they decided on their own where to sit," Noah suggested.

"Now cons," she said. "If the place is full, some folks might get overlooked if there's a waiting line. Things could get hectic with waiters trying to clear off tables and folks rushing to grab a place."

"Then let's have a hostess and a *Please Wait to be Seated* sign," he said. "See, I knew we would come up with some good ideas if we visited other cafés."

She wrote *Hostess for seating* underneath her pros and cons.

"Hello, I'm sorry it took so long for me to get here." The waitress laid the menus on the table. "What can I get y'all to drink?"

"Sweet tea," Tertia said.

"The same for me," Noah added.

"Our special today is chicken-fried steak, mashed potatoes and gravy, and green beans," she said. "I'll be right back with your drinks."

"Shall we try the special?" Tertia asked.

"I'm game if you are," Noah answered. "I make a mean chicken fry. Wanette hated it. Said it was too greasy and had too many calories. She only ate fish and chicken and only in small portions, and that had to be broiled or baked. She lived mostly on salad, and she constantly bragged that she could still fit into her cheerleading outfit when we divorced."

"Well, that's nothing." Tertia tilted her chin up in a dramatic gesture. "I can beat her brag all to pieces. All the earrings I've worn since sixth grade still fit me just fine."

Noah smiled, then chuckled, and then he broke out in laughter. "I love your sense of humor."

"I'm not joking. Not one pair of my earrings are too small." She smiled and picked up the menu. "No offense to Wanette, but I love food too much to worry about the jeans I wore in high school. Why don't we each order something different and share? That way we can test two different dishes."

He wiped his eyes on a paper napkin, and then pointed to the standard silver container on the far edge of the table. "Paper or cloth?"

"I vote for paper towels on one of those stand-up holders in the middle of the tables, and no tablecloths. That will make cleaning up easier, and we won't have to do so much laundry," she answered. "Want me to write that down?"

"Yes, please," he said.

The waitress returned with their glasses of tea and a plate of hot biscuits. "Are y'all ready to order or do you need a few more minutes?"

"I'm having the special," Noah answered.

"I'll have the fish dinner, with fries and coleslaw." Tertia handed the menus back to the woman.

"Anything else? Appetizers in addition to the biscuits?" she asked.

"These are enough for me," Noah said. "Tertia, do you want something else?"

"Nope," she answered.

"Just holler if you change your mind," the waitress said and disappeared to wait on another couple who were coming inside.

Noah buttered a biscuit and then peeled the top off an individual container of strawberry jam. "What about free appetizers?"

"I like biscuits, but I could make hot rolls to use for appetizers. Maybe with some whipped honey butter to use on them," Tertia said and then quickly added, "if I take the job."

"That sounds even better," Noah said. "But you'll have to make at least a dozen extra each day. That's how many I can put away. And what is whipped honey butter? I've been to places where they serve cinnamon butter, but not what you just said."

"That would be butter and honey whipped up together until it's light and airy." Tertia noticed that he completely ignored that *if* she had thrown out. The word was beginning to fade fast in her mind too—especially when a fresh round of heat traveled from his shoulder to hers.

———

Ophelia was sipping on her milkshake when Jake turned off the highway onto Farm Road 103 going to Spanish Fort. She had to do some fancy juggling to keep from dropping it when her phone made that screeching sound that usually warned of an Amber Alert in the area. She set the shake in the console cup holder and fumbled around in her purse until she had her hands on the phone and then read the message.

"We're under a tornado warning. One has been spotted just west of the Nocona Hills Country Club, and it's headed toward Spanish Fort," she said.

"What do you want to do?" Jake asked. "I've got a cellar out behind my trailer. We're only about ten minutes away, and we'll be going parallel to the storm until we get there."

"Let's go to your cellar then," she replied. "It's closer than the Paradise."

Rain continued to pour down so hard that the windshield wipers had trouble keeping up for the first five miles, and then it stopped so quickly that it seemed like a water faucet had been turned off. Everything went still and quiet, and the sky turned a strange shade of mossy green.

"Not a good sign," Jake gripped the steering wheel so tightly that his knuckles turned white.

"Nope, but it's not far now, and from what I'm seeing on the radar, it's going to jump the river a little east of Spanish Fort so we might not get hit." She tried to keep calm, but her voice sounded high and squeaky in her own ears.

"Some first date this is," Jake muttered.

"We sure can't say that it hasn't been…"

"Exciting? Dangerous? Disastrous?" he asked.

"The first one. A little of the second, and none of the third," she answered.

He slowed down for the last big curve. "Five more miles into town. Three to my place and shelter, and from the way those clouds are swirling, it won't be a minute too soon. And one question. Are you going to give me a second chance?"

"Yep, if you ask me," she said with a nod.

"Next Friday night? Barring a power outage, I will cook for us."

"Sounds good, but before then, would you like to come to Sunday dinner tomorrow?" she asked.

"I'll have to take a rain check on that. I've got some things to take care of at the winery tomorrow until early afternoon, and then I'm playing poker with Remy and the guys in the evening. I could make us a sandwich, and we could eat out back at the picnic table if you want to come over after church…" He stopped and pointed. "There it is, plain as day."

The funnel-shaped cloud danced along the pasture for a few seconds, then ascended into the clouds for a bit before coming right back down to the ground.

"How far do you think it is from us right now?" Ophelia's voice came out in a hoarse whisper.

"A mile at the most, but it's going slow," he answered. "I think we can beat it to my place."

Old-timers who talked about being close to a tornado often said that it sounded like the rumble of a freight train, so she figured the loud popping noise was just part of the storm. But then the truck began to swerve off to the left.

"Holy smoke!" Jake gasped. "What a time…"

To have a tire blow out, Ophelia thought as she stared at the funnel cloud. With trembling hands, she picked up her phone to call Joe Clay for help. Lightning flashed, giving her enough light to see No Service on the screen.

Jake stomped the brakes, but the vehicle went into a long greasy slide down over a slight embankment and came to a stop nose down in a ditch filled with water. He opened the driver's side door, and Ophelia opened hers. Together they might be able to push the truck back up onto the side of the road and change the tire—if the tornado didn't pick them up and dump them in the Red River.

A rock must have been down under the knee-deep water because when Ophelia's foot stepped off into the rushing stream, the heel of her shoe popped off and went floating down the ditch. She slipped out of what was left of that one and kicked the other one off.

"We'll have to have help to get the truck back out of here," Jake yelled over the roar of the storm.

"No service," she hollered and fought the swirling water trying to wash her down into a culvert under the road leading back to the winery.

Water splashed up on the running board, but she managed to get back inside, closed the door, and draped the throw back around her body. If another hard rain hit after the tornado passed by, the whole interior would be flooded. Even now the carpet was wet from her dripping feet and the tail of her dress.

Tension filled every fiber of her body, and it didn't help that she could clearly see three funnels traveling along side by side like a set of triplets. A chunk of wood flew through the air and hit the windshield hard enough to send a diagonal crack all the way across it. Then a toilet came across the sky at the speed of a bullet and landed in the ditch right beside the truck on Jake's side. Dirty water shot up like a waterspout and hit the truck with enough force to rock the whole vehicle.

"If I'd still been outside checking on the tire, that thing would have hit me," Jake gasped as he wiped his glasses clean and put them back on.

Ophelia opened her mouth, but no words came out. Then another flash of lightning from behind them filled the truck, and her door flew open. She figured the tornado had ripped the door open and would be sucking her out any second.

"Get out and hurry," Noah yelled.

"Where did you come from?" Ophelia threw her legs out, and then she was swept up into Jake's arms and carried to Noah's truck.

He hurriedly settled her into the back seat and slid in beside her. "Thank you, thank you," he said breathlessly.

"Yes," Ophelia managed to get out past the thumping in her ears.

Tertia turned around in her seat and said, "You look like a drowned rat."

"If we don't get to a shelter before those things get any closer, we may all be getting an up close and personal visit with Saint Peter in the next few minutes," Ophelia said between sucking in lungfuls of air.

"Just another two minutes." Noah had to yell to be heard above the rumble.

Ophelia wanted to close her eyes so she couldn't see all the debris flying through the air on every side, but they wouldn't cooperate. The next couple of minutes seemed to last a week. Then Noah slowed down just enough for his truck to make the turn down the short lane to his house. "There's a safe room just off the kitchen," he yelled. "I'll run ahead and get the door unlocked. Y'all come on in, and we'll hole up in there until it passes." He braked and the truck came to a slippery slide in front of the house.

All four doors of the vehicle flew open and then slammed

shut at the same time before they hurried up onto the porch. Jake tucked Ophelia's hand into his, gave it a gentle squeeze.

"Dammit!" Noah swore as he tried to find the right key and dropped the whole ring on the porch.

"Company's coming. Put on your britches," Rocky squawked from the living room.

Noah grabbed the keys and finally got the door unlocked, but not before a fake bull, probably from the front of a steak house, flipped through the air and came to rest with a loud thud in the bed of his truck.

Once inside, he grabbed the birdcage and ran across the living room and dining room and into the kitchen. "Follow me," he yelled as he opened the safe room and stood to the side to let the rest of them enter first. A gray and white cat ran past Ophelia's legs in a blur and hid under one of the two chairs lined up on the left side of the room.

The loud noise of a freight train coming right over the house was muffled when Noah closed the heavy door, set the birdcage on top of a small refrigerator in the corner, and plopped down in one of the chairs. "That was a close call. Y'all have a seat wherever you want. There's cold beer and sodas in the fridge if you'd like something to drink. I'm too jittery to get them out for you, so help yourselves."

"I'd love a beer," Ophelia said, "unless you've got a bottle of Jameson hidden somewhere?"

"That's in the kitchen, and you are welcome to it if there's anything left standing when this is over." Noah waved his hand around to take in the chair beside him and the twin-sized bed on the other side of the room. "Y'all, please have a seat."

"I'll take a beer, if you are bartending," Tertia said. "I got to admit I was even more scared than I was last Christmas when Rae braked to miss a bunch of deer."

"What happened?" Noah asked.

"Roads were icy, and we did a couple of spins before we came to a stop." Ophelia opened the refrigerator and brought out four longneck bottles. She passed them out and then sat down on the bed beside Jake.

Tertia sunk down in the overstuffed chair beside Noah. "That was nothing compared to tonight. Why are these chairs not in the living room?"

"They were about twenty years ago." Noah twisted the cap off his beer and took a long drink. "Mama got new ones and moved these in here. I never liked them—too stiff and uncomfortable—but right now I'm not complaining one bit."

Jake opened his beer and turned it up. "Me neither. Not even about my truck that's sitting in a ditch full of water."

Ophelia's hands were still shaking so badly that she couldn't open her beer. "Thanks again for rescuing us."

Jake took it from her and twisted the cap off. "I figured we were goners when that toilet came blasting through the air."

"We saw that," Tertia said. "I tried to call to see if that was y'all, but we didn't have any service. I bet the storm knocked the cell tower out south of town."

The cat slithered out from under the chair, hissed up at

the bird, and then crawled up in Ophelia's lap. "Poor old kitty cat," she said as she rubbed its fur. "What's his name?"

"Higgins after the old *Magnum P.I.* television series," Noah answered.

"And the bird is Rocky after *The Rockford Files*," Tertia added.

Rocky started whistling "Whiskey River," and the cat hissed at him again.

"I recognize that song," Jake said. "My grandpa used to listen to Willie Nelson all the time. And by the way, I don't think we've met. I'm Jake Brennan."

"Noah Wilson. I'll shake hands when mine stop trembling," he said. "I've been meanin' to visit your winery."

"Come around anytime, and I'll even give you a bottle of your choice for saving me and Ophelia tonight," Jake said. "Or better yet, join us guys for a game of poker tomorrow evening at Remy's house."

"I'll take you up on both offers if we get out of here in one piece, and thanks for the invitation," Noah said.

Aunt Bernie was going to fuss about that for sure. Jake and Remy might even be moved to the top of her "I will get even" list, ahead of Ophelia's father, Martin, and Endora's ex Kevin. And nobody ever wanted to even be on that list.

Chapter 16

NOAH EASED THE HEAVY door open. The quiet was so eerie that cold bumps the size of fire-ant hills rose up on Tertia's arms. Higgins jumped down from Ophelia's lap and stuck his nose out of the room, cocked his head to one side, then walked out into the kitchen with his tail high.

"The cat has spoken. The storm has passed," Noah said. "We can go see if anything else has been dropped in the yard other than the bull that's in my truck."

Tertia followed him out. "We can be glad that tornado season will be over when your café is built."

"*Our* café," he reminded her.

"Hey," Jake raised his voice. "You want me to bring Rocky out?"

"Yes, please," Noah yelled back. "Just set the cage on the dining room table. So far, so good. I've still got a house." He opened the front door. "But the porch roof is gone along with the posts, and so is the bull. I guess he was just visiting."

"Or maybe he heard Rocky whistling, and he doesn't like country music." Tertia wished she could put the words back in her mouth. "I'm sorry. That was too soon."

"No, it was not," Noah said. "I need something to make

me smile. I'm lucky that anything is standing at all, and that the storm didn't take my truck along with the bull. The porch can be rebuilt."

"My daddy can help with that," Tertia said. "He'll be so glad that Ophelia and I survived the storm that he will be glad to fix your porch. He's amazing when it comes to construction."

"That would be great, but I don't expect any repayment for getting all of us to safety," Noah said. "Right now, I should probably take y'all home. When daylight comes, I'll help get your truck up out of that ditch, Jake."

"Thanks...again," Jake said.

"No problem. Do you have another vehicle to use?" Noah asked.

"Got an old work truck that we use out in the vineyard," he answered. "I just hope there's grape arbors left standing."

Tertia stepped out onto the concrete porch and looked up to see stars and the quarter moon in the sky. The storm had passed, left damage behind, and evidently jumped the river into Oklahoma. "If debris wasn't strewn all over the yard, I'd think this fresh air was simply coming off a summer rain."

"I hope those three funnels didn't tear up the Paradise," Ophelia said.

"Or worse yet, the barn. Luna will cry if that fancy gazebo Daddy is building for her wedding is destroyed." Tertia took a deep breath of the cool air. Then she stepped off the porch onto the soggy lawn and opened the truck door on the passenger side. "How can everything be so calm after what just happened?"

"Mother Nature has a wicked sense of humor," Ophelia answered as she got into the vehicle right behind her sister. "Noah, you really don't have to take us home. Tertia and I could walk from here."

Noah shook his head. "I wouldn't garner many points with Miz Bernie if I let you walk home barefoot, and besides, there's no telling what's lying around out there that you could get hurt on just walking down the lane and across the road."

"What makes you think…?" Tertia started.

"I'm not blind, even though you did try to knock one of my eyes out when we were kids." Noah chuckled. "It didn't take a brainiac to be able to read her expression when I picked you up this evening. I hope I get some points when she finds out Tertia and I rescued you this evening."

"We can only hope, and I did not try to blind you. I just aimed at the biggest part of you, and back then that was your head since that held your ego," Tertia told him.

"Bernie likes me, but like I said before, I've got to win over Pepper," Jake said as he slid in beside Ophelia.

Noah got into the truck and started the engine. "I'd be glad for any help you might give me."

"Same here," Jake said.

Noah backed the vehicle up and then started driving down the lane, only to brake when he was about halfway to the road. "Looks like one of Remy's cows got loose or got…" He paused.

"That's not a real bull," Jake said. "That's the one that was in the back of your truck earlier."

"Well, we aren't going anywhere until we move him." Noah turned off the engine.

All four doors opened, and they eased out of the vehicle onto wet ground.

"Hey, we can do this," Jake said. "You ladies can stay in the truck."

"That feller looks heavy, so we'll help," Tertia told him.

"Or we can walk across the road and down the lane and Jake can crash here," Ophelia added.

"Nobody is walking anywhere," Noah declared. "That big bruiser can't be all that heavy. After all, he flew through the air like a big old marshmallow."

The bull's feet were planted in mud four inches up on his legs. Jake and Noah tried to push him out of the way, but he didn't budge. Ophelia and Tertia got in between the two men and pushed hard, but the bull stood his ground.

"What's that thing made of?" Ophelia gasped.

"Well, it dang sure ain't marshmallows," Tertia huffed.

"Metal of some kind," Jake answered breathlessly.

"We're not moving him this way," Noah finally conceded after they had tried several times.

Tertia bent forward and put her hands on her knees. "He's as stubborn as Aunt Bernie."

"Yep," Ophelia agreed. "What are we going to do with him *or* with her?"

"Y'all will have to figure out what to do with Bernie,

but I've got an idea for the bull," Noah answered. "I'm going to attach a chain to him and use the truck to pull him out of the way. If he survives the move, I'll find the café that he left behind and tell them they can come take the critter home."

Noah jogged back toward the house, circled around behind it and came back with a long length of chain. He got inside the vehicle, put it in reverse, and then turned it around. Then he and Jake looped one end around the bull's horns and attached the other end to the truck.

Jake stood to one side and motioned for Noah to go forward until the chain was tight, and then held up a fist and raised his voice. "We'll push while you pull."

Noah gave him a thumbs-up and eased forward, but the bull didn't move. Jake made a motion for him to go faster. The truck tires spun in the mud, but the bull still didn't budge.

"This puts a whole new meaning to the word *bullheaded*, doesn't it?" Ophelia panted.

"One more time?" Noah yelled out the still open door.

"Yes," all three of them hollered back.

He gunned the engine, and the tires finally got some traction. The bull let go, but it seemed like he was a real animal and didn't appreciate his horns being chained. As if he was trying to shake the chains off his horns, he weaved back and forth from one side of the lane to the other, and then came to rest in the middle of Noah's front yard.

"We did it!" Jake said.

"*You* did it," Ophelia said.

"Couldn't have…" Jake started and then stopped talking.

"A hand please," Ophelia said from a facedown position in the mud.

"I'm so sorry," Jake apologized and extended a hand toward her. "When it let go, I ran along behind it. I didn't know that you'd fallen."

The mud made a sucking sound when Ophelia and Tertia sat up. Ophelia put her hand in Jake's and tried to stand up, but she slipped and pulled him down with her.

Tertia managed to get up on her own, but when Noah ran over to her, his feet went out from under him, and he sat down hard. Tertia landed in his lap and wiped her hands on his shirt. "I would sure appreciate a good hard summer rain right now."

"I hope this is the end of bad luck." Jake rolled away from Ophelia and got to his feet. "Let's try this again."

Tertia pushed away from Noah and stood up. "I want a long bath and a warm bed after all this."

"What happened?" Noah asked as he managed to get up on the second try.

"We pushed, and the bull danced across the lane," Jake said, "and both of these ladies decided to try a mud bath to finish off our evening. You know the rest of the story."

Tertia looked down at her clothing. "I'm just glad you've got leather seats."

"Are you sure you want us…?" Ophelia started.

"Yes, I'm sure," Noah answered before she could finish

and pointed at his vehicle. "I was planning to have it detailed this week anyway. Climb in and we'll have you home in a few minutes."

Yeah, right, Ophelia thought, but she didn't say it out loud. Murphy's Law stated that if something could go wrong, it would—and they weren't home yet.

"Less than five minutes," Tertia whispered as they slogged through the mud to the vehicle and got inside.

"Don't count your chickens before they are hatched," Ophelia replied. "If Mama or Ursula were writing what we've gone through tonight in one of their romance books, their editors would say that it was too much."

"The truth is stranger than fiction, right?" Tertia asked.

"Oh, yeah," Noah agreed.

He drove the rest of the distance down the lane and across the road. Pecan tree limbs were tossed about, but nothing that the truck couldn't drive over—until they got to the last tree in the row. Noah braked hard and brought the vehicle to a long, sliding stop not six inches from the huge tree that had been uprooted and was blocking any vehicles going to or from the Paradise.

"The chickens ain't hatched yet," Tertia groaned.

"Where's a chicken?" Jake asked.

"I jinxed us when I said that we were only five minutes from home," Tertia admitted.

"And I told her not to count her chickens before they were hatched," Ophelia added. "But we're only a little way from the house, and I will watch where I step. We can crawl over the tree trunk and walk the rest of the way. Thanks for getting us this far, Noah."

"Us guys aren't going to leave you until you are safely inside the house." Jake got out of the truck for what seemed to Ophelia like the hundredth time and rounded the back end to open the door for Ophelia. "Guess the last obstacle in this horrible date is that we have to…"

"Shhh…" Ophelia put her hand in his and hopped down to the ground. She didn't even look over her shoulder at the mess she and Tertia were leaving in the back seat, but just headed toward the tree. "It's still a few yards to the house. And Mama says that in her books, the hero and heroine do not take a picnic to the river, sit down under a willow tree, and fall in love. They have to work for a happy-ever-after."

"But we didn't have a picnic or a willow tree, and we've had plenty of obstacles. Does that mean there's a happy-ever-after in our future?" Jake put his hands on her waist and lifted her over to the other side.

Noah followed his lead and did the same thing with Tertia. "I will call it a happy-ever-after if Tertia will agree to work with me when we open the café."

"I thought you didn't like blond-haired men," Ophelia said in a low voice while the two guys were climbing over the tree trunk.

"I didn't," Tertia replied, "but a woman has the prerogative to change her mind."

"He seems really nice," Ophelia said.

Both guys had joined them before Tertia could say

another word. Ophelia was surprised that one or both of them didn't fall and break a bone, or at least turn an ankle. After all, Murphy's Law had done a fantastic job that whole evening.

"Good lord, what happened to y'all?" Endora gasped when they came through the door. "Did you get caught in the middle of that tornado?"

"Kind of," Ophelia answered.

Mary Jane came out of the living room and pointed at her daughters. "You two get on upstairs and get cleaned up," she said. "I didn't know you were going to do mud wrestling."

"Neither did I. Are you sure that you are even Ophelia and Tertia, or are you a couple of vagabonds?" Luna asked.

"We're sure," Ophelia answered and turned to face Jake. He didn't look as bad as she did, but he wouldn't win the audition for a men's soap commercial. His boots sloshed with every step and his whole backside was a muddy mess. Noah hadn't fared much better. Little mud balls hung on strands of his blond hair and his formerly white shoes were now brown and very wet.

"There's a tree over the road on this end of your lane," Noah said. "If any of y'all need to get out of here tonight, I'll be glad to give you a ride. You might need to bring a couple of towels for the back seat since they're both pretty muddy."

Remy came out of the living room with Ursula at his side. "Thank you and yes. That would beat us having to climb over the fence and walk home across the pasture."

"Us, too," Shane answered. "We drove Luna's vehicle over

here when the sirens went off, so if we can just get home, I'll bring my truck back tomorrow morning to help get the tree cut up and moved."

"Okay then," Joe Clay nodded. "Noah will take everyone home, probably one group at a time, and then whoever isn't working tomorrow will meet back here to clear the path. And I appreciate all of you guys offering to help."

Bernie joined them from the living room and frowned at Noah. "Dolly just called to check in and said there is no church tomorrow. There's a tree blown over the doors, and all kinds of debris in the parking lot."

"I'm free to help most of this week," Noah offered. "When we get your place cleaned up, Joe Clay, we should go help take care of the church. We've all got trucks to haul the wood away, or folks who have fireplaces might even come and get it."

"Noah's porch is gone," Tertia blurted out. "I told him you could help, Daddy, since he kept us all from getting blown away."

"Then we'll help get that put to rights after we clean up our place and the church," Joe Clay said. "Now, you girls go upstairs and clean up. We're going to make a pot of coffee to share with these guys when they get back from taking everyone home."

"No argument here." Ophelia glanced over at Jake. "I'll see you in a little bit. Oh, and Daddy, Jake's truck is sitting in a ditch with a flat tire. Y'all might help him drag it out and take it to the winery."

"And thanks for the offer of coffee, but we aren't fit to

stay," Jake said. "We'll get these folks home, and then get on to our own places to get a shower."

Bernie laid a hand over her heart. "What happened to all of you? I want the truth, but not until y'all look like human beings again."

"Yes, ma'am." Tertia nodded.

"But you aren't going to believe all of it could happen in one evening," Ophelia threw over her shoulder and led the way upstairs.

"If we go home now, we won't get to hear the story," Luna said.

Tertia stopped on the first step and turned around. "We'll tell it again tomorrow."

"I'm not waiting until tomorrow," Endora declared. "I'll make hot chocolate and get out the peanut butter cookies. Y'all don't take forever in the shower."

"While you do that, I'm going to wander around outside for a few minutes and see if there's roof damage on the Paradise or if there's anything ruined out in the barn," Joe Clay said.

Luna and Shane were halfway out the door, but Luna turned back around. "Daddy, take pictures, so I'll know that my gazebo is still standing. I won't be able to sleep if you don't."

"I promise I will, darlin'." Joe Clay followed them out.

"Do you think Aunt Bernie will be nice now that Noah is offering to help so much?" Tertia asked when they reached the top of the stairs and were walking down the hallway toward the bathroom.

"Maybe after we tell her the whole story," Ophelia replied as she peeled off her muddy dress, stopped by her room, and put it in the dirty clothes basket. "If that comes clean, I doubt I will ever wear it again."

"It's a bad-luck dress, isn't it? Just like this shirt and jeans I'm wearing." Tertia had already removed her muddy shirt and jeans and was headed toward the bathroom with them in her hands. "I've got dibs on the bathtub first."

"You've got dibs on the shower," Ophelia snapped. "There's no way I'm waiting an hour to get this washed off my body. If this is what a mud bath feels like, I never want to do one. Besides, do you want to sit in brown water when this mud washes off us?"

"You got a point there," Tertia agreed. "I hope we don't stop up the plumbing."

"Shhh…" Ophelia shushed her. "After tonight that *could* happen."

While Tertia took a shower, Ophelia did what she could at the bathroom sink. Her sink had never had so much dirt washed down it in all the years that she lived in the house before moving out to join the air force. When she looked at her reflection, even after cleaning up as much as she could, she wondered if Jake Brennan would ever ask her out again.

"If he doesn't, I'll just have to take the initiative and ask him," she muttered, "but if the second date is anything like this, I'm going to tell Aunt Bernie that she was dead wrong about him being *the one.*"

Tertia got out of the shower and wrapped a towel around

her body and another one around her wet hair. "I've never appreciated being clean so much in my entire life."

Ophelia reached inside the shower curtain and adjusted the water. "If Noah asks you out on a real date, would you go with him?"

"I'm not sure," Tertia answered and disappeared into the hallway.

Ophelia's curly hair was matted with mud, so it took her a little longer than usual to get it all washed out. She shampooed, conditioned, and repeated the whole process a second time before she finally felt that she had gotten her hair clean. There was mud under her fingernails, in her ears and even caked between her breasts. She lathered up three times before the water running down the drain was clear. Then she stepped out and wrapped herself in one towel and put another one around her head turban style.

She went to her bedroom and pulled on clean underwear, a pair of dark-green sweatpants, and an air force T-shirt. She took time to towel dry her hair and pull it up in a wet ponytail. When she finally made it down to the kitchen, everyone was gathered around the dining room table, including Tertia.

"Okay, we're all here now," Mary Jane said. "Ophelia, start at the beginning and tell us what happened."

"Why does she go first?" Tertia asked.

"Because she's older than you," Endora answered but she stared right at Bernie. "But before you start, I want y'all all to know that I was really scared tonight, but I'm using the experience to write a story about how our cats and Pepper learned to be nice to each other during a big storm."

"Yes, they did, and I am proud of Pepper." Bernie shot a dirty look across the table at Endora.

"Okay." Ophelia sat down in the empty chair beside Jake. "Here goes. The rain hit about the time we got to Nocona…" She went on to tell her story up to the point when she and Jake were stranded in the ditch.

"My turn," Tertia said, and she finished up from that time, telling all about how the bull had flown through the air and was now standing in Noah's front yard. She embellished the rest of the tale with a good deal of exaggeration all the way until they had to jump over a tree that made those in Redwood National Park look like toothpicks. Even Aunt Bernie was giggling when she finished talking.

"Now, can either Mama or Ursula use all that in one of your romance books?" Ophelia asked.

Ursula shook her head. "No one would believe all that could happen in one evening, not even in a whole fiction book."

Chapter 17

OPHELIA WAS BACK IN her cubicle, the computer in front of her and the controls for her drone at hand, waiting for orders to come to finish the mission. She wondered if the other two controllers sharing the small room with her were affected by what their jobs entailed. But—like always—as she waited for the order to come down to push the right button to destroy a building, she reminded herself that what she did was for the greater good—it protected lives all around the world. Then she heard, "Abort mission," and let out a long sigh. She closed her eyes and waited for the adrenaline leave her body.

"Are you going to sleep all day?" Endora raised her voice.

What was Endora doing in her cubicle? Didn't she know that what went on in there was classified, and she could get in big trouble for sneaking into the room? Not only her, but also Ophelia, who could lose her job.

Her eyes popped open, but she wasn't at her desk. Sunlight flowing through the window in the balcony door bathed her face in warmth. Endora held out a cup of steaming hot coffee. But Ophelia's heart was still racing from the adrenaline rush. Then she heard the buzzing sound of chain saws and realized what had triggered the dream.

They came at longer intervals nowadays, and someday, according to the therapist, the dreams wouldn't haunt her at all.

"Thank you." Ophelia sat up in bed, wrapped her hands around the cup, and took a sip. "How long have they been busy out there?"

"Only a few minutes. Remy and Ursula, and Shane and Luna got here in time to have pancakes with us," Endora answered. "Tertia says if you don't get downstairs soon, you'll have to eat cold cereal."

"Noah and Jake?" Ophelia asked.

"They're out there loading their trucks. Remy said when they went past where y'all slid off the road last night, there was no truck there. Evidently, the tornado got it and left the bull in its place."

Ophelia shivered. "We were in that truck and could see all three of those funnel clouds coming right at us. Another five minutes and we would have been swept away too."

Endora sat down on the edge of the bed, "Jake told Remy that he was terrified something would happen to you. That's a good man, Sister."

"Why do you think so?" Ophelia set her coffee on the nightstand and slung her legs over the side of the bed. After the way Endora had thrown a pure old southern hissy fit about any of her sisters dating, hearing her say there was a good man anywhere in the world was amazing.

"When a man doesn't even think of his own life being in jeopardy but is concerned about the woman he's with—that tells me he's a good man," Endora answered. "I won't be worried one bit about you if y'all get serious."

"And Noah?" Ophelia asked.

"Don't know much about him yet, but Aunt Bernie can't be right all the time. I can see some vibes between him and Tertia. I think it would be funny if they got into a relationship since she was so adamant about not liking blond-haired men." Endora smiled and stood up. "You better get a move on if you want Tertia's pancakes. She even made her famous caramel sauce and there's whipped cream," she said as she disappeared out into the hallway.

Ophelia took another sip of coffee and thought about the dream. She had passed all the psych tests, and her therapist continued to give her the "all clear" paperwork. When she left the military at the end of the previous year, she had been warned that she might have a few issues. But she had thought that she would leave the job behind when she went home to Texas. She set the mug on the dresser and stood up. She rolled her neck a few times, then went out onto the balcony, and watched the guys working on the pecan tree that had been there for probably sixty years—maybe more. Now it was gone. Could it be that someday the nightmares would be like that tree—gone in an instant? And if so, what would make it happen?

She went back inside her room, opened the closet door, and took out a pair of old jeans and a T-shirt. Once she was dressed, she hurried down the stairs, across the foyer, and into the kitchen.

"I hear there's pancakes," she said.

"Yep, and bacon too," Bernie answered. "If Tertia and Endora don't quit putting all this good food on the table, I'm going to gain fifty pounds by next Christmas."

"Aunt Bernie, you have been a bitty little thing ever since I can remember," Endora told her.

"It's all that booze I drank when I was younger," Bernie said. "It melted all the fat right off my bones, and now I can't gain weight."

"Do you reckon I could drop twenty pounds if I drank Jameson every night?" Ophelia asked.

"Nope, and you don't want to," Bernie answered. "Jake likes your curves."

"And does Noah like Tertia's?" Endora asked.

"He'd be an idiot not to," Bernie snapped. "Just because he rescued you girls and is out there working to help Joe Clay does not mean I have changed my mind about him. He has to prove himself for me to like the idea of Tertia working for him."

"How does he do that?" Tertia asked.

"The Universe will tell him how, and then it will let me know that we can approve him as your boss," Bernie answered. "But we will probably never okay him as a boyfriend."

"Who is this 'we' business?" Tertia asked. "Do you have a superpower hiding out there in the trailer?"

"Yes, I do, and it's called my hotline to the Universe," Bernie barked.

"What if I decided to like him as a boyfriend?" Endora asked.

Bernie laid her hand on her forehead and rolled her eyes toward the ceiling. "Never. Not ever. Tertia might be able to train him, but you don't have the backbone."

"Well," Endora huffed. "Thank you so much for that vote of confidence. Maybe I won't help you with your Bernie's Advice Column you are starting on a Facebook page."

"Just statin' facts, and I'm right proud of you for showing some spunk, but Vera is a crackerjack with the computer too, and she'll help me," Bernie said. "Even with a little sass, you and Noah would not work together. I've got something else in mind for you."

"What?" Endora asked.

"It's a surprise," Bernie told her.

"What's a surprise?" Mary Jane entered the kitchen through the back door.

"Who I'm going to settle down with," Endora answered. "How are the guys doing?"

"Jake brought his three hired hands, and they all have chain saws, so it's going fast. They'll have the lane cleared by midmorning. When they get done, I told them to come inside for a break before they go to the church to clean up there. Tertia, can you whip up a couple of pans of brownies?"

"I sure can," she answered. "And if they all want to have lunch with us, I can make pots of soup. Maybe vegetable, chili, and tortilla."

"And broccoli cheese with ham?" Endora asked. "We haven't had that in forever. You didn't even make it when you were home last Christmas."

"Only if y'all help me," Tertia answered and set a plate of pancakes in front of Ophelia.

"Thank you," Ophelia said. "For your vegetable soup, I will volunteer to peel potatoes and scrape carrots." She poured melted butter over her pancakes and then topped them off with maple syrup.

"I'm here to help too," Endora offered. "We can get down the slow cookers and keep it warm all afternoon, then have the leftovers for supper."

"I'll make sweet tea," Bernie said.

"Sounds like we're all going to eat good today," Mary Jane said.

Luna breezed in the back door with Ursula right behind her. "My gazebo is fine. The barn roof isn't even leaking so we're good."

"And the tornado took away my morning sickness," Ursula said with a smile. "I would like another stack of pancakes, Tertia. What are all y'all going to do today? Remy won't let me help with the cleanup, so just tell me what to do in here. Are the rest of y'all going to go help load wood, or are we going to work on floral arrangements?"

"We'll work on wedding stuff this evening," Ophelia answered. "This morning we are cooking. Brownies first for break time, and then we're having a soup kitchen for all the working men."

Ursula looked over at Bernie. "Noah, too?"

"I promise not to poison him, but don't expect me to be hugging him," Bernie answered.

"Aunt Bernie, he's out there working hard right along with all the other guys," Mary Jane scolded. "And if it hadn't been for him, Ophelia and Jake might have been blown away with that truck."

Bernie crossed her arms over her chest. "I'm still not hugging him, but I won't sic Pepper on him. That's the best I can do."

"But Pepper likes Noah," Ophelia argued. "He attacked Jake. Don't you know what they say about paying attention to who a dog likes and doesn't like? Maybe you are wrong about Noah and Jake both."

But I sure hope not where Jake is concerned, Ophelia thought.

"Poor little Pepper was having a bad day and got my instructions mixed up. I told him to tear Noah's leg off and to cozy up to Jake. The little guy still doesn't have the English language down too good. It won't happen again," Bernie said, explaining it away.

"This seems a lot like a division of labor to me. The men out there working with chain saws, and us girls in here slaving over a hot stove." Ophelia attempted to change the subject.

Bernie ignored her comments. "You are trying to confuse me. I'm old, but I'm not stupid."

Mary Jane poured herself a glass of sweet tea and sat down at the table with Ophelia and Bernie. "You aren't old or stupid, Aunt Bernie, and Ophelia is right. My girls were taught that we all worked together. This reminds me of the historical romances I've been writing for years now. That's the way things were done back then, and very few women owned bars in those days."

"Well, thank God we've been liberated. Did I tell y'all that I would have been the first one to burn my bra, but Temple Donaldson beat me to the punch and threw hers into the big old bonfire before I could get mine off?" Bernie said.

Mary Jane shot a wink over to Ophelia. "Was Temple your friend?"

"Hell...I mean heck, no, she wasn't my buddy," Bernie declared. "She made me look like a saint, and, honey, like the words of that song on my jukebox said—'If I smell like smoke, it's because I've been through hell.' That's not a bad word, Mary Jane. It's a destination."

Ophelia tilted her head to one side. "How do you figure that you've been through hell?"

"Someday, I'll give Ursula my journals, and she can answer that for you. For now, just take my word that all the things I've done would make the devil blush with shame," Bernie answered. "Mary Jane is trying her best to clean up my soul, so I'll at least have a chance at getting past the pearly gates."

"Well, I for one would rather stay in the house and help y'all cook than go out there and load up sticks and limbs," Ursula said.

"We could save enough of the smaller stuff to have a bonfire tomorrow evening," Endora suggested. "It could be a celebration of getting our place and the church cleaned up."

"The ground is wet enough that it wouldn't be a fire hazard." Luna got in on the conversation. "And we could do hot dogs and make s'mores."

"I bet you already have a book in mind for Pepper and the cats about that, don't you?" Mary Jane asked Endora.

"Yep, just need to build one and take notes," she answered.

"Keep the fire away from my trailer. Pepper sneezes when he smells smoke," Bernie said.

"I'm surprised that he can live with you then," Luna said with a giggle. "But speaking of fire, keep the barn away from the blaze, please. My gazebo didn't survive a tornado only to be fuel for a fire."

Ophelia could understand Aunt Bernie and Luna's concerns, but they were nothing compared to the ideas that popped into her head. She remembered what her mother had said about happy-ever-after only coming after a couple jumped over hurdles and wasn't quite sure that she could live through many more disasters. She and Jake had survived a tornado. Surely there couldn't be anything worse in her and Jake's future, could there?

———

All seven men—Joe Clay, Shane, Remy, Jake, Rodney, Frankie, and Lester—removed their work boots and left them lined up on the porch. Then they padded across the foyer in sock feet.

"I smell brownies," Joe Clay said.

"And coffee," Remy said.

Shane crossed the dining room and gave Luna a kiss. "I can't smell it, but I bet there's sweet tea and milk too."

Mary Jane pointed to a table laden down with brownies and cookies and several beverages. "Y'all sit wherever you want and help yourselves. It'll be close quarters, but we can all fit."

Joe Clay took his place at the head of the table and sniffed the air. "What else is brewing in the kitchen?"

"We're having a soup day for all you guys at lunch," Mary Jane answered and then kissed him on the cheek before she took her seat beside him. "Got to keep you well fed so you won't pass out from all that hard work."

Ophelia caught Jake's eye and smiled. "Don't be shy. There's another pan of brownies coming out of the oven any minute now, so dig in."

Jake took a chair, filled a coffee mug, and then handed off the pot to Frankie. "Don't get any ideas about getting this kind of treatment at break time in the winery."

"If this is how things go at this place, I might jump the fences between here and there and apply for a job here," Rodney teased and poured himself a glass of sweet tea.

"They do make sure nobody goes hungry," Remy said. "Aren't you ladies going to join us?"

"Yep, we are," Tertia answered. "We were just waiting for this last pan of brownies to come out of the oven."

Ophelia carried another pitcher of tea to the table and then sat down beside Jake. "Thanks for all your help today and for bringing your crew over to work on their day off."

"We're having a bonfire tomorrow night," Endora announced, "and all of y'all are invited. Bring your families and a healthy appetite. And would y'all please save us a truckload of wood from the church cleanup to use in the firepit?"

"Thank you, and my family would love to come," Lester said with a serious nod. "My wife is going to want to bring something, though."

"Maybe a dessert," Mary Jane answered.

"I could bring several kinds of wine," Jake offered.

"I wish that Bo and Rae were here," Mary Jane said with a sigh.

Joe Clay patted her on the shoulder. "They will be by the end of the summer. Bernie has assured me that they will come home for Luna and Shane's wedding and stay with us for good."

Ophelia hoped that whatever universe Bernie talked to was right on that issue.

———

"What do you think the guys talk about when they're over at Remy's playing poker?" Tertia asked as she gathered around the dining room table on Sunday evening with her sisters and mother. "And where is Ursula?"

"Probably about how tired they are from all the wood business today, and Ursula is on her way. She should be here any minute," Mary Jane answered. "The job at the church took longer than your dad thought it might be. That big scrub oak at the north end of the church fell in front of the front doors and knocked out one porch post. Another one blew over from the backyard of the old store and landed in the parking lot. They still have some work to do tomorrow to get it all cleaned up."

"Remy said they will bring a couple of truckloads of wood from the church for our bonfire tomorrow night," Ursula said. "I'm sure glad that we are having the party in the evening, so I can enjoy a good hot dog with chili and onions."

"Still got nausea in the mornings?" Bernie asked.

"Not so much that I can't write, but anything more than crackers and sweet tea doesn't settle well," Ursula answered. "What are we working on today? Centerpieces? Bouquets?"

"Both of the above," Mary Jane answered.

Endora opened a bridal magazine and pointed to a picture of a bouquet. "That one looks pretty, and it has got the wildflower look that you talked about, Luna."

"It's too big." Luna shook her head. "I want something smaller but with those colors."

Mary Jane opened one of the half-dozen plastic tote-boxes on the table and took out a few silk rosebuds and half a dozen small daisies. "Like these?"

Luna shook her head. "Endora, help me."

Endora picked them up and wrapped yellow ribbon around the stems. "This is way too simple for me. I'm going to have something with more bling in it when I get married."

"I agree," Luna said. "I'm going to have all boys when Shane and I have our children."

"Where did that come from?" Bernie slipped in through the back door, with Pepper prancing along at her feet. "I always imagined you sisters carrying on the tradition and having lots of little girls."

"When boys get married, all they have to do is show up," Luna said.

"And they get to play poker while we do all the planning," Ursula added. "That's another reason to go to the courthouse. Are you listening to me, Ophelia?"

Ophelia had been busy taking flowers out of the containers and spreading them out on the table by color. "Why are you asking me?"

"You are next in line," Bernie said. "Unless I can drag Tertia away from Noah and find her a fall-in-love-at-first-sight fellow."

"No dragging necessary," Tertia protested.

Bernie pulled out a chair and sat down. "I would have thought you would want a red, white, and blue wedding since Shane was in the military, and your wedding is so close to Independence Day."

Luna whipped her long blond hair up into a ponytail. "Not me. Ophelia can do that next summer. She's our military sister."

Ophelia shook her head. "I've had enough of that. No red, white, and blue for me."

"Okay, then, all y'all. I don't want anything that is overpowering," Luna declared. "Mama, you are good at arrangements, and you know me. What do you think?"

Endora unwrapped what she had made and rewound the ribbon onto the spool.

Mary Jane picked up six calla lilies and a stem of white hydrangea. "One lily for each of your sisters, and the hydrangea with blossoms on one stem to signify unity between you and Shane. Each little blossom represents a year that you will be together. Do you want wrapped stems or into a nosegay in a holder?"

"Wrapped stems," Luna said. "Tuck some baby's breath into it to make it airy, and wrap it with dark-green ribbons. What do y'all all think?"

"Beautiful," Tertia answered. "It will be so pretty with our yellow and green floral dresses."

Bernie nodded and then said, "I believe we should tuck one of those little sample bottles of Jameson down behind the ribbon. After all, it was good Irish whiskey that put you and Shane back together last Christmas. I'm glad to loan you one that I have out in the trailer, and it could be your something borrowed."

"I was hoping that maybe"—Luna paused—"you might let me borrow your good-luck ring to tie into the bouquet for my something borrowed. After all, if you hadn't helped me through that night after Shane and I had the argument, I might not be getting married. You gave me the courage to go talk to him."

"I would be honored, but honey, nobody in this great green earth needs to give any of you sisters courage. You've all got bushel baskets full of that. Me and the Jameson just helped you see the light," Bernie said with a broad smile. "Just like my advice column on the internet is going to help lots of other couples. Vera and I've been calling and texting, and we're going to launch it right after Luna's wedding."

"That's great," Endora said. "And Sis, your garter will be something blue."

"Aunt Bernie's ring can serve as something old as well as borrowed," Ophelia added.

Bernie held up a palm, "You could use the ring and a little bottle of Jameson. That would double your chances of good luck!"

Tertia zoned out of the conversation going on around the table and let her mind go through the events chronologically from the time she had taken the walk and talked to Noah for the first time. There had been arguments with her aunt. Her sisters had gathered around her to help out. They had survived a tornado, and tonight he was playing poker with the guys.

Did she love him? Too soon to tell.

Did she like him a lot? Yes, in spite of the fact that she'd declared she would never get involved in any way, fashion, or form with a man that had blond hair—especially Noah Wilson.

How did all this happen? Well, it sure wasn't with the help of Aunt Bernie or her hotline to whatever universe she talked about.

Ophelia bumped her on the upper arm. "Tertia! Where is your mind?"

"What?" Tertia snapped.

"I was just saying that I like what you've made for the bridesmaids' bouquets," Luna said. "Were you so engrossed with what you were doing"—she nodded toward the arrangement in Tertia's hand—"that you zoned out completely?"

"Yes," Tertia said quickly and then looked down at the single calla lily with a touch of baby's breath wrapped with a wide yellow satin ribbon. "I thought the ribbon on our flower should be different than the bridal bouquet."

You sure covered that well, the little voice in her head whispered.

"Yes," Luna nodded. "Make five more just like it. While you do that, we can start making the centerpieces."

"Thank goodness you at least had a bouquet for the reception, Ursula. Joe Clay had so much fun making a shadow box for it," Mary Jane said with a sigh. "I'm not fussing at you for not having a big wedding in the fall. I understand your reason for going to the courthouse and then just having a little reception."

"But you're enjoying all this, aren't you?" Ophelia asked. "And you want the rest of us to have big weddings, right?"

"Yes, I am," Mary Jane declared. "And for all future reference, I'm calling dibs on planning my grandchild's baby shower and first birthday—not just for Ursula and Remy's baby but for all the ones that come afterward."

"You can plan the biggest splash in all of north Texas," Ursula agreed. "I'm going to get a bottle of water. Anyone need one while I'm up?"

"I'd take a beer," Ophelia said.

"Make that two," Bernie added.

"Water," Luna, Tertia, and Ophelia chimed in together.

Bernie reached down into another box and brought up a milk glass vase. "Do all the centerpieces have to be alike?"

"Nope," Luna said. "They can all be different. I just want yellow and white flowers with touches of green, so have fun with it."

Tertia unloaded several vases—all white, but none alike—onto the table. Would she use the same ones when she got married? That would depend on the time of year that she had her wedding. Fall had always been her favorite season, so maybe orange, burgundy, and yellow all blended together in quart jars. She didn't want anything as big as what they were planning for Luna's wedding, but she definitely wanted more than a quickie trip to the courthouse.

Endora nudged her on the arm. "Where is your mind? You look like you did when I woke you up again. Are you sleeping with your eyes open?"

Tertia dropped her hands into her lap and crossed her fingers on both hands. "I was thinking about how beautiful this wedding is going to be."

It wasn't a total lie—she *had* been thinking about a wedding.

———

Just last night, Tertia had been outrunning a tornado. Tonight, she slumped down onto the swing on the screened back porch. The moon hung in the sky as if everything in the whole world—no, the whole universe—was right. Stars lit up their own tiny portion like small flames at a memorial. She focused on what constellations she knew and remembered that someone had said that there were too many stars to count.

A movement caused her to shift her eyes to the left in time to see a falling star streaking through the black sky. She quickly closed her eyes and wished for a sign to help her decide about working with Noah after the café was finished. Were these vibes that she felt when Noah was close by just a physical attraction because she hadn't dated in so long? Or were they something real?

"I wish for something to help me with this," she muttered.

The squeaking door hinge announced that someone was joining her.

"I thought I might find you out here," Mary Jane said.

There was something comforting about that old blue robe her mother had belted around her waist. Tertia had cried on the shoulder when her first boyfriend broke up with her. She had cried again on the same shoulder the morning that she drove away from the house to go to college, leaving behind the two sets of twins and her mother and dad. Through the years, it seemed that when she had a real problem, her mother would appear in that same faded robe. Could this be the sign she had asked for?

"Come on out and join me," Tertia said.

Mary Jane brought out a bottle of Jim Beam and two glasses. "I thought we could both use a little nightcap after the last twenty-four hours. Your father is so tired that he's snoring in his recliner."

"I like Noah," Tertia blurted out.

Mary Jane sat down beside her, put the bottle and glasses on a nearby table, and then poured a double shot in each. "No surprise there. He's a likable man. Hardworking. Good-looking." She handed one of the glasses to Tertia and then picked up the remaining one and took a sip.

"I'm in a quandary. What if we like each other, and then we don't, and I'm committed to working with him?"

"Don't worry so much that far into the future, my child," Mary Jane answered. "Last night should teach us that we aren't guaranteed six months or a year down the road."

"Thanks, Mama."

Good advice, but not really the right sign, Tertia thought as she sipped her whiskey.

"Like and love are two different things," Mary Jane said. "They are both important. Like is the good soil that the love seed is put into. But for it to grow, you have to destroy the weeds and keep it tilled and watered. That's the like part of a relationship, and love can't grow without it. So, liking Noah is a good beginning, but it's up to you whether or not you fall in love with him. Does that make sense?"

Tertia scooted over and gave her mother a hug. "More than you'll ever know."

Her mother's phone pinged, and Mary Jane smiled when she looked down at it. "Joe Clay woke up and wondered where I was. Are you okay out here all alone?"

"I am now," Tertia assured her and held up her glass that still had most of the double shot in it. "I'm just going to sit out here and enjoy the peace and quiet for a little while before I turn in."

Mary Jane stood up and kissed Tertia on the forehead. "You've got to take that wherever you can find it in a family like ours. Good night, darlin' daughter."

"Good night, Mama," Tertia said.

Her phone vibrated right after her mother closed the door. "So much for peace and quiet," she muttered as she pulled it from her hip pocket. She expected to see a message from Ophelia or Endora, or maybe both, asking her to come out on the balcony and visit with them. But she was wrong. Noah's name popped up on the screen.

He had written: Got time to visit?

She wrote back: Sure. Want to come over and sit on the back porch with me?

The answer came back immediately. Be there in five minutes.

Tertia checked her watch. Four minutes and thirty seconds later, Noah rapped on the door.

She motioned him inside. "Want a drink?"

He held up a six-pack of beer. "I'd rather have one of these, and I'll share."

"And I will gladly take one. A double shot of this stuff is enough for me. Have a seat," she said.

He pulled the tab on a can and handed it to her. "Mind if I sit beside you?"

"Not a bit," she answered.

He set the extra four beers on the table and eased down onto the swing. "I've always loved a porch swing. Think we should replace the park benches with swings on the porch of our new café?"

Tertia could hold her liquor—much better than Endora, anyway—but that double shot of whiskey, and Noah sitting so close to her, had her mind going in a different direction than porch swings versus benches.

"Before we make that kind of decision, maybe we should talk to the insurance folks. If a toddler fell out of a swing on the property, you might get sued for everything you have or will have before you die," she finally answered.

"Good point." He nodded.

Sparks, at least on her side of the swing, bounced back and forth like a fast-moving ping-pong ball. Then he handed her a piece of paper that looked like a note. The fold lines were dingy, and the whole thing looked like something she and her friends in elementary school might have passed back and forth.

"What is this?" she asked as she took it. "It's too small to be a contract."

"I found it in an old metal lunch box that Mama used to pack for me when Grandpa took me fishing," he said. "I wrote it before you blacked my eye, but after that I was too stubborn and embarrassed to give it to you."

"Why?" Tertia asked.

"A *girl* gave me a shiner," he said, chuckling. "You can't

know how much teasing I took from my friends. No way was I going to give you *that note* after that."

She held the piece of lined notebook paper in her hands. "Why now?"

"Open it and you'll see," he said.

Tertia unfolded it once and then again. Almost two decades had faded the pencil writing, but she could still read the words that came right out of an old George Strait song, "Check Yes or No." The words were written in tight handwriting, with what looked like a drop of soda right in the middle of it. They said if she wanted to be his friend to take his hand and check yes or no. Two imperfect little squares had been drawn at the bottom of the page. *YES* was scribbled by one and *NO* by the other.

She read the note half a dozen times before she shifted her gaze from the paper to Noah. He stared right into her eyes, reached into the pocket of his chambray shirt, and removed a sharpened pencil. "I was ten years old when I wrote that. I'll be thirty in July, and I'm still feeling the same."

"What will your friends say?"

"That I'm one lucky feller to get a second chance if you check the right square," he replied.

Was this her sign, or was the advice her mother gave her what she was looking for—or both? She blinked and lowered her eyes to his mouth. She didn't want to check YES and hold his hand. She wanted to put her mark on his lips with a long, adult kiss. She pushed that thought away, took the pencil from him, and put an *X* in the box beside the

YES. Then she laid the paper and pencil on the seat between them, reached over, and tucked her hand into his.

"I'm not sure about love, but I do like you," she whispered. "So, let's just start with that for the check mark."

He gave her hand a gentle squeeze. "I'm glad. Finding that note tonight seemed to be a sign that I needed to tell you that seeing you again after all these years brought back the same feelings I had back then."

"Why didn't you just say it?"

He shrugged. "It's a guy thing. Even at my age, it's tough to admit my feelings or to accept rejection."

She handed the pencil back to him and slid across the swing to sit closer to him. "I'm afraid that even being friends might create problems if we work together every day."

"My feelings have lasted all these years. I expect anything that strong will endure a spat or two in the kitchen," he whispered.

"I hope so," she admitted.

The door from the outside swung open, and Bernie peeked inside. She frowned when she saw Tertia and Noah sitting so close, and it deepened when she noticed that they were holding hands. But she plowed right on inside the screened porch and sat down on a rocking chair, anyway.

"Come right in and have a seat." Tertia's tone was more than a little edgy. Surely this wasn't the falling-star wish coming true.

"I'm glad you are here," Noah said cheerfully. "We've been talking about something for our café, and we could use a third opinion. Do you think we should put porch swings or park benches on the porch of our new café?"

Bernie's frown disappeared. "Give me one of those beers, and I'll think while I sip on it."

Tertia was surprised that she didn't ask him to pass the bottle of whiskey over to her.

"Yes, ma'am." Noah let go of Tertia's hand, pulled the tab from a can, and handed it to Bernie. "Sorry I didn't offer you one before now."

"Not a problem now that I have one, but don't let it happen again if you want to get on my good side." She took a long sip, burped loudly, and said, "Not bad manners, just good beer."

"I agree," Noah nodded, "and I will mind my manners better from here on out."

Bernie rocked a few times and then held up a palm. "I have decided that it's all right for y'all to work on this café together, but I'm still not going to give Tertia my blessing on cooking in the place. That said, I do not think swings are a good idea. As much as I like them, they could be asking for trouble when kids are involved." She took another drink of her beer—this time without the burp.

"What's going on in here?" Ophelia peeked inside the outside door. "I saw a light when I was coming back from over at Ursula's. I'm so glad that Daddy built a stile over the fence. Even as tall as I am, crawling over five strands of barbed wire isn't easy. She sure doesn't need to be climbing over or through a fence when she's pregnant."

"Amen to that," Bernie agreed. "I was helping these two make a decision about swings or benches for the porch of the new café."

"And which was it?" Ophelia asked.

Bernie shot a dirty look over toward Tertia and Noah.

"Would you like a beer?" he asked.

"Love one," Ophelia answered and then sat down in a chair beside Bernie.

"Benches," Noah answered as he handed a can to Ophelia. "Too much danger with little kids with a swing."

"Smart," Ophelia removed the tab and took a long drink.

An awkward silence filled the room until finally Noah set his empty can on the table and stood up. "I should be going. I was out taking a walk and I ran by to talk to Tertia about café stuff. Miz Bernie answered one question for us. See you at the bonfire tomorrow, then?" he asked as he crossed the porch.

"Yes," Tertia answered. "Come on over anytime. We can always use help setting up tables and getting things ready."

"Sure thing." He waved and then disappeared into the darkness.

Bernie finished off her beer and reached over to get one of the remaining two. "I'll take this one back to the trailer. Pepper might like a little sip for his nightcap. I don't let him have a taste of Jameson anymore, but he does enjoy a lap or two of beer. You"—she pointed at Tertia with her free hand—"can be working friends with Noah, but that's all."

"I hear you," Tertia said, but that didn't mean she agreed.

Not after just simply holding Noah's hand had sent delicious little tingles through her body.

"It's a miracle!" Ophelia muttered.

"Baby steps," Tertia said with half a giggle.

Chapter 18

THE SUN WAS HALF an orange ball on the western horizon when Joe Clay lit the wood for the bonfire. Lawn chairs lined the wide concrete apron all the way around the brick firepit, and three long tables full of food were set off to the side in a U shape. Noah, Remy, Jake, and Shane had helped Joe Clay set up the food tables as well as several others for folks to sit at to eat that evening.

Now, the wood crackled, and the fire seemed to beg the folks to come on over closer and let it roast their hot dogs and marshmallows. Tertia was standing off to one side, mesmerized by the way that the slightest shift in the wind had an effect on the blaze, when she felt Noah's presence beside her.

"Y'all can sure put on an impromptu party," he said.

"We had lots of help." A flash of heat that had nothing to do with the warmth of the fire made her take off her jacket and hang it over the back of a nearby chair.

"I'd forgotten how the folks here in Spanish Fort all work together when storms happen," he said.

"Not just storms," Tertia told him. "You should have seen the turnout for Ursula and Remy's wedding reception. There's definitely good points to living in a near ghost town."

"Yep," Noah agreed. "I'm hoping that means they'll all support our café."

"They will, and so will the folks in Nocona and Saint Jo, and before long they'll be driving up here from even farther away."

Noah turned up a red plastic cup of sweet tea and took a long drink. "I hope you are right."

"Look!" She pointed up at a falling star.

"You saw it first," Noah said, "so you get the wish."

"It's my second one in less than twenty-four hours, so I'm going to give it to you," she said. "What are you going to wish for?"

"Can't tell you, or it won't come true. Has your wish come true?" he asked.

"Yes."

"Did you tell anyone what it was?"

She shook her head. "I didn't."

"Point proven," Noah said.

Joe Clay rang a cowbell and the whole area went quiet. "To friends, both old and new, past and future," he said. "The fire is hot. The food is ready. Y'all get a skewer and roast your hot dogs anyway you like them. Mary Jane says they aren't done if the outside isn't nearly black."

"That's right," she called out from behind one of the tables. "But that doesn't mean y'all have to eat them well done. This is a help-yourself affair, so don't be shy."

Lester led the way to the table. "Ain't no bashful bones in my body, and I love a good roasted hot dog."

"Shall we get in line?" Noah asked. "And you look amazing tonight. I should have told you earlier, but I was stunned right out of my manners when I looked up and saw you with the sun setting behind you."

"Thank you, and better a minute late than never," she said. No man had ever said that she was so pretty that they were stunned by her. Was that a little seed planted in the ground of *like?*

———

Jake stood up from the lawn chair where he had been sitting beside Ophelia and extended a hand toward her.

She put her hand in his and grimaced when she stood up. Her little toe was dark purple, and the bruise extended all the way to her ankle. Thank goodness the weather was good enough she could wear flip-flops. There was no way she could ever get her swollen foot into a pair of boots, or even enclosed shoes.

"Holy smoke!" Jake gasped. "The whole top of your foot is bruised. You said you stumped your toe, but you didn't say anything about breaking bones."

"Like I told you before, my middle name isn't Grace."

"You should sit as much as possible tomorrow at the winery." Jake kept her hand in his and slowed his stride to match hers as they crossed the yard. "Or do you need to take the day off?"

"I'm fine," Ophelia answered. "I've done far worse than this and didn't take time off from my job. And thank you for bringing your crew over to help. Monday is their day off."

"Being invited to this party makes it all worthwhile to them," Jake told her and then waved at a newcomer who was just getting out of his vehicle. "That's the new minister here in town. He came out to thank us, bring us out bottles of water, and help yesterday afternoon while we finished up at the church, so Joe Clay invited him to the party."

"I thought Pastor Tommy wasn't leaving for another month," Ophelia said.

"His father fell and broke his hip, so he was going to have to take a few weeks off anyway, so he just turned the keys to the parsonage over to the new guy a couple of days ago. I'll introduce you," Jake slowed down and let the new fellow catch up to them. "Hey, Parker, come on over here and meet Ophelia Simmons, one of the seven sisters of Paradise. Ophelia, this is Parker Martin. He moved here from Louisiana this past week, and he's going to be working with Henry Davis as a finish carpenter when he's not preaching."

The guy barely came up to Ophelia's shoulder. His hair was somewhere between blond and brown. Broad shoulders—probably more from carpenter work than preaching—filled out his green and black plaid shirt. Thick lashes rimmed his hazel eyes.

"Pleased to meet you," Parker said. "And thanks for the invitation to the party tonight. It's a wonderful way to get to know some of the folks here in Spanish Fort."

With that deep Louisiana accent, his words sounded like they were dripping honey laced with just a little of Bernie's whiskey.

"Welcome to town, and to the Paradise," Ophelia said, and waved Endora over. "This is my baby sister, Endora. She has an identical twin, Luna, so don't think you are seeing double all evening. Endora, this is Parker Martin, our new pastor."

"Pleased to meet you, Parker," Endora said. "Come with me, and I'll introduce you to more of the folks."

"Is the whole town here?" Parker asked.

"Quite a few of them," Endora answered as they walked toward the food tables together.

"They are kind of cute together," Jake whispered.

Ophelia shook her head. "Never happen."

"Why?"

Ophelia's mouth twitched as she fought the grin. "A preacher and an old brothel. Sounds like a country song, doesn't it?"

"I see your point, but these are modern times," Jake argued.

Ophelia tugged at his hand to get him moving. "Still never happen. Let's go get some food."

"Quit looking at Noah like one little push and you'd fall into bed and pull him down with you," Bernie whispered in Tertia's ear.

"You need to curb your imagination," Tertia said. "Don't go judging me by your half bushel."

Bernie shook her finger so hard that it was a blur. "Don't

you talk to me in that tone. Have you met Parker? With that accent, he could make a holy woman's underpants crawl down to her ankles. I bet he's hell on wheels in bed."

Heat crawled around from Tertia's neck to burn her cheeks. Only Bernie could make her blush like that. "You are talking about a preacher!" she gasped.

"I'm talking about a good-lookin' man with a sexy accent. I understand he's a finish carpenter when he's not preachin'," Bernie told her. "So, he knows how to use those big hands of his, and did you even notice the way his muscles were stretching his shirt?"

Tertia put two hot dogs on a skewer. "Ask your Universe to set him up with Bo. She's got a lovely voice and could be the music director at the church. They could fall in love at first sight when and if she comes home this summer."

"Do you realize how difficult you are?" Bernie snapped as she stabbed two hot dogs onto a skewer.

Tertia flashed a smile toward her aunt and nodded. "I'm the third child. It's in my DNA to be difficult, and besides I'm related to you!"

"I can't talk sense into you, so go on and flirt with Noah." Bernie groaned. "But when you get your heart broken, I will say, 'I told you so.'"

"Noah and I are friends, and possibly later we might work together. That part is something I'm still thinking about. You don't see me picking out wedding dresses or a cake, do you?" Tertia argued.

"It's just a matter of time." Bernie whipped around so fast

that one of her hot dogs fell on the ground. Pepper ran over to get it, but Sassy beat him to it and ran over to where the kittens were hiding under the rosebush to share it with them.

"See what you made me do," Bernie growled, "and Pepper didn't even get to have it."

"There's plenty more," Tertia told her.

Bernie cut her eyes around at Tertia. "We were taught not to waste good food, or good men that look like Parker." She stuck two more on the long metal skewer and headed toward the bonfire.

Mary Jane nudged Tertia on the arm. "Don't pay any attention to her. Like I told you before, she's probably using reverse psychology on you."

Joe Clay stepped up to her other side. "Just enjoy the evening and don't second-guess yourself. Pay attention to what your heart tells you."

"Thank you both," Tertia said and looked up to see Noah on the far side of the firepit, staring right at her. "My heart tells me to go talk to Noah. My stomach tells me it's hungry, so I'm off to kill two birds with one stone."

"Listen to both," Mary Jane told her.

Bernie was talking to Dolly Devlin on one side of the pit, so Tertia circled around the other way to stand beside Noah. More times than she could remember, her mother had told her and her sisters that anything worth having was worth fighting for. Too bad she didn't warn them that one of the biggest battles they would have to work around would be with their aunt Bernie.

"Hey," Noah said with a smile. "I was hoping you'd come over my way. This is some party."

"It's small compared to the Christmas party we throw," she answered, "Maybe you can close the café early this next year and attend it."

"I would like that, which brings me to a question. Do we close up the café at say, three o'clock on Sunday, and take Monday off?"

Tertia stuck her skewer out into the fire and turned it slowly as she thought about his idea. "I like that idea. Since we'll be open Sunday morning, we won't be able to attend church services, but that would leave us free to go to evening church. Monday could be our day to get other things done."

He nodded. "Then that's what we'll do. Speaking of church. Did you meet the new preacher?"

"Oh, yes!" Tertia rolled her eyes. "Aunt Bernie wanted to fix me up with him."

"And?" Noah raised an eyebrow.

"And I told her that Bo would be a better choice. She's a singer and plays the piano and fiddle. She could fall right into a position as music direction," Tertia answered.

Noah nodded across the firepit to where Endora was talking to Parker. "He and Endora make a really cute couple."

Tertia shook her head. "Never happen. Endora isn't nearly ready for a relationship. Looks like most of the folks are getting through the buffet line. Let's go fix our plates. I want you to try my baked beans for sure and see if you think they're good enough to serve at the café."

"That would be good to serve on the days we have ham for a special, but tonight I don't want to talk about the café," Noah said. "I want to talk about us."

"Us?" Tertia asked.

"We are friends. You checked *yes* and even held my hand, so let's get to know the adult Tertia Simmons and Noah Wilson," he answered. "The young versions of us didn't do so well, but maybe the older ones will do better."

"That would make this kind of like a date," Tertia whispered.

"Yes, it would."

She started walking toward the food tables. "Okay, then you can ask the first question."

"Why would I ask a question?"

"Isn't that what a date is all about? Getting to know someone to figure out if there's going to be a second date?" she asked.

"I guess I'm a little rusty," he said with a grin. "No, erase that. I'm a whole lot rusty. I only dated Wanette all through high school and college, and then we got married."

"Really?" Tertia asked.

"Really," he answered. "After that horrible breakup, I just backed away from women. But if asking questions is what we do, then I'll start with, why did you go into coaching when you like to cook?"

"Because I was good at softball, and I got a full-ride scholarship." She talked while she made herself two hot dogs with chili and cheese.

Noah scooped a spoonful of baked beans onto his plate and took a bite. "These are amazing, so yes, let's put them on the menu for the days when our special is ham. We'll serve it with your baked beans, and hot rolls, and my potato salad. And maybe apple pie."

"I thought we weren't going to discuss café stuff."

"We won't after this, but these beans are really good," Noah said. "Next question. Are you going to regret leaving coaching behind?"

"Not for one minute," Tertia answered. "I've been ready to hang up the catcher's mitt and come back to this area for a couple of years."

"Why didn't you?" He finished making his plate and looked around for an empty spot at a table.

"I'm not sure, but then Ursula paved the way," she answered and nodded toward an empty table.

Noah followed her across the yard. "I thought Endora and Luna moved back before Ursula."

"They did, but that was because Endora's fiancé cheated on her. She took it hard, and getting over the whole thing has been tough on her. There were two positions open at Prairie Valley School, so Mama talked them into coming back here. Both Endora's ex and her best friend that he cheated with worked at the same school she did," Tertia explained. "Ursula came home with no job to give herself a year to write. That's going out on a pretty shaky limb. So, anyway…" She set her plate on the table and sat down. "That kind of gave me the courage to do the same. My turn to ask you a question. Why didn't you go to chef school since you love food so much?"

"Guys in my family don't even mention doing something like that." He sat down beside her.

"Why?" she asked. "Most of the greatest chefs in the world are male."

"It is what it is." He shrugged. "Coaches or bank presidents or heavy equipment operators are what all my cousins are. I loved to spend time in the kitchen with my grandmother. She was an awesome country cook. My mama can put a meal on the table, but it usually comes from cans or boxes."

"How about Wanette? Or is that too personal?" Tertia asked.

"We're getting to know each other, so ask anything you want," Noah answered. "Like I told you, Wanette was a picky eater—always afraid that she would gain an ounce. She made salads, but she did not cook at all, period. Her main objective in life was being beautiful. Mama tolerated her. Granny didn't even do that."

Tertia could feel the chill from Bernie's staring at her even before she shifted her eyes from Noah to the table next to them. She smiled and waved, and Bernie gave her a big dose of stink eye.

"Daddy told me that he's coming over tomorrow for y'all to put your porch back together," she said and then bit into her hot dog.

"That's right, and Parker is coming to help. He says it's

payback for us doing so much at the church," Noah answered. "I guess we'll have to wait to start cooking until…"

"Until the next day." She finished the sentence for him. "But I could bring over some party leftovers about noon for y'all to snack on at lunchtime."

"That sounds great," Noah said.

"Hey, are y'all saving these seats for us?" Luna asked from a few feet away.

"Of course, we are," Noah answered. "How's the store coming along?"

"We're planning to have a grand opening in the middle of June," Shane set his plate down, then pulled out a chair for Luna. "That way we can get any kinks ironed out before the wedding."

"How about the café?" Luna asked.

"Slower than I'd like, but then when it opens, I hope we stay busy," Noah answered. "Tertia and I decided that we wouldn't talk business tonight."

Luna tucked a strand of blond hair behind her ear. "Rotten wind plays havoc with my hair, but I shouldn't complain. It could have rained and ruined our plans."

"Or came another tornado," Noah said.

Tertia shivered.

"Need my jacket?" Noah asked.

"No, thank you. I'm good. Thinking about how close we were to that storm still gives me the hives." If she was honest with herself, she would have to admit that there was more to that little shiver than what happened two nights ago.

Noah's knee grazing hers under the table started it, and then the night breeze sent the scent of his cologne her way. Like Aunt Bernie said about the new preacher, that was enough to make a holy woman's underpants crawl down around her ankles. Forget Parker; that's the effect Noah seemed to have on Tertia.

"I forgot to tell you that I got in touch with the café in Henrietta where that bull came from. They said that they didn't want it back because the café was totally destroyed and they weren't going to rebuild it," Noah said.

Shane chuckled. "Does that mean you're going into the cattle business?"

"Only the kind that doesn't require feeding," Noah replied. "Actually, I thought maybe I would set the old boy out in front of the new café. After all, this was part of the cattle drive trail back in the day. I'd still like to turn the old store into a museum someday."

"Do you own it?" Shane asked.

"I inherited it along with my grandpa's property." Noah picked up his second hot dog and took a bite. "My original plan was to put the café in that building, but it wouldn't pass inspection and it wasn't big enough."

"Between all of us in this generation, we're going to put Spanish Fort back on the map," Luna declared.

There they were talking shop, Tertia thought. Maybe friendship was as far as her relationship with Noah was destined to go. That idea disappointed her, but it would suit Bernie just fine and dandy.

"Mind if I join y'all?" Parker asked.

"Not at all," Luna replied and motioned for him to sit down.

"I've sure met a lot of folks tonight," he said. "I just hope I can put half their names with their faces when they come to church. Endora told me there are seven of you sisters. Are you all here tonight?"

"Just five of us," Tertia answered. "Bo is in Nashville, and Rae is in the panhandle of Oklahoma, but we're hoping they will be back around these parts by the end of the year."

Ursula and Remy came over and joined them, and then Ophelia and Jake.

"How long has it been since all seven of you sisters were back in Spanish Fort?" Parker asked.

"We were here for Ursula and Remy's wedding reception and Mother's Day, but only for a short while," Ophelia answered.

"It's been about fifteen years since we all lived here at the same time," Ursula added.

"I only have one sister, and she lives in Canada on a wheat farm," Parker said. "I can't imagine having six siblings living around me. That would be wonderful."

"Sometimes it was," Luna said. "And sometimes not so much."

The conversation among all of them skipped from one story to another as they entertained Parker with tales of having so many sisters in one house. Tertia caught a few words here and there. But mostly she got lost in her own roller coaster of thoughts. Noah fit in very well with the family—except with Aunt Bernie. Even Pepper liked him. Would Rae and Bo really come home? And if they did, would Bernie meet them at the door with a marriage license in one hand and dragging Parker along by the arm with the other one?

Chapter 19

Tertia pointed to the bar. "Sausage gravy in the slow cooker so it will stay warm. Biscuits on the stove. Muffins on the table. Y'all help yourselves," Tertia said when her parents came into the kitchen together the next morning.

"I love biscuits and gravy, but then you know that." Joe Clay kissed her on the cheek, then poured two mugs of coffee and set them on the table.

"Thank you, darlin'." Mary Jane sat down and picked up her mug. "Just a muffin for me this morning. I swear, the way you girls have been cooking, I'm going to gain ten pounds."

"We could pay them guys that they've been seeing to hurry up and take them off our hands," Joe Clay teased. "That way we could go back to toast and coffee for breakfast, a quick sandwich for lunch, and a light supper."

"Daddy!" Tertia air slapped him. "You can't sell us off like one of your wood projects."

"Don't intend to as long as you keep cooking like this." He grinned.

Mary Jane slathered butter on her cranberry orange muffin. "Speaking of food, we have a lot of leftovers, so why don't you guys come on over here for lunch today? Seems like a lot of trouble to cart food over to Noah's place, when y'all can just walk across the road and eat here."

"There weren't as many hot dogs as I thought there would be, but I can make up some hamburger patties, and we'll have both." Tertia planned out loud as she fixed her own plate. She would also whip up a couple of peach crisps to stretch out the leftover desserts.

Aunt Bernie came in the back door at the same time Ophelia and Endora entered the kitchen from the foyer. Ophelia was dressed in jeans and a cute little blouse. Endora still wore a pair of pajamas and had bags under her eyes.

"One of you slept well," Bernie pointed at Endora. "But you look like warmed-over sin on Sunday morning after a rough Saturday night."

Endora covered a yawn with the back of her hand. "I haven't even been to bed. I finished my first book about an hour ago and sent it to Mama's agent. If she can't sell it, then I plan to self-pub."

"And I'm on my way to work." Ophelia grabbed a muffin and headed back out toward the foyer.

"So, other than Ophelia going to work and Endora going back to bed, what's everyone else doing?" Bernie split open two biscuits, covered them with gravy, and carried her plate to the table.

"I'm helping Noah fix his porch. Remy and Shane and Parker are going to pitch in and help this morning," Joe Clay answered.

"Working on the final two chapters of my work in progress," Mary Jane replied. "I want to get it done and ready to send to the publisher by the end of the week so I can have a whole month free to finish planning Luna's wedding."

"And you?" Aunt Bernie looked right at Tertia.

"I'm going to make lunch for all the guys who are working on Noah's house," Tertia answered. "Mama suggested they all come over here, rather than us having to tote food over to them."

Bernie had to be fuming, but she hid it well. The old gal couldn't fuss at her because it had been Mary Jane's idea to invite them—not Tertia's.

"At least I can get to know Parker better and decide if he'll make a good husband," Bernie said.

"He's a preacher, for God's sake," Tertia scolded. "Why wouldn't he make a good husband?"

"Even preachers can be lousy in bed," Bernie answered.

"How do you know?" Tertia asked.

"Don't ask if you don't really want to know," Bernie snapped.

"I don't want to know," Joe Clay said, "so let's change the subject."

"Yes," Endora agreed and blushed.

———

At exactly noon the guys all paraded into the kitchen through the back door and, one by one, followed Joe Clay's lead when he washed his hands at the kitchen sink. Tertia had laid everything out on the bar separating the kitchen from the breakfast nook. "Y'all help yourselves and find a place to sit wherever you can," she said as she filled glasses with ice and set two pitchers of tea on the table, along with several bottles of water.

"I want to thank all y'all for the help this morning, and thank you, Tertia, for fixing lunch for us," Noah said.

"It was a joint effort," Tertia told him, "but you are welcome."

"Parker, would you say grace?" Joe Clay asked.

The kitchen went quiet while Parker said a quick prayer, and then Joe Clay led the way again when he picked up a disposable plate and made himself two hamburgers.

"Would it be rude if we sit on the screened porch?" Noah whispered.

His warm breath on her neck caused a little rush of heat to flow through her body. Her voice sounded kind of high and a bit squeaky in her own ears when she said, "Not at all."

She and Noah both carried their plates out the back door onto the porch, set them down on the table between the two rocking chairs, and then sat down at the same time.

"So, how did the morning go?" she asked.

"Faster than I expected," Noah answered. "I just have to paint the posts and put the shingles on the roof now. If I'd been doing all the work by myself, it would have taken me a week or more. I'm going into town to buy a couple of squares this afternoon. You want to go with me?"

"Love to," she answered with a nod.

"I figure I can finish up the rest of the job tomorrow

morning, and then we can start to cook in the afternoon." He stood up and rolled the kinks out of his neck. "I really like this screened porch. I'm going to talk to Henry about having my deck fixed like this. I like to sit outside in the evenings, but the river is a perfect breeding ground for mosquitoes."

"That's why Daddy fixed this one up for Mama all those years ago. After a day cooped up in the office writing books all day, she loved to be outside in the evenings, but she didn't like fighting with bugs."

Instead of sitting down in the chair he had just vacated, he leaned forward, tipped up her chin with his fist, and brushed a soft kiss across her lips. When it ended, he rose up and sat down beside her. "I've been wanting to do that for days, but someone always gets in the way."

Tertia had not been speechless very often in her life, but she was at that moment. She had thought about more than just kisses with Noah, but she hadn't expected a sweet kiss to send hot desire shooting through her body.

"Too soon?" he asked as he sat down.

"No," she whispered. "I just wasn't expecting it to affect me like it did."

"And how is that on a scale of one to ten, with ten being the best?" Noah asked.

"Fifteen," Tertia answered.

Noah flashed a smile and nodded. "I was thinking sixteen or seventeen, but fifteen is good."

"Hey, y'all, mind if we join you?" Luna asked as she pushed the door open.

"Not at all," Noah answered and winked at Tertia.

"We don't mean to interrupt," Shane said as he sat down on the swing and balanced his plate on his knees. "I had to get Luna out of the dining room before she exploded."

"What about?" Tertia asked.

"Aunt Bernie is meddling," Luna said. "I think Endora might like to talk to Parker, maybe just as a friend, but Aunt Bernie is hogging the conversation and telling him all about Bo. I love her, but she needs to back off."

"Amen!" Tertia said.

"As a bartender, she was probably used to a lot of excitement in her life," Noah said between bites, "and I bet that she misses all that. She can meddle all she likes, but when the last word is said, it's up to you sisters how you live your lives."

"I agree," Shane said, "but then I'm one of the lucky ones. She had me and Luna matched up from the beginning."

"I'll change her mind about me," Noah declared.

"Good luck, and if I can help, just let me know," Shane said.

Tertia hoped that Bernie did change her mind, or maybe swear that she had used reverse psychology like Mary Jane had suggested. But when it came right down to it, Bernie's liking Noah or not liking him wasn't the deciding issue in Tertia's relationship with him.

———

Compared to the previous Tuesday, this one went slower than any day Ophelia had ever experienced. She actually wondered if the clock had stopped several times throughout the day and had fallen asleep a couple of times while she waited for the doorbell to ring. She reminded herself that folks all over the area were still busy cleaning up what the weekend storm had left behind, so they weren't thinking about buying wine. Jake had been one of the lucky ones. The wind from the tornado had flipped his grill over and blew a couple of lawn chairs away, but it had not damaged his grape arbors or even stolen a single shingle from the winery roof. Electricity had been restored to his trailer as well as the winery, and production was going on as if nothing had happened.

Tomorrow Ophelia intended to bring her mother's latest book to work with her. She hadn't had time to read the last two that had been published, and slow days like this one would be a perfect time to catch up.

"Ready to close the door and go home?" Jake asked as he came from the back of the shop.

"It has been a slow one," she told him.

"If you get bored up here, come on to the back and visit with us guys. The doorbell is fixed so we can hear it from that area. I should have told you sooner." He crossed the room and flipped the sign around to show that they were closed.

Ophelia slung her purse over her shoulder and met him as he was coming back. They were only a few feet apart when she stumped her already bruised toe on the table where the wine had been. She started to fall, but Jake caught her and pulled her close to his chest.

"Do you think the third time will be the charm?" he asked.

"Third time?" Adrenaline rushed through her body almost as badly as it had when three funnel clouds were waltzing toward them.

"First time you fell into my arms was because of slick grass. Second time is right now," he replied.

"Why would the third time be a charm?"

He let go of her and cupped her face in his hands. "Because that would be when I kiss you."

She looked up into his eyes. "Why wait until the third?"

She barely had time to moisten her lips before his eyes fluttered shut and his mouth closed over hers. Her pulse jacked up, and time stood still as the heat built up to the boiling point between them. Ophelia had wondered what it would be like to kiss Jake, but nothing had prepared her for the rush of steam building up in her body, or the desire to push him through the door into the reception room and make out with him for hours.

"Holy smokin' hell!" he muttered when he finally took a step back. "I can hardly breathe."

"Me either," she panted.

"I wasn't expecting"—he stopped and sucked in a lungful of air—"for a simple kiss to knock my socks off."

"If that was just a simple kiss, then I don't know if I'm ready for a hot kiss." She was so breathless that her words came out one at a time.

"Want to go home with me and share a cold shower?" His grin was downright wicked.

She shook her head. "If I got in the shower with you, the water would boil. I expect I'd better go home and take a cold one all by myself." She felt as if she was floating, rather than walking when she started for the door. But if she'd spent another minute so close to Jake, they wouldn't be thinking about a cold shower at all—more like how quickly they could make it to a table in the reception room.

Jake slipped her hand into his, and another steamy burst of heat shot through her body. "I'll walk you out to your truck." She tried to control the sexy pictures popping into her head, but it didn't work.

His voice was deeper than before, giving testimony that he really had been affected by the kiss as much as she had. That exclamation he'd uttered hadn't just been a pickup line. "You might need my help again if you take a tumble."

"I could fake a fall," she teased.

"Any time," he said as he opened the door and led her out onto the porch. He helped her get settled into her vehicle, brushed a kiss across her cheek, and then took a step back. "I'll call you later tonight and see you tomorrow morning."

"Maybe if it's as slow as it was today, I'll come to the back room and learn the art of making wine," she said.

"I'll be glad to teach you." Jake closed the door.

She kept an eye on him in the rearview mirror, and he didn't turn around to go back to the business until she turned onto the road. She slowed down to a crawl and wiped her forehead in a dramatic gesture. "Whew!" she said as she took a long breath and let it out slowly.

The drive to the Paradise took twice as long as normal because she was trying to process her feelings before she was bombarded by however many sisters were at the house. And of course, her mother and Bernie would take one look at the smile on her face and ask a million questions.

To her surprise, no one was on the porch, and she was able to sneak upstairs to her room. Once inside, she gently closed the door and fell back on her bed. "Dammit! I wish Jake was right here beside me," she muttered. "But that's hormones talking. We haven't known each other long enough for that to happen."

She almost groaned when she heard a gentle knock on her door and sighed when Tertia peeked inside. She needed a few more minutes to think—alone!

Tertia came into the room, closed the door behind her, and stretched out on the other side of the bed from her sister. "Noah kissed me twice, and I liked it, a lot."

"You sound like a teenager," Ophelia said.

"I know!" Tertia groaned. "Is this rebellion because Aunt Bernie doesn't like Noah, and maybe because I'm turning thirty soon?"

"Thirty is not old!" Ophelia argued. "It's the new eighteen, don't you know?"

"Then that would explain the way I feel. I had to talk to someone. I'm not sure I've ever felt like this, and considering how I've felt about Noah Wilson all these years, that says a lot."

"Aunt Bernie isn't going to like it." Ophelia chuckled.

"But then it's your life, not hers. And one or two kisses do not mean a trip down the aisle at the church."

Tertia popped up to a sitting position. "You are so right. The second time around might not make my hormones whine. How are things going with Jake?"

"He kissed me," Ophelia whispered and then wished she had kept the news to herself. "Please don't tell anyone. I'm still processing the whole thing. I've been in relationships, but a few hot lingering kisses never made me want to throw caution to the wind and take a man to bed right then and there."

"Me, either," Tertia whispered, "but when Noah kissed me a few minutes ago, I got the same reaction. Are we both crazy, or has it just been too long since our last relationships? You are past thirty, and I'm staring it right in the eyes, and here we are, acting like we just got our first kisses at sixteen."

"I was fourteen," Ophelia said with a soft giggle.

"You hussy!" Tertia picked up a throw pillow and threw it at her sister.

Ophelia caught the pillow and threw it back at her. "I was an early bloomer. You just took a while to catch up."

Tertia sat up and propped her back against the headboard. "I might have been slow when it came to romance. After all, I was a tomboy for years, but I made up for it later. Still, nothing has prepared me for the effect that Noah is having on me."

"And you weren't ever going to date a blond-haired guy," Ophelia said.

"Or make out with one either. Remember that old saying: *'Be careful of the words you say. Keep them soft and sweet. For you never know which ones you'll have to eat.'* Or something like that?"

"Mama used to quote that to us when we were hateful to each other," Ophelia answered with a nod. "We're both having to eat our words. I wasn't going to work for Jake or date him either. But I can't help but wonder if it will be really awkward if I'm working with him, and then we break up?"

"I've been wondering the same thing, but we don't get fancy glasses that let us see into the future."

"Sometimes I wish we did," Ophelia said with a long sigh.

"Don't we all," Tertia agreed.

Chapter 20

WEDNESDAY MADE UP FOR the slow day on Tuesday. By closing time, Ophelia's feet were aching and the cash register was overflowing. At six o'clock she flipped the sign in the window, kicked off her shoes, poured the last of the tasting wine in a plastic cup, and perched on one of the barstools behind the checkout counter. The door to the back room opened, and it didn't take a clinical psychologist to see from the expression on his face that his day had not been nearly as good as Ophelia's.

He didn't even speak to her but took a bottle of elderberry wine from a cubicle, popped the cork, and drank it warm right from the bottle. "Looks like I have no choice but to sell the winery," he said as he hiked a hip on the second barstool.

Ophelia was almost too tired for a goodbye kiss that afternoon. She sure wasn't up for joking about something as serious as the future. "That's not funny!" she snapped. "I've had a long, busy day. My feet are hurting, and I'm tired. Don't tease me."

"I'm as serious as a sober judge." Jake took another long swig from the bottle, set it to the side, and pulled a magazine from under the counter. "I was going to surprise you today and tell you that I had a vendor who could put my wine in a lot of Texas convenience stores, and even in some grocery stores around these parts. Then this came out, and he called and backed out on me."

"A magazine can't do that," Ophelia argued.

Jake turned to the back page and stabbed a review with his forefinger. "This goes out to millions of households. Right here is a one-star review from a well-known critic for the Brennan Winery. He says that my strawberry wine is subpar, and the watermelon tastes worse than cheap punch."

"When was he even in here?" Ophelia asked.

"According to the date that he says he came in for a tasting, it was before you came to work," Jake sighed again. "I've had a couple of interested folks wanting to buy the business before now. One from an existing winery down south of here, and another from a man from Napa Valley in California who would like to relocate. I'm sure neither of them are interested after that thing." He glared at the magazine.

"Aren't most of your sales local?" she asked.

"Yes, but…"

She shook her finger at him. "No buts…and think about it. How many people in this whole county subscribe to that magazine?"

"Probably none, but what if this is a sign that I shouldn't…?" he started.

"Do you want to sell?" Ophelia asked.

Jake shook his head. "But this morning, Lester, Frankie,

and Rodney all gave notice. Seems like every sign is pointing me out of Spanish Fort."

Ophelia could feel her almost perfect world dropping out from under her so fast that it made her dizzy. "Why are they leaving?"

"Lester's wife and Frankie's run a little taco wagon and take it around to different towns each day of the week— Nocona, Saint Jo, and Henrietta, plus Bowie and a couple of others. They've wanted to expand into a café for a while and a place came up for sale in Henrietta. The bank loan got approved yesterday. The whole family is going to move over there and work in the new place. It opens a week from next Monday, so they'll only be here until the Friday before that. When it rains, it pours." He turned up the bottle again.

Rather than sympathizing with Jake, Ophelia's Irish temper shot to the top. "So, when things are going good, you are happy. But when a little obstacle gets in your way, you throw in the towel and quit? Is that the way you approach everything?"

"I thought you would…"

"What?" she snapped as she slid off the stool. "Hand you some crutches so you won't fall down and wallow in your pity party? Get drunk with you and whine because things aren't going good right now? We were saved from a tornado, for God's sake. Your grape arbors were spared and are producing wonderfully well. The cash register is overflowing from today's sales. Who needs a vendor? You are doing well right here." She started toward the door.

"Where are you going?" Jake asked.

"I'm going home. You need to do the same and count your blessings rather than diving into one day's failures. So, one critic didn't like your wine. Boo-hoo! So, your crew is leaving. Conor is coming to help, and I'm willing to learn, plus there's folks begging for jobs in this part of the world. When you get done whining, call me. I'll be here tomorrow morning ready to work if you haven't decided to sell the place. If you do, then just send me a text, and I'll go find a job somewhere else," she told him as she slammed the door behind her.

You could have been a little more sympathetic, the aggravating voice in her head scolded.

"What if he just cuts and runs every time the going gets tough? Why waste my time on a man like that, even if his kisses do melt my insides? He'll just leave after our first big argument," she muttered as she put the truck in gear, stomped the gas pedal, and slung gravel all over the porch as she drove away.

Looks like you'll never know the answers because you just burned all the bridges with your hot temper. The voice in her head was definitely Aunt Bernie's that time.

She came to a stop at the end of the gravel road and slapped the steering wheel so hard that her palm smarted. "Maybe so, but better to burn them now than cross over the rotten thing and find out that I'd made a big mistake by getting into a relationship with someone who can't fight for what he wants."

She made a left-hand turn with the full intention of going home and sneaking up to her room to cool off. But when she came to the short lane to Ursula and Remy's house, she came to a long, sliding stop and made another left-hand turn. She was still too angry to go home, and she didn't want to hear about how wonderful Tertia's day had gone while she and Noah were trying out new recipes. Or worse yet, listen to Aunt Bernie fuss at her for not being more sympathetic.

Remy's truck was nowhere in sight, but Ursula's vehicle was parked out front. Ophelia decided that if they were both gone, she would sit on the porch until she calmed down. She really wasn't ready to talk about the argument with anyone, anyway. She eased her truck in beside Ursula's SUV and sat there for several minutes before she finally turned off the truck engine, threw open the door, and marched across the yard.

She sat down on the porch swing, pulled her legs up, and wrapped her arms around her knees. As if the inanimate object knew that she needed something to distract her, the chains creaked as it barely moved back and forth, easing the anger a tiny bit. Not enough that she wanted company, but she had no choice in that matter when her sister opened the door and brought out two glasses of sweet tea and a plate of cookies on a tray.

"What has Jake done?" Ursula set the tray on the swing and then sat down on the other end.

"What makes you think he's done anything?"

"I heard you drive up, saw you stomp across the yard,

and I know you, so spit it out before you explode," Ursula answered.

"I may have just lost my job."

"Well, if you did, I'll hire you to help Remy in the hayfield this summer," Ursula said, "but what makes you think you've lost your job?"

"Because I threw a hissy fit." Ophelia groaned and went on to tell Ursula what had happened. "All I could think about was the fact that he didn't stick it out through tough times, and you know that there's a lot of difficult things that come up in any relationship. And long-distance ones..." The adrenaline rush had died and left her weepy.

"Usually fizzle out." Ursula finished the sentence for her.

"Yes, but I really felt something for him when he kissed me yesterday," Ophelia said with a long sigh. "I've never gotten a heat rush as hot as that one."

"Now who's whining?" Ursula fussed. "If you want something, fight for it. If you have doubts, shut the door and never look back at what might have been."

"You sound like Aunt Bernie," Ophelia said.

"Nope, that's straight Endora," Ursula told her. "When I had a problem with Remy, that's pretty much what she told me."

Ophelia laid a hand on her heart. "I'm shocked. That had to have been last winter when she was still trying to pull up out of her depression over being cheated on."

"Yes, it was, and I was just as surprised as you are," Ursula admitted. "Want a beer or a glass of tea? Or maybe stay with me and Remy for supper? I've got a tortilla soup in the slow cooker."

"I better not stay for supper. Endora has been so good at taking over supper duties that I don't want to disappoint her by not showing up." Ophelia picked up a glass of tea and took a long drink. "And I suppose that one or two or half a dozen of those cookies won't spoil my supper too much. When is Remy coming to the house?"

"About dark, which is a couple more hours," Ursula answered.

Ophelia took a cookie from the stack, bit into it, and thought about the next step. Did she go back over to the winery and confront Jake right then, or just show up for work the next morning?

"What's your advice? Go back and fight tonight, or wait until tomorrow?" Ophelia asked.

Ursula ate half a cookie before she answered. "When I was angry with Remy, I went home with a broken heart and thinking all kinds of mean things about him. Endora set me straight, and so I came back over here and cleared the air. But my situation was about another woman and wasn't like yours at all. When Luna and Shane had their fight about her tiptoeing around Endora, she and Aunt Bernie polished off a lot of whiskey, and then she went to talk to him the next morning. I'd say in your situation, maybe you should let him stew about things until tomorrow. The shock of every-thing that happened will be past, and he might be thinking about alternative ways. Maybe you should have a few drinks with Aunt Bernie. It might not cure the anger, but it would mellow you out so you could sleep tonight."

Ophelia couldn't think of a single scenario where drinking would help with the problem. "I could tell him that a magazine is like a newspaper. Once it's read, it's tossed aside to either be a liner for a birdcage, or else used to start a fire."

"That's right, and there's not much opportunity for jobs around here, so he shouldn't have trouble hiring other folks to work," Ursula added. "And you could mention that Mama doesn't get in a tizzy when she gets a one-star review on her books."

"I could, but if I have to be the strong one every time problems arise, I'm not so sure that I'm up for it," Ophelia declared. "I might need to lean on him at times."

"This could be a one-time moment of doubt for him," Ursula suggested.

Ophelia cut her eyes around at her sister. "Whose side are you on?"

"Yours, forever amen," Ursula said. "We are sisters but think about what you would say if the tables were reversed, and I was mad at Remy for wanting to sell the ranch and move away from Texas."

"Let's hope it's a one-time thing and not the norm," Ophelia said.

———

Tertia sprinkled freshly grated Parmesan and a little parsley on the green beans she had prepared to go with Noah's crumb chicken that day. Chatpata baby potatoes were ready to serve, and two small salads waited in the refrigerator. The table was set and glasses were filled with ice and sweet tea.

"We should publish a cookbook with all our recipes in it," Tertia said as she carried the two sides to the table.

"No way," Noah said in an edgy tone.

She set the bowls down and turned to face him. "That was pretty definite."

"Yes, it was and is."

That mean tone reminded her of the fight they had had back when they were kids and he was a bully about her mother owning a former brothel. A bit of anger surfaced but she really wanted to give him the benefit of a doubt. They weren't kids anymore, and maybe he just had a bad day.

"What's going on with you?" she asked. "Did I say or do something to upset you?"

"There are some things you have to understand if you are going to work for me." His tone was cold and indifferent. "And there are rules that you'll have to follow."

"I just thought we could sell the cookbook, along with the locally grown jellies and jams," she said. No more *our* café, but now he was saying that she would be an employee that had to follow rules. Where did all this come from and why now?

"Not just no, but hell no." Noah raised his voice. "I don't want folks to be able to make my food at home. I want it to be a treat for them to come to my café and…"

"Noah, I got the recipe for the green beans and potatoes

off the internet and just tweaked them a little bit so they would be slightly different," she reminded him.

"The customers won't know that." His tone was still harsh. "We don't give away recipes. If someone asks, we just say that they are old family recipes that we can't share. That is rule number one. Understand?"

She had argued with him about saying *our* café and *our* food in the past, but it riled her when he suddenly said *my* café and *my* food. Aunt Bernie had been right—his ugly side had surfaced. Not only did Tertia not like it, but she wouldn't tolerate it for a single minute.

"Do you understand?" he asked again.

"I'm not going to black your eye this time, Noah Wilson"—she pulled off her apron and tossed it on the cabinet—"but nobody talks to me the way you are doing. I don't have to work for you or help you anymore. I quit. You are on your own."

"I've had a bad day," he tried to explain. "Henry won't be able to start work on my café for another week."

"That's a lousy excuse, and there is never a reason for you to take your frustrations out on me. I'm going home and sitting down to supper with my family."

She marched out of the house and didn't even slow down when Rocky whistled at her and yelled that company was coming. Maybe Noah should teach him to say that company was leaving and probably would never come back again. She wouldn't be working with Noah anymore. He could take his café, his attitude, and his supper and go straight to hell with all of it. He could test his own recipes without her help and build his own café without any more input from her.

"You've got more personality than he does," she told the statue of the bull as she passed by it. A crow flew down from a nearby tree to light on the bull's horns and cawed loudly.

"You don't have a dog in this fight, so hush," she growled and kept walking. At the end of the lane, she stopped to let a vehicle pass.

"Hey, you need a ride?" Ophelia stopped her truck and rolled down the passenger-side window. "I'm headed home. Crawl in and ride with me the rest of the way."

Tertia climbed in the truck and folded her arms across her chest.

"Bad day?" Ophelia asked.

"Good day," Tertia answered. "Horrible last fifteen minutes. I don't want to go home. Can we go down to the old store and just talk for a few minutes?"

Ophelia nodded and drove past the lane to the Paradise. She parked in front of the old store, turned off the engine, and turned around in the seat. "Get it off your chest now, or have to listen to Aunt Bernie gloat when we get home. I just came from Ursula's, where I had to either talk or explode, and it's pretty evident that Noah has made you mad enough to chew up railroad spikes and spit out staples."

"I've always had a secret dream of getting a cookbook published," Tertia said through clenched teeth. "Mama and Ursula are writing romance books. Endora is working on books for children. And I want to work on a cookbook, maybe several."

"Why does that make you angry?" Ophelia asked.

Tertia could still feel hot adrenaline rushing through her veins. "It's not the cookbook idea. I'm determined to do that now, no matter what Noah Wilson says. And you can bet Aunt Bernie is going to crow over this." She gave her sister a detailed play-by-play of the argument that she and Noah had just had. "His tone was downright nasty, and he talked down to me. I'm not a submissive little woman that will take his hatefulness."

"Did you black his eye?" Ophelia asked.

"No, but I damn sure wanted to," Tertia answered. "Only this time, I would do more than just give him one black eye like I did when we were kids. I just realized that what he said back then made me mad, but it was his smart-ass attitude that really set me off enough to punch him."

Ophelia took a deep breath and let it all out in a long *whoosh*. "We've been paddling our canoes in parallel creeks."

"What does that mean?" Tertia hated to be wrong or to hear those four words—*I told you so*—but no one was going to talk to her like Noah did.

"Kisses yesterday," Ophelia said with half a shrug. "Fights today."

"You and Jake?" Tertia's eyes popped open so wide that they ached. "I thought y'all were going to be like Ursula and Remy—so perfect together that you never had an argument."

"Didn't happen," Ophelia said. "Aunt Bernie might have been right about Noah, but she was wrong about Jake."

"Good lord!" Tertia almost forgot about Noah. "Tell me what happened."

Ophelia gave her the short story and then shrugged again. "Do you think we could keep our arguments a secret?"

"Maybe for a day or two, but when I don't go to Noah's to test recipes or invite him to Sunday dinner, there will be questions," Tertia answered. "I really thought Noah had changed, and I would have never thought Jake would let something like a stupid critic's opinion of his wine affect him that way. I'm mad at Noah, and I probably won't work for him, but I don't have a doubt that he would carry a whole line of Jake's wines in his new café."

"I bet Shane will, too," Ophelia nodded. "That would be two places other than the winery itself. And chances are that I won't have a job either after the fit I threw, and there will be questions there too. But hey, better to burn the bridge now than to cross it and wish we had stayed on the other side, right?"

"Maybe you and I should put a pastry shop in the old store building, and I'll sell my cookbooks there," Tertia said and then shook her head. "That won't work. Noah owns that place now, and after the hissy I pitched, he probably would burn it before he'd lease or sell it to me. But nothing says we couldn't buy one of the empty houses in town and start a business."

"Look at us," Ophelia finally smiled. "Nothing gets a Simmons sister down, especially not an argument with a man."

"Think either of them will apologize?" Tertia asked. "Not that I'm ready to forgive Noah, but it would be nice if he was man enough to admit he is wrong."

Ophelia started the truck engine. "We won't hold our breath because neither of us…"

"Look good in that shade of blue," Tertia finished her mother's old saying.

Ophelia pointed the truck toward the south and headed to the Paradise. "Another one of Mama's sayings. As soon as Aunt Bernie ferrets out what happened today, she will be trying to fix one of us up with Parker."

Tertia giggled, and then laughed out loud. "As tall as you are, and as short as he is, he would have to carry around one of those little step stools to even kiss you."

"Put a smile on your face, Sister," Ophelia said as she turned into Paradise lane. "Aunt Bernie won't be the only one to drag out a soapbox. Endora will preach at us too, and say that she was right about men being scoundrels."

"I'm smiling, see," Tertia flashed a fake grin at her sister. "Maybe we'll get one evening of peace before they figure things out."

Chapter 21

"Do I stay, or do I go?" Ophelia asked her reflection in the mirror that Sunday morning as she got ready for church. She had tamed her hair somewhat, and big bouncy curls floated down her back. For church that morning, she had chosen a straight denim skirt that came down to her ankles with a side slit up to her knee and a shirt printed with tiny little shamrocks. Green inlays were cut into her white cowgirl boots.

Tertia came into the bathroom and went straight to the sink and started putting on her makeup. "Go or stay where? Church or the winery? Do you think that shirt will bring you good luck?"

"I'm going to church, but things have been so very businesslike at work for the past three days that sometimes I consider putting in my notice." Ophelia answered. "Then I rethink the whole thing, and I'm determined that I'm not going to lose this battle even if I feel like I'm leaving a funeral every day when I walk out of the place. And yes, I wore this shirt special today in hopes it will bring me good luck."

"What would good luck look like?" Tertia asked as she leaned into her mirror and applied lipstick. She wore a multi-colored gauze skirt with a bright-orange tank top and matching sandals. "If Jake sells the winery, and you move on to find someone else, is that good luck? Or is it good luck if you and Jake make up and go on to have great-grandkids together?"

"Is that my only two options?" Ophelia turned around and leaned against the long vanity.

"One never knows until it happens, and then it takes us ten years to figure out if it was good or bad luck," Tertia answered. "Has Jake said anything about his plans?"

Ophelia raised one shoulder in half a shrug. "Nope, we are professionally polite. 'Good morning,' and 'Have a nice evening,' are basically what conversations we have each day."

Tertia twisted her curly brown hair up off her neck and held it there with a large clamp. "Are you ever going to talk about it?"

"The ball is in his court," Ophelia replied. "How about you and Noah? Any communication?"

"Nope, not a word, zilch, nada, nothing," Tertia answered. "How long are you going to work at the winery if things don't change this next week?"

"I'm determined to outlast Jake Brennan," Ophelia answered and took a step toward the door. "And, Sister, your skirt is tucked up in your panties."

"Are you teasing me?" Tertia whipped around and checked her backside in the long mirror on the back of the door to find the hem of her dress tucked into her bright-red lacy bikini underwear.

"I wouldn't joke about something like that," Ophelia said and then pulled her sister's dress free. "But if you got all the way to church without anyone noticing, and Noah was there…" She giggled.

Tertia followed her sister out of the bathroom. "I'm not sure he would even be kind enough to say anything about something like that. Thanks for not letting me embarrass myself. Are you ready for the family's questions when Noah and Jake don't show up for Sunday dinner?"

"Nope, I'm not, but today won't be a big problem. Remember that we're having a potluck to welcome our new preacher. Everyone will be so busy that they won't even realize we aren't sitting with Noah and Jake," Ophelia answered.

"Saved by a slow cooker of baked beans," Tertia smiled. "And a blackberry cobbler for Daddy. Maybe if we are 'lucky'"—she air quoted the last word—"neither of them will show up today, and we'll get another week's reprieve."

Ophelia crossed the long hallway and started down the stairs. "That would fall under the *miracle* category." She came to a dead stop on the third step from the bottom and realized that Jake was standing there, staring right into her eyes with his cowboy hat in his hand.

She felt Tertia's hand land on her shoulder, probably more for balance than for support, but it helped all the same.

"Good morning," Ophelia said.

"Good morning to you. Endora told me to wait right here, and you would be down in a few minutes," Jake said. "I should have called first, but I was afraid you would say no. Would you go to church with me this morning, and then out to dinner so we can talk?"

"Say yes," Tertia whispered.

Ophelia shook her head.

"I understand," Jake said.

Tertia gave her shoulder a hard squeeze. "Get it over with."

"All right," Ophelia said, "but we have a potluck after church today to welcome Parker to the church and our town. I need to be there and help with that."

"I had forgotten that was planned. I could go to the potluck, and then maybe talk afterward?" Jake looked so miserable that Ophelia wanted to hug him—until she remembered the argument.

"That might work." Ophelia finally nodded.

Jake held out a hand, and she put hers in it. The chemistry was still there, to her surprise. She figured that the chill of the previous couple of days would have frozen any future vibes.

"Thank you," he said, but his eyes still looked sad. Did that mean he had sold the winery and was going to tell her not to come to work on Tuesday?

He held the truck door open for her without saying a word, and they rode in silence to the end of the lane. "Conor and his girlfriend, Lucy, will be here in time to help me harvest the crop in a few weeks. Until then, it will just be the two of us. I've been on pins and needles that you will turn in your notice or simply not show up for work."

The thought was crazy, but all Ophelia could think at that moment was that Bernie was going to be disappointed that

Conor wouldn't be up for grabs in her matchmaking schemes. Then that idea vanished, and she figured that Jake was about to tell her that she'd better look for another job pretty soon.

"Lucy's father works for Grandpa in his wine-making business, and she knows quite a bit about the business. They'll be moving in the trailer with me," he said.

"That's great news." Ophelia's tone sounded hollow even in her own ears. Did that mean Lucy would take over the front of the winery when she arrived? "Does that mean he's buying the business from you?"

"That's a fair question after the way things have been the past few days," Jake answered. "But no, the winery is not for sale. However…"

Ophelia was ready for him to say that she wouldn't be needed anymore when Lucy and Conor arrived. "However, what?"

"However, Conor would like to invest in the winery and make it even bigger—be a partner so to speak. He would put up the money for more grape arbors and an addition onto the warehouse part of the business so we can store more barrels. And Lucy wants to expand to include white grapes." He pulled into the church lot and nosed into one of the few parking spots left. "What do you think?"

"I told you the first day I walked into your winery that I don't know jack squat about making wine." Ophelia wondered exactly why he was even asking her opinion. "We should go on inside. Services begin in five minutes, and we can talk about this later."

Jake nodded, got out of the truck, and like always, opened the door for her. He did not try to hold her hand as they crossed the gravel parking lot, but he did guide her down the center aisle with his hand on her lower back. The church was so full that there were only places to sit left on the front pew. Parker took his place behind the lectern at the same time Noah entered the sanctuary.

"Looks like we've got a full house today, Noah, but if everyone on the front pew scooted down just a little, there would be room for one more. The scripture tells us it will be a tight squeeze by the time Tertia gets here. There she is now. Come on down to the front, Tertia," Parker said. "Noah is waiting for you."

Ophelia's heart went out to her sister. Poor Tertia had no option other than escaping back to the fellowship hall and leaving the door open so she could hear the sermon. When everyone scooted down, Jake's shoulder was pressed firmly against Ophelia's, and he held the hymnal they would have to share.

"Welcome to everyone this fine, sunny morning," Parker said. "I don't know all of you yet, but I'm so glad to see a full church this morning. Before I deliver my message, I'm going to turn this over to our song leader, Miz Dolly Devlin. Let's lift our voices so that everyone in Spanish Fort can hear us." He sat down on the deacon's bench to his right, and Dolly marched up the aisle to take her place. "Let's have a congregational singing this morning with hymn number 63."

Jake had picked up one of the two hymnals lying on the

pew when he sat down, so he opened it to the right page and shared the book with Ophelia. Noah did the same with the one he had in his hands and held it over toward Tertia. Ophelia couldn't have cut the tension swarming around the four of them with a machete. Several elderly folks, mostly with hearing problems, sat on the pew with the four of them and had no idea that the world wasn't perfect between the two couples.

God has got a sense of humor almost as big as my Universe does. Bernie's voice popped into Ophelia's head.

This is not funny by any standard—in heaven, on earth, or anywhere in between, Ophelia argued silently.

The song ended. Noah and Jake held the hymnals in their laps since there was no place to put them. Parker stepped up to the old oak lectern and smiled. Ophelia could almost read Bernie's thoughts, even though she was sitting several rows back with the rest of the family.

"I'd like to say welcome again, and to tell you that I'm grateful to be here in Spanish Fort. As some of you know, this is my first position as a full-time preacher, but I'm a lot like Paul in the Bible. When he went to a new place, he worked to earn his keep, and I will be helping a local carpenter"—he waved at Henry—"here in town. But my congregation comes first, so when and if any of you need me, I'm just a phone call away. That said, open your Bibles to the fifth chapter of Matthew, and let's visit a while about forgiveness."

I agree, Aunt Bernie. Ophelia rolled her eyes toward the

ceiling. *God does have a sense of humor, or else He is speaking loudly to all four of us this morning.*

Ophelia leaned forward just enough to catch Tertia's attention and winked. Tertia barely shook her head, but the meaning was clear. Parker could preach until eternity dawned without his message getting through to Tertia. She had not forgotten Noah's bullying when they were kids, and she might never forgive him for the way he talked to her a few days ago. Of all seven sisters, Tertia was the funny one, but she could also hold a grudge forever.

=====

Tertia set her jaw, clenched her teeth, and swore she would freeze the vibes she felt at the touch of Noah's shoulder pressing against hers. Sure, sitting beside Noah and sharing a hymnal with him would convince folks that they were a couple, and that would keep the questions at bay for a while longer. But if he was feeling the same chemistry that she was—which she doubted from the way he held himself so stiffly—he could just take a flying leap at a rolling doughnut in a blizzard.

Parker's soft southern accent was very different from the big booming voice that the old preacher had. Even though Tertia wasn't listening to a word Parker said, his southern tone had a soothing effect on her thoughts as she wrote out several recipes in her mind. She was going to publish a cookbook by Christmas, even if she had to self-pub it and sell her wares out of the trunk of her car.

She was jerked back to the present when Parker said, "I'll ask Joe Clay Carter to give the benediction and say grace for the meal we are about to partake of, and then we'll sit still just a minute or two to allow the ladies who are preparing our potluck dinner to leave first."

When she saw her dad stand up to pray, Tertia bowed her head and reined in her thoughts even further. His prayer was short, and the *amen* came before Parker reached the back of the sanctuary to shake hands with all his congregation. Tertia had never been so glad to stand up and head to the fellowship hall with the ladies who would be helping with the dinner. But the heat from Noah's shoulder didn't disappear just because she was away from it.

Ophelia looped her arm in Tertia's and whispered, "We survived, but I could hear Aunt Bernie giggling because we had to sit on the front pew."

"I love Jesus for not letting me go up in flames—both from the heat I felt sitting so close to Noah, and for my wandering thoughts. I got to admit I didn't hear a lot of the sermon," Tertia said out of the side of her mouth. "But I did hear that he was preaching on forgiveness, and I'm not buying into that—not even if Noah Wilson walks through a bed of hot coals to bring me a box of chocolates and a dozen red roses."

Ophelia was the first one to the double doors into the fellowship hall, so she opened both of them wide. "Not even if he dropped down on his knees and begged?"

Tertia removed her sister's arm from hers and went straight to the kitchen, where she took two bibbed aprons from a hook. She handed one to Ophelia and put the other one over her neck, then tied the waist strings in the back. "He was too proud to apologize as a kid. You don't change the stripes on a zebra."

Ophelia took the apron that Tertia handed to her and slipped it over her head. "I believe that's spots on a leopard."

"What...ever!" Tertia did a head wiggle.

Endora walked past them and slipped an apron over her outfit—a red-and-white-polka-dotted dress with a white collar. "Wasn't that a lovely sermon?"

"Are you ready to forgive your two exes?" Tertia asked.

Endora frowned. "Two? There was only Kevin."

"And Krystal. She is now your ex-friend, but she had an ongoing affair with him," Ophelia reminded her.

"I'm working on it. The forgiveness is a lot easier than the forgetting, isn't it?" Endora said with a nod.

"Yes, it is," Tertia agreed, "but you've come a long way in the past six months."

"I've had a lot of help from my family," Endora said with a smile. "Now, we better get busy. We've got a bunch of folks to feed today."

"Amazing how the mention of a potluck brings more folks to church," Ophelia whispered.

"Feed 'em naturally and spiritually." Endora went around the end of the long row of tables and began to take lids off of the casserole dishes and slow cookers. "And besides, if the church grows, then maybe the community will too. Wouldn't it be something if we got a post office again?"

"It could happen." Tertia tried to keep an upbeat tone, but it wasn't easy. Still, there was no need to spoil Endora's positivity—especially after all the negativity she had overcome. "Looks they're fixin' to start coming in, and Parker is leading the parade." She nodded toward all the folks starting to come into the fellowship hall.

"I just love gatherings like this." Endora's bright smile was met with one from Parker as he entered the room before any of the congregation.

Ophelia nudged Tertia on the shoulder. "Think there might be a possibility there between those two?"

"Not if Aunt Bernie has her way," Tertia answered. "She's got him earmarked for Bo."

"We are living proof that she's been wrong before," Ophelia said.

Parker went to a table right inside the room and picked up a microphone. "Thank you to all the ladies who did this so I could get to know more of the church family. Thank you to everyone who insisted that I was first in line today since this was done to welcome me to Spanish Fort. I have to admit, I never expected such a warm welcome. Now, let's dig into all this good food and enjoy the fellowship amongst ourselves."

Tertia scanned the folks waiting at the door for Parker to finish and caught sight of Noah. He looked miserable, but she didn't feel sorry for him. His attitude had caused him to be unhappy, so he could deal with it.

"Okay, girls," Mary Jane said, "Ophelia, you are on tea duty. Tertia, you can take care of water. Endora, grab a pitcher of lemonade. Ursula and Luna can stay behind the tables with me to help however we are needed."

"I'll go to the kitchen with Dolly as soon as we eat and help wash up the casserole dishes as they are emptied," Bernie offered.

Tertia waited until a few people were seated to pick up a pitcher of water and begin her rounds. When she reached Noah, he held his red disposable glass full of ice over his shoulder for her to fill. She fought the urge to miss the glass and pour water down the back of his neck, but then he looked up at her with sad eyes.

"Can we talk?" he asked.

"What good would it do?" she whispered and went to the next table.

Bernie shook her head when Tertia offered to fill her glass. "I'm waiting for tea, but what was that all about? Are you and Noah fighting? You should have listened to me. I told you that a skunk can't ever get rid of the stink on him."

Dolly clucked like an old mother hen gathering in her chicks. "Poor old Noah. I feel sorry for him."

"Why?" Tertia asked.

"He's had a whole streak of bad luck ever since he was in school, and the first thing was Wanette," Dolly whispered. "Now, he'll most likely have to go back to coaching. I was sure looking forward to having a restaurant right here in Spanish Fort."

"That's what he gets for being a bully," Bernie said out the corner of her mouth.

"What was Aunt Bernie telling you?" Ophelia asked when she and Tertia met in the kitchen to refill their pitchers.

"She's figured out something is going on with me and Noah. Dolly says he's had some bad luck as far as the café goes and may have to keep his coaching job," Tertia answered. "Good thing I hadn't made up my mind about working with him, isn't it?"

"Disappointed?" Ophelia asked.

Tertia nodded. "Got to be honest and admit that I *am* disappointed. That was my dream job, and making the cookbook was important to me. Both have been dashed, but hey, I didn't have my life all lined out when I left coaching and came back here. I've still got a year to get things figured out."

"You can always sub, like I did," Ophelia suggested.

Tertia shook her head. "I'm done with teaching in any form or fashion. I'm going to follow in Endora's footsteps."

"And write children's books all summer?" Ophelia asked.

"No, I'm going to invent recipes, test them, and write a cookbook." Tertia picked up her pitcher of water and headed back out of the kitchen. "One more round and then Mama says we can eat."

"I'm so ready. Do you think you might talk a few of the church women to share their recipes with you?" Ophelia asked.

"Hey, that's a great idea. We could make a Spanish Fort church cookbook and sell it as a fundraiser for the church. We could title it *Famous Funeral Dinners*." Tertia was excited just thinking about it. "I'll volunteer to be the head of the committee and get the cookbook all ready for publication."

"Sounds like a plan, and you can work on your personal one at the same time. That should keep you busy when we're not working on Luna's wedding," Ophelia said and carried her pitcher of tea out of the room.

"Wedding plans are usually only on Sunday evenings, so I'll have plenty of time through the week." Tertia was already planning several alternatives to the title as she made a final round to see if anyone needed a water refill.

———

Ophelia expected Jake to take her home after the potluck, but he made a right out of the church parking lot and drove straight ahead. "Luna and Shane are at the Paradise, so why are we going to their house?"

"Shane said we could borrow his willow tree down by the river," Jake explained. "He said that's where he and Luna made up after a big fight that they had back before Christmas."

"Why did you tell Shane about it?"

"Because he came in to buy a bottle of wine and asked me if someone died," Jake answered. "When I told him about the review and everything else, he said I should talk you into coming down here with me to talk things through."

"Well," Ophelia crossed her arms over her chest. "We didn't actually have a fight, just a difference of opinion."

The road to the river was two bumpy ruts with knee-high

grass and weeds growing up in the middle. Jake had to slow down to let a couple of bunnies cross from one side to the other. "Then why does it feel like we are about to break up?"

"One date doesn't mean we were a couple. It means that we figured out we are not compatible," she said.

He braked at the end of the road, got out of the truck, and opened the door for her. "Maybe not, but it was beginning to feel like we might be—at least, to me."

She slid off the seat and planted her feet on the ground. She had already lost one pair of expensive high heels to the tornado, and the ground was soft around the river, so she was glad that she'd worn her boots that day.

He laced his fingers with hers and nodded toward a huge weeping willow tree. "That's where we are going."

Dammit! I don't want just holding his hand to affect me this way, she thought. *Why can't my heart want someone else?*

Maybe Parker? Aunt Bernie's voice was back in her head.

Ophelia set her jaw in a firm line. She was not one bit interested in a man who barely came up to her shoulder, and besides all that, she couldn't see herself as a preacher's wife.

Jake let go of her hand and parted the long, drooping limbs as if they were curtains. "Ladies first."

Luna had told her the story of how she and Shane had settled their argument under the old willow tree. Ophelia could understand where two people could settle their differences when she stepped into an area that was so ethereal that it took her breath away. The massive tree grew right up in the middle of a wide circle of ground packed down as hard as concrete. The only sounds were tree frogs and birds blending their voices like a church choir and the occasional splash out in the river when a catfish flopped up out of the water.

Ophelia sat down and braced her back against the massive tree trunk. "I can see why Shane and Luna like this place. It's like the rest of the world has disappeared with all its cares and problems."

Jake eased down close enough that he could share the tree trunk with her. "It's sure peaceful, isn't it? It's a perfect place for us to clear the air."

He waited so long to say another word that Ophelia thought maybe he'd changed his mind. "Do you want to go first, or should I?"

"This is your party, so have at it," she said.

"I'm not a quitter, never have been," Jake declared, "but when all that came crashing down on me at the same time, I wanted to throw up my hands and give up. I'm sure we've all been in that place a time or two. I thought I needed your support that day, but after a couple of days of stewing about the situation"—he paused—"and listening to Lester, Frankie, and even Rodney fuss at me, I realize you were right to lower the boom on me."

She opened her mouth to say something, but he shook his head. "I'm not finished. I'm not a mama's boy, but I did call her last night after I talked to Conor and asked him if he could move up here before we harvest the grapes. She really let me have it over that review and reminded me that the next one might be a five-star. She also told me that if I really liked you, I was foolish not to apologize for the way I have acted these past few days."

"And," Ophelia finally said.

"I'm sorry," he said.

"Does that mean you really like me?" she asked.

"It does," Jake admitted.

Ophelia slipped her hand into his. "Okay, then, apology accepted. I'm not sorry for the way I behaved, Jake. I'm a strong woman, but I'm not going to continue to go out with a man who might live in phases."

"Phases?" he asked.

"That's someone who lives in six-week or even six-year phases and then moves on to another one. I want someone in my life who is steady. I can support a dream, but I'm not going to be in a relationship that is constantly changing. That would be like starting to build a house, only to get it halfway finished and move away to start another dream. Does that make sense?" she asked.

He gave her hand a gentle squeeze and moved over closer to her. "Yes, it makes a lot of sense, and I agree with you. I remember an old song my granny used to listen to back when she had cassettes. Have you heard 'My Elusive Dreams'?"

"Aunt Bernie likes that song, and yes, the lyrics exactly match what I was thinking that day. I like you. I might even fall in love with you, but I'm not willing to follow your whims all over the world."

"I understand," Jake agreed with a nod, "and any man worth his salt wouldn't ask a woman to do that."

"Next time you have a bad day, I promise that I will give you ideas on how to fix it rather than exploding," Ophelia said. "And speaking of that, I think that Shane would be glad to sell your wine in his new store, and I bet that Noah would let you put a display in his café. Once folks catch on, they'll start asking for it in other places. So, who needs a vendor? We can do our own marketing and not have to give up a percentage of the profits to a third party."

She didn't want to talk about wine or arguments. As if he read her mind, Jake turned to face her and smiled, right before his mouth landed on hers in a long, lingering, hot kiss. The idea of vendors, grape harvests, people moving in with Jake, and every other idea in her head disappeared. She and Jake were the only people in the world and were living in a little bubble surrounded by limber willow limbs and a pair of doves cooing somewhere close by.

Chapter 22

DARK CLOUDS COVERED THE sun, so instead of sitting on the balcony and watching a brilliant Texas sunset like Tertia often did at the end of a day, she kept an eye on the swirling clouds and a few streaks of lightning that zigzagged through the sky.

"Looks like we might get rain," Ophelia said as she came out of her bedroom and joined her sister.

"The weatherman agrees with you, but he says it'll just be rain. No hail or tornadoes." Tertia nodded. "What happened when you and Jake left the church this afternoon?"

"We cleared the air, settled things, and we have a date for next Saturday. Right now, he's over at Remy's at the Sunday night poker game, and you and I are supposed to be downstairs talking about Luna's wedding," Ophelia answered. "Mama sent me up here to get you."

"I guess this is where we paddle our own canoes and your river or creek goes in a different direction than mine does," Tertia said with a long sigh.

"What are you talking about?" Ophelia asked.

"Remember when you said we were paddling canoes on parallel creeks? We got kissed the same day, had arguments the same day…"

"Oh, that," Ophelia butted in before her sister could finish. "What will be, will be…"

Tertia stood up and finished Ophelia's sentence. "And what won't be, might be anyway."

"That's right," Ophelia told her. "Let's go talk weddings, and both be glad that wedding cakes and flowers are not in our immediate future."

Tertia followed her sister into her room. "Luna gets to keep all the thunder to herself, and you can be next in line. Are you going to do it up big, or just have something simple?"

"Jake and I just survived our first disagreement. We're not ready to think about marriage." Ophelia made it to the middle of the room when a streak of lightning seemed to land on the balcony and thunder rolled so close by that it rattled the windows. She stopped so fast that Tertia ran into her back and both of them had to grab a corner of the dresser to keep from falling.

"What happened?" Tertia asked. "Did a mouse run across your foot, or is there a spider hanging from the ceiling?"

"I always imagine that the sound of…" Ophelia stopped in the middle of the sentence. "You know that I flew drones. It's classified what I did, but I always imagined that when I pushed the red button, the sound was something like thunder. I couldn't hear it, of course. The whole thing was just images on a computer screen."

Tertia flipped the switch to turn on the light. "Do you want to talk about it?"

Ophelia shook her head. "I stopped because I expected a panic attack when I heard the noise, but it didn't happen. I don't feel like my chest is caving in, and I don't want to hide under the bed until the attack passes."

"Just exactly what happened when you and Jake made up this afternoon?" Tertia asked.

"We didn't have sex if that's what you are asking, but I would be more than willing to fall into bed with him if that would make the nightmares and panic attacks disappear." She took another step toward the hallway.

Tertia air slapped her on the arm. "That would be using Jake, and so very wrong. You can have sex with him for many reasons, but not to stop your bad dreams."

A hard knock on the door took their attention from the subject. Tertia expected one of her sisters or her mother to have answered it before they reached the foyer, but no one was there. Evidently, they were making a playlist for the wedding reception because music came from the living room. Tertia recognized the Aaron Watson song, "When I See You," and hoped that someday, someone would play and sing that song for her—maybe even draw her into his arms and dance with her.

Ophelia threw open the door to find Noah standing on the other side of the old-fashioned screen door. "Looks like we might still be running parallel," she whispered to Tertia. "I'll give you the same advice you gave me—go with him." Then with a wave she disappeared into the living room.

"Noah?" Tertia greeted him, but didn't invite him in.

"Tertia, we need to talk," he said.

"I don't think we have anything to say to each other." Her heart went out to him for the misfortune, whatever it was, but that was business, and she had to protect her own feelings.

"You might not, but I do," Noah said. "Will you just come sit with me on the porch and let me say my piece? After I do, I'll leave and never bother you again."

"I can do that," she agreed and stepped outside, "but there's a storm brewing so we might do better to sit in your truck."

"I agree," he said and hurried off the porch to open the passenger door for her.

She slid into the passenger's seat and kept her eyes glued on the clouds rolling in like burnt marshmallows over the roof of the Paradise. When he took his place behind the wheel, he just sat there for several minutes.

"Well?" she asked when the first big drops of rain splatted against the windshield.

"I'm sorry," he said. "For every stupid mistake I made the other day, and for being so ugly when we were kids. My mama told me that I should walk across the road and apologize to you back then, and she told me the same thing when she and my dad came to see me yesterday. So, here I am, apologizing for taking my frustrations out on you. It was wrong, and I promise to never do it again. I've never been so lonely—not even when Wanette left me for another man—as I've been since Wednesday. I've probably ruined anything that we might have had, but I want you to know that I'm sincere in what I'm saying."

"What frustrated you so bad?" Tertia asked. "If I'm going to forgive you, I should hear the whole story."

"I can't build the café."

Tertia could feel the pain in his voice. "Why?"

"I thought I was okay financially, even with the application for a bank loan. I'd need to borrow about a third of the cost, and I could use the land for collateral, but the bank sent out an appraiser and..." He shrugged in defeat.

She pressured. "And what?"

"My debt-to-income ratio is only borderline strong enough for a loan that big, and too many oil wells were drilled around that ten acres of land. The water well I would have to have drilled would be salty. No good water. No café," he answered. "I had just gotten the news that afternoon and was trying to figure out a way around it. I didn't want to tell you because that meant I probably wouldn't see you again."

"And there we were making a recipe for a café that wasn't ever going to be," she said. "And me rattling on and on about making a cookbook."

Another shrug. "I asked my dad why he even built a house in Spanish Fort if there were problems with salty wells. He said that he had everything tested before he built on the land that Grandpa deeded over to him. He found out that there's an underground stream of good water flowing about twenty feet down not far from the back of my house, so we're good on that land, but the place where we were going to build the café is good for grazing, just not building anything on that requires water."

"Is there another place that you could build?" She wondered how much of the town that the stream took care of, and if that would be a reason why Spanish Fort was almost a ghost town.

"What if…?" she started and then stopped.

"Go on," Noah said. "I can see the wheels turning in your head like they did when you were looking at the plans for the new café."

"Can we drive over to your house?" she asked. "I've been in it, but I didn't get the grand tour, and you might not even agree with my what-if."

"Why now?" Noah asked. "Does this mean you are going to give me a second chance? I'm just a coach, but we can always enjoy spending time together."

"I've got an idea, but before I voice it, I'd like to really look at the place. You do have a tape measure over there, don't you?"

"Of course, and a hammer and a screwdriver," Noah answered as he started the engine and drove from the Paradise to his place.

Tertia didn't give him time to be the Texas gentleman and open the door for her. As soon as the truck stopped, she hopped out in the pouring rain and ran to the porch. Noah was right behind her, and he unlocked the door. "Am I forgiven for being a jackass or not?"

She pushed inside and nodded. "You are forgiven, but don't you ever talk to me in that tone of voice again."

"I promise I won't," he agreed. "Now tell me what you have in mind."

She walked through the whole three-bedroom, three-bath home, measuring each room as she went and writing the sizes down on a notepad that she picked up from the dining room table. "Okay," she said, "here's what you could do. The kitchen and dining room could be closed off, maybe with swinging doors. The dining room could be the food prep area. The safe room could be a storage room, and you could put a commercial freezer in there as well."

"You are talking about making this house into a café?" His eyes widened out, and he slapped his palm against his forehead. "The living room could be the dining area. The foyer could be where the hostess could set up shop. But what about the bedrooms?"

"Houses in other countries are often turned into cafés," she said. "The bedrooms could be opened up for extra tables and guests when the dining room is full. One bathroom can be for men. One for women. The third one would be for employees. We could build a wall in front of the bathtubs in each room, and put a door on the other end, and use that area for storage. This could work if it would pass inspection to be remodeled into…"

"We could knock out the walls to two of the bedrooms and make the living room bigger to seat more people, and then use the smallest one for a break room for the employees." His tone said that he was really getting excited. "The remodel would take less time and money than building a new place. But where would I live? I've given up my apartment in Saint Jo, but I could ask if they would let me keep it, and then I could commute."

"Or you could have one of those prefab homes brought in and park it out back, maybe along that tree line way back there so it would be private," she suggested. "It shouldn't take long to drill another well for the house and get electricity brought out to it from the road. You might not even have to ask the bank for a loan if you could locate a repossessed one, and that could be less than what it was going to take for Henry to put up the new café."

Noah grabbed Tertia around the waist and spun her around several times. "You are a genius."

She was panting and dizzy when he set her back on her feet. "I don't know about that, but it seems like a plausible plan."

"I would have never thought about making the house into the café or of buying a prefab home, either one. Please say you'll help me cook, hire a staff, and pick out a house. You are my good-luck charm, Tertia."

"Let's don't get in a big rushing hurry about everything. First, we have to be sure we can trust each other again, and if we can get through a week or two without arguing." The walls had finally stopped spinning, but her words came out one or two at a time in between pants.

"We are both passionate people," Noah said. "We will argue."

"Then we'll see how we each react to disagreements for

a couple of weeks. We've got a lot of actual planning to do, and you have to talk to Henry about knocking out walls and remodeling, and making sure there are no zoning laws in Spanish Fort."

"Fair enough," Noah agreed. "Is it too soon to kiss you? Maybe as a thank-you."

She took a step closer to him and kissed him on the cheek. "Thank you for knocking on my door and apologizing."

"I'll take what I can get and be satisfied tonight with baby steps." He grinned. "I'm going to call Henry tonight and tell him to put me back on the list. Will you go with me tomorrow to look at one of those prefab homes?"

"Of course, I will," Tertia answered. "Jake might even tell us where to start. He lives in a trailer back behind his winery."

"Would it be totally rude of me to take you home and go over to Remy's poker game?" he asked. "I could talk to Jake tonight. I'm too excited to wait until morning."

"It would not be rude at all," she answered. "I'm supposed to be helping make the wedding playlist for the music tonight anyway."

"Damned old rain. I hate storms," Rocky screeched from the living room.

Noah draped an arm around her shoulders and started for the door. "Don't mind him. Dad used to say that every time it thundered. Oh, and look at that!"

"What?" Tertia asked.

"The bull is already in the right place and won't have to be moved."

"But your front yard is going to probably have to be graveled for a parking lot."

Noah kissed her on the forehead. "I've heard that there is a silver lining in every storm cloud. *You are* my silver lining, Tertia. And the gravel parking lot just means we have less to mow."

Chapter 23

"Looks like we're having a grand opening for a major hotel in New York City." Ophelia helped load boxes and boxes of cookies into Ursula's SUV that Friday morning.

"That wouldn't be nearly as important as a convenience store in Spanish Fort, Texas," Ursula said. "A big hotel in New York City would just be another place. A store in Spanish Fort is the only one, and therefore a bigger thing."

Ophelia threw up both palms. "I'm not arguing. I'm as tickled as everyone in this area to be able to buy gas and emergency supplies right here in town. I was simply stating a fact that there's enough cookies here to feed an army of hungry men."

Ursula held up one finger. "Harry Dalton." Another finger went up. "Everett Sampson." A third one. "Dillard Andrews."

Ophelia laughed out loud. "Now that you mention it, maybe I ought to use the kitchen at the winery and make another six or seven dozen this morning. Just those three could eat two dozen each, and they'll bring Walter, Bill, and Coy with them."

"And might even set up a domino game on one of the tables we're setting up between Luna's place and the new store!" Ursula told her. "Isn't life great in a small town?"

"Even better in an almost ghost town," Ophelia said. "I've got to go to work. See y'all as soon as I can."

She took a deep breath and let it out slowly as she drove away from the Paradise. She made a mental list of everything in the boxes in her back seat. The house had been a hive of hustle and bustle since before daylight, and she had loaded what she needed for the party at the winery before breakfast.

"Gift bags and cards," she said out loud. "Cookies, decorations, tablecloth. I'm forgetting something. I know I am." She pictured the reception hall and one by one thought about the ways she intended to decorate it.

She fussed at herself to stop overthinking. If she forgot something, the little five-person party at the winery would still be a surprise for Lester, Frankie, and Rodney. Bless their hearts, they had agreed to stay on one more week past when their original last day would be. They deserved to be sent off in style to open their new café in Henrietta.

Luna and Shane's party would be much, much bigger, probably more on the scale of a huge class reunion. Ads had been placed in area newspapers, and the entire population of Spanish Fort—all one hundred of them—had told their relatives and friends the good news about a store finally coming to town. Hourly prizes that included a couple of bottles of Brennan wine and ten-dollar gift certificates for gas would be given away starting at ten o'clock that morning. The grand prize was a fishing trip for four to be awarded five minutes before closing that evening.

Tables had been set up in the space between Luna and

Shane's house and the store for folks to sit around to visit and enjoy cookies and either sweet tea, lemonade, or bottles of cold water. Pizza would be served at noon, and hot dogs and burgers that evening. The whole family would be taking shifts serving that day. Jake was even closing the winery at noon, and after they had their little going-away celebration, Ophelia and Jake would be taking a turn at helping with the grand opening.

For just a split second, Ophelia was a little jealous that the rest of her family would get to spend the whole day together, but then she remembered that she had a job she loved.

"And a boyfriend that I could so easily fall in love with," she whispered.

Jake was waiting for her on the porch and hurriedly crossed the yard to open the door for her. "Good mornin'. You are so sweet to think to do this for the guys."

She nodded toward the back seat. "We were baking for the open house anyway, so it was no trouble."

He opened the door and grabbed one of the boxes. "This is heavy. There's no way we'll eat all these today."

"What we don't eat, we'll bag up with a bottle of wine and send one home with each of the guys as a going-away gift," she told him. "I brought three gift bags that have THANK YOU written on the outside, and three good-luck greeting cards. You can put their final checks in the cards."

"You are amazing," Jake whispered.

"Mama trained me well, but thanks for the compliment."

She picked up the second box that held all the party supplies, and followed him to the porch and then inside. "In between customers this morning, I'll get everything ready for the party. Tertia is picking up a couple of dozen pizzas for the grand opening, so I told her to get two extra for us. They'll be here just before noon."

"Thank you for thinking of all this," Jake said. "My grandpa would say that you are a keeper."

Ophelia set the box she was carrying on the table beside Jake's. "Like I said, Mama raised me well, so the credit goes to her, and maybe to Endora for making the cards and a banner for us. We'd better get out of here before they catch us. We want it to be a surprise."

Jake wrapped her up in his arms and held her tightly against his chest. "Do you really think we can hold down the fort here with just the two of us for the next couple of weeks?"

Ophelia leaned back and looked into his eyes. "I really do. We don't have anything but Dolly's birthday party on the calendar for the rest of June. By the time we have another big thing to plan, Lucy and Conor will be here. And speaking of holding things down with just the two of us, Tertia offered to come help out in the front. Right now Henry and his crew are remodeling the house, so they can't do much in the way of testing recipes and she has some free time."

"That would be great. Tell her that she can start on Tuesday," Jake said.

"I was thinking tomorrow would be better since we've

got that birthday party for Dolly booked in the reception room from two to four," she reminded him.

Jake's eyes fluttered and his lashes came to rest on his cheeks. "Yes, definitely," he whispered just before his lips covered hers.

"Hey, Jake." Lester's voice came over the intercom. "We need you to make a decision back here."

Ophelia took a step back. "That's our cue to get to work."

"Maybe after the reception for Dolly tomorrow, we could have a real date?" He slipped her hand into his and led her out of the room.

"Without a tornado?" she asked.

"I checked the weather, and it's supposed to be hot and no storms." Jake brought her hand to his lips and kissed the knuckles. "See you at noon if not before."

"I'll have everything ready." She covered the hand he'd kissed with her other one, and was surprised that it wasn't nearly as warm as it felt.

"Delivery for party number one." Tertia carried a couple of flat boxes into the winery about thirty minutes before noon.

"Thank you, thank you," Ophelia said. "How's the grand opening going? Still have a few cookies left?"

"So far, so good," Tertia answered. "Harry brought a box of dominoes, and folks are having a grand time telling fishing stories and talking about old times. They even talked Aunt Bernie and Dolly into playing a game with them."

"That's great," Ophelia led the way back to the reception room. "Just set them on any table."

"This looks awesome, Sister," Tertia said. "The bunch of us sisters could be party planners."

"No, thank you!" Ophelia shook her head. "That's exhausting work, and speaking of work, Jake wants you to come help out here, starting tomorrow."

"That's great," Tertia said. "I'll be here, but right now, I've got pizza to deliver down the road. Oh, and one more thing, Walter is going to check into leasing the old store for a kind of senior citizens' place where they can go play every day. Good things are going to happen around here."

"They already have," Ophelia waved over her shoulder.

She had no sooner left than Ursula came into the shop. "I need a bottle of watermelon wine. Endora and I were making up the gift bags and found we were one short."

Ophelia hurried across the room, grabbed a bottle, and handed it to her sister. "Tertia just left. If you'd been five minutes earlier, I could have sent it with her."

"I stopped by my house," Ursula smiled. "This pregnancy makes me have to go to the bathroom every thirty minutes, and there was a line at the store. Parker showed up this morning and stuck around to help out. Looks like we've adopted him into the family. Think maybe Aunt Bernie is right and he'll fall in love with Bo?"

"No, I do not!" Ophelia answered. "Study him when he's around Endora. I think he's got eyes for her. I'll see y'all soon as we close up."

Ursula waved over her shoulder. "You could be right about Endora and Parker, but it won't happen fast like me and Remy or you and Jake."

"I hope so," Ophelia whispered, and then checked to see if everything was ready for the going-away party. She thought of a going-away party and a grand opening the same day. One was leaving, and the other was putting down roots. She and all six of her sisters couldn't wait to get out of the tiny community or away from the Paradise to start living their individual lives. But when it was time to put down their roots, they all wanted to be right back in Spanish Fort. Then her thoughts went to what Ursula said about the romance happening fast for her and Jake. Ophelia hoped her sister was right, because she was so ready to take her relationship with Jake to the next level.

Jake winked at her and smiled when he threw open the double doors into the reception area. Lester stopped at the door and shook his head in disbelief. Frankie wiped a tear from his eyes. Rodney gave Ophelia two thumbs-up and a big smile.

"We feel so bad to leave you as it is," Frankie's voice quivered, "and now you go and do something like this for us?"

Jake patted Frankie on the shoulder. "This was Ophelia's idea. My part was just to write your paychecks and tell you that when we get done eating, your week is finished. Ophelia and I need to get down to the grand opening and help out, so we're all going home when our party here is done. Now dig in and let's make one last memory together."

Frankie dragged a handkerchief from the back pocket of his jeans and wiped his eyes. "Thank you both. We feel pretty special, don't we, Poppa?"

"This is not a last memory," Lester declared. "This is just the beginning of a new journey, and we will be returning to Spanish Fort to visit from time to time."

"That's so sweet." Ophelia handed Lester a plate. "But for now, let's have pizza before it gets cold, and then cookies."

"Thank you," Jake whispered in her ear. "I know I've already said it, but it seems so little."

"You are welcome."

Until you are better laid. There was no doubt in her mind that the giggles she heard came straight from her aunt Bernie.

━━━━━━

"I could kick myself for being too stubborn to walk across the road and apologize for being rude when we were kids," Noah said as he tied off a bulging trash bag and threw it in the back of his truck.

"Why's that?" Tertia asked.

"Look at all the fun your family has," Noah answered. "I could have been a part of this for all these years, and most likely saved myself a lot of heartache."

"We are what our past makes us," Tertia told him. "That's why I quit coaching. I felt like I was wasting time."

Vega, Texas, had not offered a lot of dating opportunities, and Tertia had a rule about dating anyone within the school system. That rule became written in stone after she saw what happened to Endora. But she did go out with a local doctor, an auto mechanic, and a couple of other guys during the years she taught there. None of them had ever talked about their feelings, and when the breakup came, they sure didn't knock on the door and ask for a second chance.

"I can sure agree with you on that, and for the record, I do not intend to waste what time the present and the future give us," Noah said.

"Amen," Tertia agreed and then pointed to the table where the snacks were laid out. "The cookie trays are almost empty. We should go refill them before the next wave of folks come by." She slipped her hand into Noah's, ignored the stink eye that Bernie shot their way, and together they headed across the lawn and into the house.

"Hey," Ophelia called out as she and Jake crossed the yard. "How's it going?"

"Fantastic," Tertia answered. "I thought we would be eating leftover cookies until Luna's wedding, but if we have a dozen left, it will be a miracle."

Ophelia and Jake stopped walking at the bottom of the porch steps. "Maybe when we start serving hot dogs and hamburgers at five, that'll stretch out what cookies there are. Where is everyone else?"

"Remy is pumping gas today. Ursula is running the cash register, and Mama and Daddy are giving out all those cute little fishing lures with the store name on them."

"Endora?" Jake asked.

"She and Parker were here for the noon rush on the pizza,

and now they've gone to the church to bring in a few more folding chairs," Noah answered. "This is turning out to be a bigger event than any of us thought it might. Even the lady who runs Horn's Corner, a little convenience store over near Burneyville, drove over to visit. They've been trying to remember how long it's been since there was any kind of business in town, but no one can come up with an exact year."

"Does anyone remember when the old store was closed up for good?" Ophelia asked.

"One old-timer said his grandfather remembered it being open," Noah replied. "But that would have been decades ago."

Noah opened the door and stood back to let the ladies go first. "You are going to enjoy all the stories that are being told. Aunt Bernie is having a ball listening to them and adding tales of her bar. Plus, she's getting to know a lot more people."

"Next thing you know, she'll be looking at the old store building to put in a bar," Ophelia said.

"Shhh…" Tertia put a finger over her lips. "She might hear you, and besides Walter is wanting to put a domino hall in there. Parker said that if that doesn't work, the old guys can use the fellowship hall for a senior citizens center through the week. There come Endora and Parker with the chairs now. They're going to hand out fishing lures until supper, and Mama and Daddy are going to be on serving duty."

"And we take over to man the store so Luna and Shane can eat and mingle with the folks, right?" Jake asked.

Tertia nodded. "We'll be back at the tables in a few minutes. If you hear a funny story, remember every word to tell us later."

"Will do," Jake said.

Noah stopped inside the front door and wrapped his arms around Tertia. "We can get a lot done in a few minutes."

She rolled up on her tiptoes and moistened her lips. "Such as?"

"This for starters..." His mouth closed over hers.

Five minutes later when she came up for air, they had somehow moved to the sofa and she was sitting in his lap. Her heart pounded, and her pulse raced. She could hardly breathe and her hormones were screaming for more than kisses.

Not here, not now, the voice in her head whispered.

She agreed with the warning. When and if she and Noah took the next step, it shouldn't be a hurried thing. Reluctantly, she stood up and took a step backwards, stumbled over the leg of the coffee table, and fell flat on her butt. Noah jumped up, tripped over her feet, and landed with his head in her lap. The back door hinges squeaked, and Luna and Shane's two half-grown dogs bounded into the room. Mutt came to a long, sliding stop on the hardwood floor and licked Noah up across the face. Tertia covered her face with her hands to keep Holly from doing the same.

Tertia removed her hands when she heard her mother ask, "What's going on in here?"

Her neck felt as hot as her insides, and then the blush moved around to her face.

Noah pushed the dogs away, sat up, and then stood. He extended a hand to Tertia to help her. "We came to get more cookies, and…"

"There's a perfectly good sofa right there," Joe Clay said with a chuckle. "I'm sure Luna and Shane wouldn't mind you sitting on it."

"I stumbled and fell," Tertia explained.

"And then my feet got twisted up in hers, and I wound up flat on my back," Noah said.

"I raised beautiful girls, not graceful ones." Mary Jane winked at Tertia. "We are here to get another box of lures and a case of water. Are you kids all right? That had to be a pretty nasty fall."

"The only thing hurting is my dignity," Tertia answered.

"I could say the same thing," Noah said with a nod. "But on a different subject, I think having a grand opening like this and serving food all day is a wonderful idea. I'm going to do something like this when we open the café."

Joe Clay picked up a box with promotional fishing lures in it. "Do you think you'll have a house ready to move into soon?"

"I haven't even told Tertia this yet, but"—he took a deep breath—"I'm checking into having my grandparents' house moved rather than buying something else."

Joe Clay nodded in agreement. "Sounds like a smart idea. Where is it located now?"

"About halfway between my place and Nocona. I could live there and drive, but I'd rather live where I could just walk across to the café," Noah answered. "It's an old two-story farmhouse. The bones are good, but the inside might need some cosmetic help. If that's feasible, the movers could easily get it up here and set it in place by our grand opening for the café. What do you think, Tertia?"

"It would sure come with a lot of memories," she told him.

"Lots of good ones," Noah admitted, "and more could be layered on top of those."

Tertia thought she knew what he was saying, and hoped she was right.

"Why don't you take a couple of trays of cookies out and tell me more about this idea? Where are you planning to set it?" Joe Clay asked.

Noah picked up a tray of cookies in each hand. "I'd love to, and I'll help greet the folks while Miz Mary Jane catches her breath."

Joe Clay led the way out the back door with both dogs at his feet. "Glad y'all took a tumble in here. If you had dropped two trays of cookies in the backyard, these two mutts would have been glad to scarf them right down. And if Bernie had seen y'all all tangled up together, she would have fried both of you right into the dirt."

Mary Jane sat down on the sofa, leaned her head back, and closed her eyes. "I need a few minutes away from the crowd."

Tertia sat down beside her mother. "Mama, Noah is

acting like the café is ours, not his, but I haven't even told him for sure that I would work for him. And I don't know what to say about him living in his grandparents' old farmhouse."

"Honey, in his mind, you two are already in a committed relationship—both as business partners and otherwise. Now the ball is in your court as what to do with that. Forget your aunt Bernie. She's just putting on a show, and like I said before, she's going to claim credit for the match if it works out. Just figure out what you want to do and go after it."

"I want to be sure, but my heart tells me that it's falling in love with Noah," Tertia whispered.

"Then tell him," Mary Jane said without opening her eyes. "I love all this, but I'm used to spending hours in my office where the only noise I hear is the clicking of the keyboard and the voices in my head arguing about the plot."

"The wedding is going to be even bigger," Tertia reminded her mother. "We start on Friday with the spa stuff they're setting up in the living room, and the hairdressers arrive on Saturday morning."

"I will live through it," Mary Jane said, "but if you and Noah ever decide to get married, let's go to Las Vegas and let an Elvis impersonator to do the honors."

"Will you and Daddy and my sisters go with us?" Tertia asked.

"Of course, and that's all," Mary Jane said with a long sigh.

"And Aunt Bernie, of course."

Mary Jane reached over and patted Tertia on the shoulder. "She will be there. She wouldn't miss all those bars for anything in the world, or to gloat that her reverse psychology is what put you and Noah together."

"If you are wrong, and she boycotts my wedding, she and Pepper can stay home and take care of the cats." Tertia closed her eyes. "Not to worry, though. I'm not getting married for a long time. Ophelia will be the next one down the aisle. Or maybe Endora and Parker."

"They do seem to have some chemistry between them, don't they?"

"I think so, but Endora will need to be doubly sure before she enters into a relationship, so it will be a long time before it gets hot enough to boil," Tertia answered.

―――――

Ophelia's feet were aching by the time she crawled into Jake's truck at nine o'clock that evening. "It's been a great day, what with the party we gave the guys and the grand opening, but I'm really tired."

"But the night is still young," Jake said. "Want to go to my trailer, prop up our feet, and have a beer while we watch a movie on television?"

She covered a yawn with the back of her hand. "I might fall asleep, but a beer sounds really good."

Jake put his truck in gear and headed away from town. "If you do fall asleep, I'll wake you up in time to eat breakfast."

"Who's cooking? Me or you?" she asked.

"I make a mean stack of pancakes," he answered as they passed the turnoff to the Paradise.

"That actually sounds good for a midnight snack," she said. "I was so busy that I never did get around to having a hot dog or a burger. Seems like the evening rush of folks was even bigger than what was there all morning and afternoon."

"You got it, darlin'." Jake grinned. "I'll make pancakes and bacon as soon as we get to the trailer."

"Thank you," Ophelia said. "We can even call this our tornado makeup date night. And thank you for closing shop and helping with everything today."

Jake turned down the gravel road, drove around the winery down the path back to his trailer, and parked in front of it. He got out and, as always, opened the truck door for her. "You are welcome to both, but if we're passing out thanks, I believe I owe you more than you owe me. You planned the whole going-away party for the guys and let me be a part of your family the rest of the day."

"We'll just call it even."

He took her hand in his and led her up onto the deck. A big dog came from around the end of the place and lay down at her feet. "This is Stubborn, or Stubby for short. He and I both welcome you to the Brennan home. It's not fancy or the size of the Paradise, but it's home."

She bent down and scratched the animal's ears. "He looks like a stubby with that nub for a tail. Why did you name him Stubborn?"

"He was too stubborn to leave," Jake answered. "The first three days he was here, I refused to feed him in hopes that someone would claim him, or else he would just go away, but every morning he showed up on the deck again. I would say, 'You are a stubborn rascal,' and he'd just wag his tail. Then I saw him running pesky animals out of the grape arbors, and I decided to give him table scraps. Now I'm buying fifty-pound bags of dog food."

Jake stepped around the dog and threw open the door. "Come on inside and make yourself at home while I wow you with my cooking skills."

She expected a small single-wide trailer, but this was so much more.

"Does your expression mean that you don't like the place, or that you are surprised that I'm a neat freak?" he asked as he left her inside the open living space and went straight for the refrigerator.

"Both," she answered. "I didn't realize this was a double-wide, but then I've never driven all the way back here. All I could see from the winery was the front of the place."

"I looked at the smaller ones, but they were too cramped to suit me." He took eggs and milk from the fridge and set them on the cooking island. "Master bedroom is on the left over there. Two bedrooms and a bath on your right. That's where Lucy and Conor will be living when they arrive. I talked to him again last night, and he said that they would like to move a prefab home like this down the pathway toward the farm pond. I sent pictures of a couple of areas, and Lucy really liked the idea of living in that place. It's spring fed, so the water is pretty and clear all the time."

"You're going to have a community of your own back here," Ophelia said. "What can I do to help you?"

"You can put on a pot of coffee, unless you'd rather have beer with your pancakes," Jake responded. "I'll handle the rest for a kiss."

She planted a soft kiss on his cheek.

He slipped an arm around her waist and pulled her to his chest. "Darlin', that's *not* a kiss. This is a kiss!"

She didn't even have time to moisten her lips before his mouth settled on hers in a kiss so passionate that it practically curled her toes. When it ended, he took a step back and poured flour into a bowl.

"I agree," she said breathlessly. "That *was* a kiss."

He wiggled his eyebrows and grinned. "I've got lots more that I will share with you anytime you want."

"Be careful what you offer," Ophelia flirted.

"It's not just an offer. It's a promise that you can collect anytime, night or day or anywhere in between," Jake said. "You want more kisses before or after pancakes?"

Ophelia wanted more than kisses and had since they had made up after the argument they had several days ago. There had been kisses, hand-holding and lots of romantic flirting, but he hadn't made a move to take it to the next level. An instant visual of the two of them tangled up in the bed she could see through the open door into the master bedroom made her break out in a hot flash.

That's your biological clock, not a hot flash. Bernie was back in her head.

Go away. This isn't the time or place for you to be here, she thought.

"Who are you arguing with?" Jake asked, "And who is winning."

She filled the coffeepot with water and set it to the side. "How do you know I'm fighting with anyone? Maybe I'm just hungry."

He removed his glasses, cleaned them on a tea towel, and leaned in closer to her. "Nope, your stomach isn't growling. That look says you are doing some internal arguing."

"Busted!" she said with a grin. "I was fighting with myself over the issue of being a brazen hussy."

"Oh?" he frowned.

"I think my heart is going to win the battle. I was thinking maybe we could have dessert first."

"Why, Ophelia Simmons, are you...?" He chuckled.

"I am," she said.

"Thank God!" He laid his glasses on the counter, swept her up in his arms, and carried her to the master bedroom. "I've been dreaming about this for the past two weeks."

"Me too," she said as she kicked the door shut with her bare foot.

Chapter 24

"Good mornin'," Tertia said from the swing on the front porch. "Did you forget something? Like the way home last night?"

"I knew the way," Ophelia answered and sat down on the other end of the swing. "I just didn't come home. Why are you up and around before dawn? Did you just get here, too?"

"No, ma'am," Tertia replied. "Our canoes didn't run on the parallel course last night, but I did tell Noah that I would work with him, and he told me that he was falling in love with me."

Ophelia was more than a little jealous of her sister. Sure, she'd spent the night in Jake's bed, had a midnight snack of pancakes after a round of the hottest sex she'd ever known, and then another round that put the first one to shame, but neither of them had said the three magic words.

"And," Tertia went on, "we talked about moving his grandparents' house back behind the café. Henry says it's doable, and that he'll do whatever remodeling we want done."

"Does that mean you'll be moving in with him?" Another

little burst of jealousy ran through Ophelia's heart with a cloak of guilt following right behind it. She and Jake had not even thought about taking that step. Now that Conor and Lucy would be staying with him, it probably wouldn't be a possibility.

Tertia raised one shoulder. "He hasn't asked me, but everything is 'we' and' our,' not 'me' and 'mine.' If and when he does ask, I'm going to say yes. How about you?"

"Our canoes have separated, Sister," Ophelia answered with a sigh. "Conor and Lucy will be living with him until they can get their own place set up. "

Tertia nodded. "I understand Look at that sunrise. That's a good omen, right?"

"What's a good omen?" Bernie came out of the house with Pepper on a leash.

She wore a hot-pink silk robe over purple-and-white-checkered pajamas and a pair of fluffy orange house shoes. She looked like the manifestation of the sunrise behind her. Was Bernie the omen that Tertia had mentioned?

"Why are you two up so early, and why didn't you even put on a pot of coffee?" Bernie asked.

"We're watching the beautiful sunrise, and I bet you know how to make coffee," Ophelia answered.

"I do, and I did, and I smell a rat." Bernie sniffed the air, and then she tied Pepper's leash to one of the porch posts. "Which one of you...or did both of you spend last night with your boyfriends?" She eased down in a rocking chair and propped her feet up on the porch railing.

Ophelia raised her right hand. "That would be me. Just call me Abraham. I cannot tell a lie."

"Hmphhh," Bernie snorted. "That's a lie within itself, and it's George who couldn't tell a lie!"

Ophelia dropped her hand. "White lies do not matter, and for your information, I am owning my sexuality, and I get that from you, Aunt Bernie. For future reference, I may spend more nights over there in the next couple of weeks. Or"—she lowered her voice to a whisper—"I might break the 'no boys allowed upstairs' rule and sneak Jake up to my bedroom when Conor and Lucy move in with him."

"Or you could just meet him out in the barn. There are several sofas out there that would do for a night of passion," Tertia said.

"Is that what you and Noah do?" Aunt Bernie asked.

"No, ma'am, we kind of like the bed of his truck. He throws a futon mattress back there and…" Tertia's eyes sparkled. "But so far he hasn't done that. However, when we get ready to have sex, the barn sounds like a good place." She turned toward Ophelia. "And if we get there first, I'll hang a 'Do Not Disturb' sign on the door. But once he gets the house moved in across the road, I'm going to take my furniture out of the barn."

"What does your sofa look like? I wouldn't want to be the one to break it in…" Ophelia started.

"It's the dark-gray one with carved wood across the back."

"Okay, okay!" Bernie snorted. "My job is done for you two. Ophelia, I knew you would wind up with Jake the day we walked into the winery. My Universe has come through for me. And Tertia, I played you like I used to do when you were a little girl."

"You did what?" Tertia gasped.

Bernie giggled softly. "You wouldn't eat carrots so when I came to visit, I told you that I was glad you wouldn't eat them because that way I could have all of them out of the pot roast. You weren't going to let me do that, so you ate them. I knew that Noah was right for you even before he came to offer you that job. Dolly told me all about him, and I just knew he needed a good strong woman like you. And besides, Pepper likes him. Never doubt the intuition of a dog—especially a Chihuahua."

Tertia narrowed her eyes toward Bernie. "Did you really use reverse psychology, just like Mama said you might?"

"You can turn off that nasty look. Of course I did, and you are welcome. It was easy, and I didn't even tell Mary Jane. Dolly is the only one who knows. So, now I'm on to matching up Bo with Parker, and finding someone for Rae."

Ophelia shook her head. "You've done well four times, but you might as well hang up your cap with Universe written on the bill. Parker has eyes for Endora."

Bernie smiled. "I know that, and you know that, but Endora hasn't figured it out, and a little jealousy thrown into the plot might work just fine."

"Not between sisters," Ophelia argued. "If you've got to drag out the jealous card, do it with someone else. Besides Bo isn't going to be interested in a preacher, and for sure, not Rae."

Bernie stood up and untied Pepper. "Good boy for not hiking your leg on the porch post. We'll take a little stroll around that bush in the backyard that you are partial to. You girls should go on inside and start some breakfast. I'll be back in a few minutes, and I wouldn't mind having some of your pecan caramel waffles, Tertia. I'm going to miss you when you move across the road."

"We'll put those waffles on the breakfast menu at the café, so you can come over anytime and have them," Tertia told her.

"I'll keep that in mind, and once again, you are both welcome," Bernie said.

"I swear she's walking on air," Tertia said when her aunt disappeared around the end of the house.

"Don't you kind of feel sorry for Bo and Rae? They'll be here in another week to help get everything polished off for the wedding, and I guarantee you she will be sitting on the porch waiting for each of them when they drive up," Ophelia said.

Tertia pushed up out of the swing. "Nope, it's their turn, and I don't feel a bit sorry for them. I just hope that Aunt Bernie has as much luck with them as she did with me and you—even if she does use reverse psychology on them both."

"Who do you think they might wind up dating?" Ophelia stood up and followed her sister into the house.

Tertia crossed the foyer and flipped on the light switch in the kitchen. "I have no idea. The pickin's are getting slim around these parts. Maybe they'll meet someone who comes to Shane's store for a fishing trip."

"Oh, no!" Ophelia raised her voice. "It has to be someone in this county. I'm ready for us all to be together again."

"Me too." Tertia got out the waffle iron and plugged it in. "In a month Luna is getting married. I've decided that sometime in the future when Noah and I tie the knot, we're not having the big hoopla. Mama said we should go to Las Vegas and get an Elvis impersonator to do the job."

Ophelia giggled, and then laughed. "Let's make it a double!" She held up her little finger.

Tertia locked hers into it. "That's a pinkie swear between sisters that can't be broken. But let's keep it as our little secret."

Ophelia broke away and gave her sister a sideways hug. "I agree. We might not even tell anyone until after the trip is over."

Chapter 25

One month later

OPHELIA ROLLED OVER TO find Jake propped up on an elbow staring at her. His eyes looked even dreamier when he wasn't his wearing glasses, but then she thought he was sexy no matter what he was wearing or how little. She reached over and combed his hair back with her fingers. "I'm going to miss you tonight," she whispered.

"Not as much as I'll miss you." He drew her to his side and kissed her on her neck, and moved up to her eyelids, then her cheek, and finally her lips. "I can't believe all of you sisters are taking the whole day today and until sunset tomorrow to get ready for this."

She glanced over at the clock and wiggled out of his embrace. "It's the culmination of months of planning, and Mama says we are going to be pampered. And darlin', I'm supposed to be there in fifteen minutes. Pedicures and manicures are on the agenda this morning for all of us and massages this afternoon. The living room is being turned into a spa." She pulled on her underwear and then her jeans and shirt. "Hairdressers are coming in tomorrow morning, and the makeup ladies will be there at noon. After that, it becomes a dressing room for all of us."

"I hope we have all daughters," he said. "Sons just have to show up in time to stand in front of the altar and say vows."

Ophelia bent to find her second flip-flop hidden under the edge of the bed. "Oh, really. So, we're talking about children now?"

"I love you, Ophelia Simmons," Jake said, "and I want to grow old with you, and have babies with you, and then sit on the porch and watch our grandchildren play. So yes, we're talking about children. Do you want a big family?"

Ophelia shoved her foot into the flip-flop and kissed him on the forehead. "Hold that thought while I decide if I'll settle with half a dozen, or if I want to go for the full twelve. I'll see you at the wedding tomorrow evening. I'll be the tall one with red hair."

Jake blew her a kiss. "You, darlin', will be the most beautiful one there."

"No, Luna will be because she's the bride, but I appreciate the compliment." Ophelia kissed her fingertips and blew on them to send the kiss across the room before she left.

Tertia was waiting on the porch when she arrived at the Paradise. "It's already a madhouse in there. I'd forgotten what it's like to have all seven sisters at home at once. Noah has been begging me to move in with him, and I'm going to. Endora can share the house with Bo and Rae. Noah's house is livable since we moved his bedroom furniture into the biggest upstairs bedroom, and Daddy took my stuff over there last week from my old place in Vega, so I'm saying yes as soon as this wedding is over."

"When are we going to Las Vegas?" Ophelia whispered.

"How about the week before the café opens? Maybe the second weekend in September? Are we really going to do that?" Tertia asked.

"Jake says for me to name the day, and he'll make the arrangements," Ophelia sat down on the swing. "Are we crazy to even think of getting married after such a short relationship?"

Tertia sat down beside her and handed off her coffee mug that was half-full. "Probably, but then I love Noah, and he proposes at least every other day."

Three cats were a blur as they ran past the sisters and huddled up together under a rocking chair. Pepper came around the end of the house in a dead run and went right on past the porch to the other side of the house.

"Too bad we aren't like Sassy, Poppy, and Misty." Ophelia chuckled.

"How's that?"

"We could hide under a chair until sometime in September," Ophelia answered. "But since we can't, we might as well go on inside and have breakfast with the family. Who's cooking this morning?"

"Endora, but everything else is catered after that. Mama says that she's not paying out all that money for expensive mani-pedis to have us break or chip our nails while we're cooking."

"Our mother is one smart lady," Ophelia said as she stood. "I wonder how many of the last three sisters will elope like we're planning to do?"

Tertia got to her feet and opened the door for Ophelia. "Endora won't. She's getting so involved in the church that she'll want a little service there when the time comes. Parker has asked her to teach children's church, and she's getting a quilting bee going a day a week for the older folks. And she told me yesterday that she's in charge of the first ever Christmas program this year."

"I can't believe that she turned in her resignation at the school."

Endora met them halfway across the foyer. "If y'all are talking about me, you can believe it, and I'm happy that I did. I told myself if a publisher bought my first children's book that I would quit and devote my time to what makes me happy. It sold, so I did. Now you'd better come on and have some breakfast. We're all around the table, and Luna is getting nervous."

"Cold feet?" Tertia asked. "She should have just gone to the courthouse or eloped."

"Not cold feet, but she hasn't written her vows yet. Shane has had his done for weeks, and she's afraid hers won't be as good as his. I told her to just throw away any written words and speak from her heart."

"That's awesome advice," Tertia said.

Endora gave her sister a gentle push toward the kitchen. "Go convince her of that."

Ophelia opened her eyes the next morning and realized that it had been weeks since she'd had a nightmare. She popped up in bed so quickly that the room took a couple of spins before things settled down. "I'm happy," she muttered.

"Yes, you are," Tertia said.

At first she thought Tertia's voice was just in her head, but then she got a whiff of coffee and turned to see her sister sitting cross-legged at the foot of her bed. She held out one of the steaming mugs in her hand. "Good morning, happy sister."

Ophelia took it from her. "Thank you. I'm happy because I just realized that I haven't had a nightmare in a long time. Jake has cured me."

"No, darlin' sister, love chased them away just like it kicked doubt and fears out the door for me and Noah," Tertia told her. "I hope Aunt Bernie's Universe tricks work on Bo and Rae."

"Why not Endora?"

Tertia took a sip of her coffee. "She doesn't need it. She's carving out her own future and doing a fine job of it."

Luna bounced into the room wearing a white silk robe with BRIDE embroidered in hot pink across the back. She handed each of them an identical one with SISTER written across the back. "I'm getting married today!"

"So, we are not maids of honor, but sisters of honor," Ophelia said.

"That's right. I can't believe that today is finally here."

Luna smiled, took Ophelia's coffee from her hands, and helped herself to a couple of sips.

"You are welcome," Ophelia said when Luna handed the mug back to her.

"Sisters share," Luna said. "It's already like a hive of bees in the living room. Granny and Grandpa Marsh were parked out in the yard in their RV. They must've gotten here late last night. Grandpa walked over to Noah's house. The guys are all gathering there for breakfast. Granny and Aunt Bernie are off in a corner catching up. The aunts and uncles and cousins will be arriving in time for the wedding. They're all staying in a hotel in Nocona."

"Do you think the fellowship hall will be big enough to hold everyone?" Ophelia asked.

"It's a beautiful day," Luna answered. "We'll put tables out in the yard if it gets too crowded. I wouldn't mind having my first dance with Shane on the grass in my bare feet."

"And beneath the stars," Tertia said with a long sigh. "I wish I was getting married today."

"Why don't you?" Luna asked.

"No license," Tertia reminded her. "And remember, you and Shane had to be together to apply and then wait seventy-two hours before you could file them."

"That's just for the government. You could get married today while everyone is here, get the license next week, and redo the ceremony at the courthouse. You would have two anniversaries, so maybe Noah would remember one of them," Luna argued.

"You would share your wedding day with me?" Tertia asked.

Luna reached for Tertia's coffee and took a sip. "Sisters share coffee, secrets, happiness, tears, and wedding days. So, do you want to get…?"

Tertia shook her head. "Thank you, but this is your day."

"It can be my day," Luna protested, "but it could be your night. After Shane and I have our first dance as a married couple, we could announce that there are going to be two more weddings tonight."

"She makes a good argument," Ophelia said and held up her pinkie finger. "But you'd have to propose to Noah and not even give him time to think about it."

"He's already proposed to me," Tertia told her. "More than once, but this is entirely too fast. We've got a café to get ready to open, and our house still needs lots of work, not to even mention the yard, which looks horrible right now."

"Well, if you change your mind, just let me know so I can tell Parker," Luna said. "I'm off to deliver the rest of the sister robes. I love it that we're all together."

"Hey, did you get Mama and Aunt Bernie robes?" Ophelia asked.

"Of course." Luna turned to leave the room. "'Mama' is on the back of hers, 'Granny' is on the back of Granny Marsh's, and 'Boss' is on the back of Aunt Bernie's. She loves it and says that it makes up for her not getting to be a bridesmaid."

Ophelia waited until Luna was out of the room and she

could hear her talking to Bo before she whispered, "I release you from our pinkie swear."

"Thank you, but it's so fast, and…" Tertia stopped and took a deep breath. "I might consider it if you and Jake are ready to jump over the broom too."

"I'm not jumping over a broom. As clumsy as I am, I'd fall on my face."

"If we got married tonight, it would be kind of like jumping the broom. It wouldn't be legal in Texas until we redid it at the courthouse, but the ceremony would be done with, and…"

Ophelia butted in and finished Tertia's thought. "We wouldn't have to do all this planning when you're going to have a café to run, and I've got something almost every weekend at the winery from now until September."

"And we wouldn't have to think about dresses or flowers. We'd each already have a bouquet and a catered dinner," Tertia added. "But I shouldn't spring this on Noah."

"And I'm not going to…" Ophelia's phone rang before she could finish.

Tertia slid off the bed and took a couple of steps toward the door. "I'll see you downstairs."

Ophelia answered the phone on the fourth ring. "Good mornin'."

"Mornin' to you, darlin'," Jake said. "I just called to say I love you, and that I'm so jealous of Shane right now that I'm turning leprechaun green."

"Oh, really?" Ophelia threw back the covers and slid out of bed. "And why is that?"

"Because he's getting married, and I want it to be us," Jake answered.

"Is this a proposal?" Ophelia asked.

"No, but if it was, would you say yes?" Jake asked.

"Ask me and we'll see. The sisters all headed down to breakfast. I should go," she said.

"I know the bride can't see the groom until the wedding, but that doesn't go for bridesmaids and friends, does it?" Jake asked.

"Not in my world," Ophelia answered, "and Jake, I love you too."

She followed the other six down to the foyer and listened with one ear to all the talk of the plans for the day. She heard something about Joe Clay and all the guys getting the gazebo set up out in the backyard. But her thoughts were on what a crazy idea it was to even think about Luna's suggestion, and yet, she couldn't get it out of her mind.

She didn't stop at the table where breakfast was laid out but went out to the screened porch to take a peek. The gazebo was set in the right place and all the guys were standing back discussing something. The chairs had all been placed on two sides with a center aisle. Florists were like worker bees dashing around getting everything in order.

"It's going to be beautiful, isn't it?"

Mary Jane's voice startled Ophelia so badly that she jumped. "You snuck up on me, Mama, and yes, it is beautiful. The whole yard looks like something out of one of those bridal magazines."

"I always thought Luna and Endora would have a double wedding," Mary Jane said.

The idea that she and Tertia had paddled in parallel canoes when it came to their love lives came to Ophelia's mind. "Maybe they each needed to take a different path. They're still close and share so much, but they need to have something separate, like Rae and Bo do."

"You are right," Mary Jane agreed.

"I'm surprised that you aren't taking notes for your next book from all this wedding stuff." Ophelia caught sight of Jake and waved.

"I've already done that. My next story is going to be about a wedding planner during Prohibition who runs a secret moonshine business on the side. It'll be set in Texas in the nineteen twenties. The first wedding planners only started in 1919, so it was a brand-new profession at the time. I'm so ready to delve into it, and honey, I've gotten a lot of fodder for it from all this planning."

"You amaze me, Mama," Ophelia said.

"Thanks, honey, but I'm going back into the house. I see Jake coming this way, so I'll give y'all a few minutes alone."

Ophelia gave her mother a quick hug. "Thank you—for everything you do for all of us."

"You are so welcome, but it would *not* hurt my feelings one bit if you just eloped. I used to think that I wanted every one of you girls to have a big wedding like this. Luna hasn't even been a little bit of a bridezilla, but..."

"I understand," Ophelia said.

"You are first one in line for the hairdresser in thirty minutes," Mary Jane reminded her and then closed the door behind her.

Jake knocked on the door leading into the screened porch and then came inside. "It's looking fancy out there, isn't it?"

"Just beautiful," she managed to get out before he dropped down on one knee, pulled a velvet box from his pocket, and opened it.

"Mary Ophelia Simmons, I feel like we've known each other for years, and I know that you are my soul mate. Would you marry me and make me the happiest man on earth?" he asked.

She stared at the set of rings and nodded. "Yes," she whispered.

That's a sign for sure that you need to take Luna up on her offer, Aunt Bernie was back in Ophelia's head and sounded over the moon with excitement.

Jake removed the engagement ring and slipped it on her finger. "I'll let you decide when and how big of a wedding you want, but I sure wish I was in Shane's shoes today," he said as he stood up and sealed their brand-new engagement with a kiss.

"How do you feel about tonight?" she asked.

———————

"Noah is here to see Tertia," Endora yelled from the front door.

Tertia's curly brown hair was up in curlers the size of

orange juice cans. She was still wearing the red-and-white-striped boxer shorts and orange tank top that she'd slept in the night before when she heard her sister's voice. But she didn't care how she looked; she ran to the door with the silk SISTER robe flapping behind her. She pushed open the door, wrapped her arms around Noah's neck, and kissed him.

"I missed you so much last night," she whispered when the kiss ended.

"I don't ever want to wake up without you beside me again," Noah said. "You make me happy, and my life is finally complete with you. I've asked you to marry me a dozen times, but today I'm asking for real."

"Yes, I will marry you," Tertia answered.

"You said once that you didn't want an engagement ring because of all the cooking we'll be doing. I hope you meant it," Noah said as he brought out a small box from his pocket. He popped it open to reveal two matching wide gold wedding bands. "I don't want to be engaged. I don't even care about a big wedding, but if you want one, I'll wait for you to get it planned. I just want a life with you, Tertia. "

"I love them!" she squealed. "I don't care about a long engagement or a wedding. I want a marriage, and I want us to wear these rings that match. Luna came up with an idea this morning. If you don't want…"

"If it involves marrying you, I'm all ears," Noah said.

She hoped that Luna had been serious about her offer to share her evening with her, and that Ophelia meant it when she released her from the pinkie promise. Who would have thought that the double wedding would not be between the two identical twins, Luna and Endora?

―――――――

Ursula led the way down the aisle just as the sun had begun to drop behind all the mesquite trees to the west of the Paradise. She took her place on the left of the gazebo, then each sister followed her, according to age. On the other side, Shane waited—a bit nervously—with Remy acting as his best man. Parker stood at the back of the gazebo with his Bible in his hands.

Bo stepped out of the line of beautiful women and picked up a microphone. Luna appeared like an angel in her white dress and a circlet of roses around her blond hair, flowing down past her shoulders. Bo began to sing a song that she'd written especially for the day titled, "Forever with You." Everyone stood as Joe Clay led Luna down the aisle.

When the song ended, Bo laid the microphone down and took her place again.

"Who gives this woman to be married to this man?" Parker asked.

"We don't give our girls away," Joe Clay answered. "But we do share them, and we are glad to take the men they choose to live with for the rest of their lives into our family." He kissed Luna on the cheek and sat down beside Mary Jane on the front row.

Ophelia heard a sniffle and noticed that Aunt Bernie was dabbing her eyes with a lace-trimmed hanky. Joe Clay had pulled out a handkerchief from his pocket, wiped his eyes, and then handed it to Mary Jane. After all the planning and preparation for such a lovely day, the ceremony was over in a few minutes. Parker pronounced them husband and wife just as a gorgeous Texas sun set behind them. Ophelia hoped that every picture the photographer took at that moment turned out well, because her mother really liked her pictures.

"The family would like to invite everyone here this evening to the church fellowship hall for a reception," Parker said as Luna and Shane made their way down the aisle toward the house. "The bride and groom will join all y'all right after they pose for a few more pictures."

The photographer worked fast since she was losing light by the second, and in only fifteen minutes, she finished her job. "Y'all have been amazing to work with, and if it's all right with the bride and groom, I would like to use some of these pictures for my portfolio."

"Fine by me," Shane said. "Shall we all go to the reception?"

"Yes," Ophelia said and scanned the crowd until she found Jake. She locked eyes with him and weaved through the chairs until she was beside him. "Ready?"

"Never been more ready," he said with a grin. "Why is Bo in such a hurry?"

"She has to get to the church before we all do. She is in charge of the playlist and has to introduce the bride and groom when they arrive. Man, I'm glad we aren't going to go through all this."

"Me too," Jake whispered and offered her his arm, "but I'm even more glad that we aren't waiting. Shall we go?"

She tucked her arm into his and nodded.

Folks were being served a plate dinner when the wedding party arrived at the reception, and Bo had the microphone in her hands. When Mary Jane gave her the nod, she turned it on and said, "Ladies and gentlemen, I give you Mr. and Mrs. Shane O'Toole." Then she pushed a button on her phone and "From This Moment On" began to play as the bride and groom entered the room.

Luna let it play out through the first verse and chorus, and then she took the microphone from Bo and motioned for her to turn off the music. "I want to thank you all for sharing my special day with me. Thank you, Daddy, for walking me down the aisle and always being there for me. Thank you, Mama, for…too many things to even list. Thank you, Aunt Bernie, for getting me through some tough times. And thank you to all my sisters for sharing everything with me. Speaking of sharing, Tertia and Ophelia shared their coffee with me this morning, so it seems only right that I share my wedding cake with them."

"I hope you're sharing it with all of us," Remy laughed.

"I am, but since it's time to cut the cake so all y'all can have a piece of it after you have your dinner, well…"

Parker came from the back of the room and stood in front of the cake table.

"Well, what?" Joe Clay asked.

"All of you get to attend three Simmons sisters' weddings

tonight," Luna answered. "Mine that you've just been to, and now you can share in the joy of seeing Noah and Tertia exchange vows, and Jake and Ophelia do the same." She handed the microphone to Parker.

"I thought this was going to be after the first dance," Jake said as he led Ophelia toward the front of the fellowship hall.

"I did too," Ophelia said out the side of her mouth, "but I'm not arguing with Luna, and it is kind of nice that we have a wedding cake."

"I agree," Tertia said as she and Noah joined them.

"Thank you, Lord!" Mary Jane said somewhere behind them.

"Amen!" Joe Clay added.

Ophelia heard a few muffled giggles, and then Parker said, "Family and friends, we are gathered to witness two more weddings here tonight. I've never had a part in a triple wedding, but I understand there's three more sisters who aren't married at this time so it might not be the last."

Acknowledgments

As always, I have many people to thank for this book. First, my readers for asking for it. Then Deb Werksman and all the folks at Sourcebooks for giving me the opportunity to write about the sisters. My gratitude to Folio Management for representing me, and to my agent, Erin Niumata, who has been on this journey with me for more than twenty-five years. Thanks to my family, and to Mr. B, my husband and soulmate, who has stood beside me through all the ups and downs of living with an author. Every one of y'all have made me the author I am today, and I'm sending out virtual hugs to each and every one of you.

About the Author

Carolyn Brown is a *New York Times, USA Today, Wall Street Journal, Publishers Weekly,* and #1 Amazon and #1 *Washington Post* bestselling author. She is the author of more than one hundred novels and several novellas. She's a recipient of the Bookseller's Best Award, Montlake Romance's prestigious Montlake Diamond Award, and a three-time recipient of the National Reader's Choice Award. Brown has been published for more than twenty-five years. Her books have been translated into twenty-one foreign languages and have sold more than ten million copies worldwide.

When she's not writing, she likes to take road trips with her husband, Mr. B, and her family, and she plots out new stories as they travel.

Website: carolynbrownbooks.com
Facebook: CarolynBrownBooks
Instagram: @carolynbrownbooks

Also by Carolyn Brown

What Happens in Texas
A Heap of Texas Trouble
Christmas at Home
Holidays on the Ranch
The Honeymoon Inn
The Shop on Main Street
The Sisters Café
Secrets in the Sand
Red River Deep
Bride for a Day
A Chance Inheritance
The Wedding Gift
On the Way to Us

Lucky Cowboys
Lucky in Love
One Lucky Cowboy
Getting Lucky
Talk Cowboy to Me

Honky Tonk
I Love This Bar
Hell, Yeah
My Give a Damn's Busted
Honky Tonk Christmas

Sisters in Paradise
Paradise for Christmas
Sisters in Paradise

Spikes & Spurs
Love Drunk Cowboy
Red's Hot Cowboy
Dark Good Cowboy Christmas
One Hot Cowboy Wedding
Mistletoe Cowboy
Just a Cowboy and His Baby
Cowboy Seeks Bride

Cowboys & Brides
Billion Dollar Cowboy
The Cowboy's Christmas Baby
The Cowboy's Mail Order Bride
How to Marry a Cowboy

Burnt Boot, Texas
Cowboy Boots for Christmas
The Trouble with Texas Cowboys
One Texas Cowboy Too Many
A Cowboy Christmas Miracle

REVENGE IN A COLD RIVER

"The storytelling is dazzling, as it always is in a Perry novel. . . . Like the great Dickens novel *Our Mutual Friend*, the Monk series has a deep, almost primal bond with London's river, which disgorges all sorts of objects, including human bodies, with each tide. . . . [An] uncommonly atmospheric mystery."

—*The New York Times Book Review*

"Fascinating and addictive . . . Another strong historical mystery that is true in both culture and manners to its Victorian setting."

—*New York Journal of Books*

"Perry is a master storyteller whose writing encompasses rich detail and nuance. . . . [*Revenge in a Cold River*] is her best to date."

—*The Star-Ledger*

CORRIDORS OF THE NIGHT

"[A] suspenseful, twisting narrative."

—*Historical Novels Review*

"Anne Perry has once again evocatively and meticulously conjured up Victorian London. . . . This is one of her best as she continues probing . . . the dark impulses that haunt all human souls."

—*Providence Journal*

"Pulls no punches and depicts Victorian London in all its corrupt glory."

—*Bookreporter*